# THE RIGHT TWIN

They pulled onto a little turnoff and headed into a thick grove of trees. The grove gave way to a meadow of late-spring wildflowers and tall grass. Smack-dab in the middle of the meadow sat a stone bench that looked like it had been there for hundreds of years.

Bo glanced at her, his face full of light. "I found this place years ago when I was out exploring with my *bruderen*."

"It's beautiful," Omi said. "And exactly why did you bring me here?"

"Not yet."

She nearly jumped out of her skin when he took her hand and tugged her to the bench. He motioned for her to sit, then ambled a few feet away and broke a Purple Prairie Clover from its stem. He came back to the bench, sat down next to her, and handed her the flower.

What was he up to? She didn't dare hope that it was exactly what it looked like.

"Omi, I've been an idiot."

"You brought me all the way out here to tell me this?"

"I brought you all the way out here because I wanted to be alone." He grew even more serious. "Omi, I was completely fascinated with Ruth. She's fun and exciting and . . . I guess I've already told you. But something happened to me that night we kissed. It was like I got hit by lightning." Doubt saturated his expression. "Please tell me I'm not the only one who felt that way . . ."

**Published by Kensington Publishing Corp.**

# Happily Ever After on Huckleberry Hill

## THE MATCHMAKERS OF HUCKLEBERRY HILL

# JENNIFER BECKSTRAND

## ZEBRA BOOKS
### Kensington Publishing Corp.

www.kensingtonbooks.com

ZEBRA BOOKS are published by

Kensington Publishing Corp.
119 West 40th Street
New York, NY 10018

All Kensington titles, imprints, and distributed lines are available at special quantity discounts for bulk purchases for sales promotion, premiums, fund-raising, and educational or institutional use.

Special book excerpts or customized printings can also be created to fit specific needs. For details, write or phone the office of the Kensington Sales Manager: Kensington Publishing Corp., 119 West 40th Street, New York, NY 10018. Attn. Sales Department. Phone: 1-800-221-2647.

First Printing: November 2023
ISBN-13: 978-1-4201-5530-3
ISBN-13: 978-1-4201-5531-0 (eBook)

10 9 8 7 6 5 4 3 2 1

Printed in the United States of America

# Chapter 1

Anna Helmuth sat in her rocking chair knitting a chunky winter scarf for her husband, Felty. It was only March, and Felty wouldn't need a new scarf until September, but she was all caught up on her other knitting so she might as well get a *gute* start on her next winter projects. She'd found a new, delightfully soft and fuzzy kind of yarn at the store last week, and she'd bought every cherry-red skein they had. Felty wasn't the only one who'd be getting a new red scarf for Christmas. With the amount of yarn she had, she could probably scarve the entire district, even the little babies. She should definitely knit faster, especially since knitting wasn't the only project she had planned this year.

"Felty, dear," Anna said, purling like her knitting needles were just an extension of her fingers. "I've been thinking about which of our grandchildren needs our help the most this month."

Felty, Anna's husband of more than sixty years, peered over his newspaper. "They're giving Andy Lapp a card shower to pay for his gall bladder. I'm going to send him some money."

Anna glanced up from her knitting. "The *gmayna* is

buying Andy's gall bladder? I thought it wasn't working anymore."

"*Jah*, that's why they had to take it out."

"Of course you should send some money. What are we here for but to help our fellow man?" She came to the end of a row and smoothed her hand along the half-inch width of scarf she'd already finished. It was going to be beautiful. And soft. And chunky. "Speaking of serving our fellow man, our grandson Bo desperately needs our help."

No sound on the other side of the room but the soft turning of a newspaper page. Sometimes Felty got so engrossed in reading the obituaries that he didn't even hear Anna when she talked to him. This was not one of those times. It was obvious by the way Felty sort of ducked his head behind the newspaper that he didn't want to talk about the grandchildren's problems. Anna simply couldn't let him skirt his responsibilities to the rising generation. "Troubles only get bigger when you avoid them, Felty," she finally said, with just a hint of scold in her voice.

Felty sighed, folded his paper, and set it on the side table. Then he gave Anna that crinkly, merry smile that always made her heart beat a little faster. "*Ach*, Annie-banannie, you know how much I adore you."

"I do, but what does that have to do with our grandson Bo?"

"You already have plenty to do, what with your knitting and your cooking and your chickens yet. You've already helped thirteen of our grandchildren find spouses. No one can say you haven't done your duty."

"I've actually helped fifteen grandchildren find mates, but we have one hundred and three grandchildren. That's less than twenty percent. There's still a lot of work to do."

Felty raised his eyebrows. "You were always *gute* at math."

"Then you can see why I'm concerned."

"*Ach, vell,* more than half of our grandchildren are too young to get married, and many grandchildren were married before you started your matchmaking schemes."

Anna laughed. "Schemes? *Ach,* Felty, that makes me sound so devious."

"For sure and certain they have all been the *gute* kind of schemes, and you've only been sneaky in a sweet, grandmotherly sort of way."

Anna didn't mind being devious when Felty explained it that way. "I suppose I have been devious, but only with everyone's happiness in mind."

"Of course, but I worry that you'll run yourself ragged doing for our grandchildren what they are perfectly capable of doing for themselves. Every one of my grandchildren is good-looking, smart, and kindhearted."

Anna couldn't disagree with that. "Not a scrub in the bunch."

"They should be able to find spouses for themselves."

"But, Felty, it never hurts to help out."

Felty pushed his glasses farther up his nose. "It *often* hurts to help out. I would never disagree with you for disagreement's sake, but just last year, you broke your wrist trying to get Martha Sue married."

"I broke my wrist because I tripped."

She loved Felty, but sometimes he was too persistent. He counted on his fingers. "You've been stuck in a runaway RV, our tent burned down, and Titus's Christmas goat ate one of your pot holders. Rachel Shetler permanently stained our floor with a huckleberry pie, Reuben yelled at you, and seven of your chickens died."

Anna frowned when she thought about her poor chickens. "That was my fault. I shouldn't have taken them camping." But there was no use crying over spilled milk or chickens. "Making matches for our grandchildren isn't easy, and chickens can sometimes die, but you can't tell me the effort isn't worth the trouble. Think of all the love and joy we've spread around with our scheming, not to mention how many extra great-grandchildren we have because we've been sneaky."

Felty fingered his salt-and-pepper gray beard. "You can never have too many great-grandchildren."

"So you see, I have to keep making matches for my grandchildren. Love is worth every risk."

Felty didn't look convinced, but he gave up arguing. "I don't know where I'd be without you, Annie."

"Probably married to Rosie Herschberger."

"*Ach*, Rosie couldn't hold a candle to your cinnamon rolls. It never would have worked out."

Anna giggled. "Especially since she married my *bruder*."

"Especially because of that."

"Let's talk about Nebo," Anna said, setting her knitting in her lap. Some discussions required her full attention. "I've been doing a lot of thinking, and he should be our next project."

Felty leaned forward, as if he'd just thought of a wonderful *gute* idea. "*Ach*, this is the perfect solution for both of us. Bo already has a girlfriend, so we can pretend we helped him and take a break from matchmaking. You and I should start a new hobby."

"A hobby? Felty, who has time for a new hobby? Our time should be spent helping our grandchildren."

"But Bo . . ."

Anna huffed out a breath. "I admit he already has a girl

he's interested in, but my big toe is acting up. That's a sure sign he's going to need our help. We should have a backup plan if she breaks his heart."

Felty furrowed his brow. "What's your backup plan?"

"I won't know until I talk to Bo and determine what his needs are."

"Maybe he'll just need you to come to the wedding."

Anna swatted away that suggestion with her knitting needles. "Wishful thinking. He's going to need more than that. I'm going to find out what it is."

"In the meantime, let's start a new hobby."

Anna wasn't fooled. Felty wanted her to start a new hobby so she'd forget all about Bo, but Anna was a very devoted *mammi* and she would not let Bo down.

Felty would have to start a new hobby without her.

# Chapter 2

Bo Helmuth walked into the Mischlers' house, and Naomi Coblenz tried not to stare. She also tried not to swoon or drool or make a fool of herself in one of the many ways it was possible to make a fool of herself in front of him. It was completely fitting that Nebo Helmuth was named after a mountain. He was tall and solid, with firm muscles and a square, determined jaw. Naomi drew her brows together. She couldn't be altogether sure his muscles were firm, but they certainly made every shirt he wore look too small, as if he would tear right through the fabric if he flexed hard enough. What would it feel like to be wrapped in those strong arms?

Naomi's face got warm. She shouldn't be thinking such thoughts, especially about her *schwester*'s boyfriend. She averted her eyes and pretended to be very interested in the huge rag rug that covered at least half the Mischlers' great room. It would have taken hours and hours and scraps and scraps of fabric to make such a thing. It was beautiful. Whoever made it had used blues and greens with the occasional white and yellow accent, and it looked like a meadow full of wildflowers. It was a shame more people didn't notice the rugs at their feet. This one was quite interesting, and it took Naomi's mind off handsome you-know-who.

*Ach, vell*, at least temporarily.

Naomi, or Omi, as everyone called her, despaired of ever being able to put Bo Helmuth from her mind. He was intolerably handsome—so handsome that every girl in the *gmayna* had a crush on him—and he was built like a freight train, his edges only softened by his curly wheat-colored hair and his deep brown, puppy-dog eyes that brimmed with sympathy and kindness. Omi was also drawn to him because he was quiet and of a sober disposition. She wasn't especially fond of *die buwe* who couldn't stop talking or thought everything was a joke or fancied themselves more important than anyone else in the room.

Bo's worst quality was that he only had eyes for Omi's twin *schwester*, Ruth, and their relationship would progress to engagement as sure as rain fell in April. Unless Omi moved to a different state, Bo Helmuth would be a part of her life for a very long time. It made her feel excited, sad, and guilty all at the same time. The Bible said not to covet your neighbor's *fraa*. Was it wrong to covet your *schwester*'s boyfriend? To wish it was you he smiled at and came to the house to visit? To be fair, Omi had admired Bo Helmuth from a distance ever since fifth grade. It wasn't as if she could turn off her infatuation like flipping a switch, even for Ruth's sake. Surely she'd become accustomed to Bo's presence if he married Ruth. Surely she wouldn't care a speck that Bo was her *bruder*-in-law. Omi watched as Bo greeted two of his friends and bloomed into a dazzling smile. She pursed her lips. She'd leave the moving-to-another-state option open just in case.

Ruth and Bo hadn't been dating forever. The first time

he'd asked to drive her home from a gathering was in November, so it had only been four months. But a boy never asked to drive a girl home unless he had serious designs on her. A girl never said yes unless she felt the same. A courtship could take many months, but an invitation to drive someone home said, "I'm thinking very seriously about marrying you."

"Can I help?"

Omi had been trying so hard not to look at Bo Helmuth she hadn't seen Marilyn come up beside her. Marilyn was her best friend, next to Ruth, and she always seemed to appear when Omi needed her most. Omi pried her attention from Bo and remembered the tablecloth in her hand. She should probably stop staring at rugs and boys and start helping out. "*Ach, jah, denki*. Verna asked me to spread the tablecloth before we sing so the table will be ready for eats afterward."

Marilyn grabbed one side of the cream tablecloth. She and Omi spread it over the table and smoothed out the wrinkles. Marilyn smiled. "Plenty of handsome *buwe* here tonight. Danny Mischler can't stop looking at you, Omi. Maybe he'll ask to drive you home."

Omi laughed quietly. "He's only looking over here because he thinks I'm Ruth."

Marilyn cocked an eyebrow. "*Ach*, Omi, you are just as pretty as Ruth. You two look exactly alike. *Exactly*. Why do you put yourself down like that?"

Omi squared her shoulders. "I'm not putting myself down. I'm trying to be realistic and humble. Everybody considers Ruth the prettier of the two of us, even though we look exactly alike."

Marilyn's eyebrow rose farther up her forehead. "That's the silliest thing I've ever heard. You don't have a proud bone in your body. Ruth gets more attention because she's high-spirited and bouncy, but she's not prettier."

The corners of Omi's mouth slowly curled upward. "Bouncy?"

"*Ach*, you know what I mean. The loudest bird in the forest attracts all the birdwatchers, but that doesn't mean her song is any prettier than the other birds. You're more reserved and less willing to draw attention to yourself. Some *buwe* like your type better."

Not Bo Helmuth.

Omi clenched her teeth. She'd be much happier if she quit using Bo Helmuth as her measuring stick. He wasn't the only *bu* in the district, and he and Ruth were as *gute* as engaged. Try as she might to pretend Bo didn't exist, she was fully aware of every move he made, every person he talked to, and every place in the room he stood.

Laughter coming from across the room drew their attention. There she was. Ruth and two friends had found Bo, and the three of them surrounded him and were laughing hysterically. Bo wasn't "bouncy" or high-spirited like Ruth, but his grin was so wide, it looked as if it would fly off his face.

Marilyn gave Omi a knowing smile. "I adore your *schwester*, and I like you even more."

Omi put her arm around Marilyn's shoulder. "You are the best kind of friend, always trying to make me feel better about myself."

"Is it working?"

Omi giggled. "It's the thought that counts."

Marilyn elbowed Omi in the ribs. "You are impossible!" They both laughed, and Marilyn stopped trying to convince Omi of anything. Marilyn glanced toward the kitchen. "Does Verna need more help?"

"I don't know."

"I'll go see."

Retreat seemed like a *gute* idea. Omi followed Marilyn into the kitchen where Verna Mischler and her *dochter* Lea were shaping dough into pretzels. Verna was a sweet woman who always had a permanent worry line etched right between her eyebrows and a paper napkin balled in her fist like a security blanket. Her *dochter* Lea was a cheerful, *gute*-hearted girl, pleasingly plump and well into her thirties. Lea was too old to attend gatherings anymore, so she helped her *mamm* in the kitchen. Omi adored Lea because she smiled with her whole face and made everyone feel *gute* just to be around her.

Lea looked up from the butcher block and gave a little squeal. "Marilyn and Omi. Two of the sweetest girls in the *gmayna*."

Omi smiled. "Not sweeter than you. How is your toe?"

Lea lifted her foot and wiggled it for Omi's benefit. "Better. It's still black and blue and swollen, and it still hurts to put weight on it." She giggled. "I guess it's not better, but I don't want to complain. It's my own fault for missing that stair."

Marilyn curled her hands around a bowl of dough. "Have you been making pretzels all day?"

"*Nae*," Lea said. "You can't make the dough too early, or it will overrise. Mamm figured it out down to the last minute." She motioned to seven timers lined up on the counter ticking merrily, each one with a number—one through seven—taped to the top. "Mamm bought five extra timers just to make sure we wouldn't ruin a single batch."

Verna grimaced. "Maybe I shouldn't have spent all that money, but I want everything to turn out well. It's my first time hosting a gathering."

"How can I help?" Marilyn said.

Verna wiped her hand on the towel slung over her

shoulder and eyed timer number one. "We've put the first batch in the oven. All the pretzels will be done by the time the singing is over, but they won't all be warm. If only I had two ovens . . ."

Always so unsure of herself, Verna wrung the napkin in her fist with both hands. Omi tilted her head to one side. Maybe she was a little like Verna. "No need to worry. Your pretzels are *appeditlich* hot out of the oven *and* cold."

Verna accepted the compliment with a slight smile. "I made enough dough for six dozen. Do you think that will be enough?"

"Six dozen?" Marilyn said. "I should think so, but Omi is the expert."

Omi shook her head. "I'm no expert."

Marilyn gave Omi that look again. *It's not proud to acknowledge the truth.* "Omi, you work at a bakery. You know how many doughnuts to make every morning down to the last one."

Omi giggled and made a show of counting on her fingers. She quickly estimated how many of *die youngie* were gathered in the great room and divided it into six dozen. Verna was always concerned about having things just so, and Omi wanted to put her mind at ease. "Everyone loves your pretzels. They'll get eaten no matter how many you make, but six dozen should be enough if *die buwe* don't make hogs of themselves."

Verna wrung her hands. "I hate to run out. Let's hope *die buwe* will mind their manners."

In an effort to not be in the same room as Bo Helmuth, Omi started to fill the sink with water. She could spend a *gute* fifteen minutes washing dishes and not worry about Bo at all.

"*Nae, nae,* Omi," Lea said, taking the dish soap from Omi's hand and shooing her through the doorway to the great room. "Mamm and I will clean the kitchen. You and Marilyn go have a *gute* time."

"Are you sure?"

Lea smiled wryly. "Omi, we have seven kitchen timers. We'll be fine. You can help set out pretzels and mustard after the singing."

Before Omi was out of earshot, Verna said to Lea, "I'm going to make two more batches just in case."

Oh, dear. Verna wouldn't have enough timers.

Marilyn was sure to have a *gute* time. She had a boyfriend in Pennsylvania, and she was expecting a proposal this summer. Marilyn didn't have to impress *die buwe* or ignore her *schwester*'s boyfriend. She just got to sing and eat pretzels. Omi wouldn't have a *gute* time, no matter how much she liked to sing or eat pretzels.

Ruth caught Omi coming out of the kitchen and grabbed her hand, her eyes alight with the excitement of being in love. "*Cum*, Omi. You and Marilyn need to sit by me so we can do the harmony. I can't hear it without you singing in my ear."

Ruth heard the harmony better than Omi did, but it warmed Omi's heart to think that she was still as important to Ruth as Ruth was to her. Omi grinned and squeezed her *schwester*'s arm and pulled Marilyn toward her with her other hand. "Let's sit by Lillian. She's *gute* at picking out the harmony too."

Ruth put her arms around Marilyn and Omi and pulled them so close they bumped heads. They giggled hysterically, and Ruth let go and rubbed her eyebrow. "Sorry! I'm just so happy to be here where there are so many handsome *buwe*."

Marilyn glanced at Omi, a teasing glint in her eyes. "Danny Mischler was staring at Omi."

Omi's face got hot, mostly because it wasn't Danny she cared about. "He was not. He was looking for Ruth."

Ruth's eyes flashed with amusement. "Was he?" She slid her arms around the other two and pulled them close again, but not close enough to knock heads this time. "Raymond Fisher brought his cousin from Cashton," she said in a breathless whisper. "He's so handsome, I think I'm going to faint."

Omi tried very hard not to be annoyed. Wasn't it enough for Ruth to claim one handsome boy's heart? Did Ruth have to make every boy in Wisconsin fall in love with her? Of course she did. For Ruth, the more admirers the better. "Well, don't faint now or we'll have to take you home and miss the singing."

"I wouldn't dream of it." Ruth squeezed Omi's arm affectionately. "I think we should try three parts on 'Oh, Happy Day' and 'Life's Railway to Heaven.'"

Omi frowned. "Even though we might end up singing some sour notes?"

Ruth nudged Omi toward the benches. "You can't get to the sweet notes if you don't try a few sour ones first."

The three of them passed by Bo Helmuth on the way to the benches, and Bo smiled at Ruth as if it was the first time he'd ever seen her. Bo's sleeve brushed Omi's arm as he went by, and Omi nearly floated off the ground. *Ach*, she hated being so weak, so enthralled by a *bu*, but there was no denying her feelings, even if she didn't like them.

*Die youngie* quieted, and they began to sing. Ruth tried to sing three-part harmony on every song, and Omi followed as best she could. Sometimes the harmony sounded *gute*, other times it didn't go so well, but Ruth wasn't discouraged. She kept right on singing, trying different notes, some higher, some lower than the melody. It was one of the things Omi admired most about her *schwester*. She wasn't afraid to try new things, even if she failed or made a fool of herself. Ruth had ten times more courage than Omi ever would. That's why *die buwe* liked her.

Omi enjoyed singing and harmonizing, but it was no fun watching Bo give Ruth adoring looks from across the room. It was even harder seeing Ruth blush and bat her eyes as if Bo's attention was completely unexpected. Omi couldn't find much pleasure in singing while Ruth enjoyed the looks and smiles that Omi so desperately wanted for herself.

Guilt crawled under Omi's skin. She loved Ruth better than her own soul, but she was so jealous she could barely see straight. She was a terrible, horrible person as well as the worst *schwester* in the history of *schwesteren*. She should seriously consider never coming to a gathering again. And moving to a different state.

After the singing, Omi practically ran to the kitchen to help serve pretzels, just to get away from Ruth and Bo. What she didn't see couldn't upset her, at least that was what she told herself. Verna was studying a timer, and Lea was sprinkling salt on a fresh batch. "Lea, do you want me to start taking pretzels to the table?"

"*Jah*. Take these two plates, and I'll bring the mustard and honey."

With a plate in each hand, Omi marched into the great room. Bo was talking to someone as he walked backward and nearly crashed into her. She caught her breath as he turned just in time, saw he was about to collide with her, and with that smooth, catlike grace, grabbed one of her plates before she dropped it. He smiled apologetically. "*Ach*, Omi, I'm sorry. I didn't see you there."

Of course not. He never saw her. "It's okay. I'm often overlooked."

He lost all trace of a smile. "*Ach*, I'm sorry. I didn't

know . . ." He trailed off, obviously unsure how to reply to such a pathetic remark.

Omi took a deep breath. What a petulant, childish thing to say! It wasn't Bo's responsibility to pay attention to her. Why was she so bitter all of a sudden? *Ach*, *vell*, it wasn't all of a sudden. Only since Bo had taken an interest in her twin *schwester*. She knew why jealousy was called "the green-eyed monster." She almost didn't recognize herself. It was time to stop acting like a baby.

She cleared her throat and attempted a self-effacing smile. "I'm kidding. Of course I'm kidding. I meant that I'm short, and you're so tall, you overlook just about everybody."

A smile dawned on Ben's face like a sunrise. "You're tall enough, Omi, and you know I'd never overlook you."

It wasn't true, but his smile was so attractive, she forgave him for the little fib.

He still held the plate of pretzels. "Do you want these on the table?"

She gathered her wits and pretended Bo was just another *bu* in the *gmayna*. But even though she tried to imagine him with buck teeth and pimples, she couldn't keep her heart from galloping. "*Jah*. Lea is bringing out the dipping sauces."

Bo took the other plate from Omi and set both plates on the table. "I'm sorry I almost made you drop the eats yet. Verna would not have been happy about that."

"*Nae*. She's already fretting she won't have enough."

"I'm afraid she'll give herself an ulcer with how much she worries."

"Me too."

Bo tilted his head to one side as if to see Omi better. "It's wonderful kind of you to lend Verna a hand. Most of *die youngie* don't notice things like you do, but you're always the first one to help after church or a singing."

His words tasted like warm chocolate in her mouth. Maybe he didn't always overlook her like she had accused him of doing. She should probably tell him that she hadn't done much. She hadn't made pretzel dough, and they hadn't even let her wash dishes. She should tell him that Lea was Verna's biggest help and Marilyn almost always pitched in too, but selfish as it was, she wanted to keep the praise all to herself this once. "*Ach*, it's nothing. I like to be useful."

His smile got wider, showing off those dazzling white teeth. "And you're humble too."

She giggled and held up her hand. "Stop, or you'll tempt me to be proud." Why was he being so complimentary? It was Ruth he liked.

"I'm only telling the truth. For sure and certain Emma appreciates your help with the *buplie*."

Now she *had* to stop him. "You're making me out to be a better person than I am. Helping Emma is a pleasure. I love babies, and Emma is one of my closest friends. Of course I'm eager to help."

"All the same, it's a blessing to my whole family."

Much as she had wanted Bo to notice her, Omi didn't know what to do with all the praise. For sure and certain, her face had turned a very unattractive beet red, and there were probably beads of sweat sprouting on her forehead. "Emma is very dear to me."

His expression turned her spine to jelly. "I'm *froh*."

Emma was Bo's *schwester*-in-law, married to Bo's *bruder* Ben. Emma was a few years older than Omi, but they were almost as close as *schwesteren*. Emma also had a twin, though he was a boy, and Omi and Emma both understood how sometimes your life could be overshadowed by a more vivacious sibling. Emma's second pregnancy had been rough, and the delivery had been even harder. Omi had done all she could to help Emma, especially during those first few months after she'd given birth. Emma's husband, Ben, was as solid and serious and soft-spoken as Bo, but he had multiple sclerosis and couldn't be as much help with the *buplie* as he wanted to. Omi went to Emma's two nights a week to help feed, bathe, and put *die kinner* to bed. It wasn't much, but it gave Emma a little rest.

Bo glanced around the room. "Where's Ruth?" And just like that, the connection between them snapped. Omi would always be the forgettable twin sister.

"I don't know. I've been in the kitchen."

Bo seemed to lose interest altogether. Scanning the room, he turned and walked away, without another word or glance in Omi's direction. *Ach, vell,* it had been nice for a minute, but she certainly couldn't have expected any more than what he'd given her.

Omi kept an eye on the pretzel table, refilling the honey and mustard bowls when they were empty, spying on Bo as he wandered around the room searching for Ruth. He stopped to talk to several of *die youngie*, but Omi could tell his main purpose was to locate Ruth. Omi couldn't see her *schwester* either. Where was she?

Suddenly, Marilyn was by her side with a bewildered look on her face. "Ruth needs you in the bathroom."

Omi glanced in the direction of the back hall. "The bathroom? Is she sick?"

Marilyn stretched her mouth across her teeth. "I don't think so. She's acting strange."

"That doesn't sound *gute*."

"I know," Marilyn said. "When Ruth acts *strange*, she usually has some sort of mischief up her sleeve."

Omi rolled her eyes. "Or some adventure." After her

encounter with Bo, she wasn't in the mood for an adventure. Hadn't singing in three-part harmony been adventure enough?

Marilyn pressed her lips together and stared at Omi. "I know you don't want to go in there, but she said to hurry."

Of course she did. To Ruth, everything was either not worth bothering about, desperately urgent, or wildly important. But maybe she really was sick. Omi shouldn't think unkind thoughts about her *schwester* until she knew what was going on.

She'd been so engrossed in her conversation with Marilyn, she hadn't noticed Bo until he was right next to her. "I still can't find Ruth. Have you seen her?"

Omi's smile stuttered. "Um, she's in the bathroom. I'm going to check on her."

Nothing made a *bu* back away faster than the thought of a girl in the bathroom. Bo cleared his throat. "*Ach*, okay. I'll wait here."

*Gute* idea, Omi wanted to say, but he would have heard the irritation in her voice. Couldn't he survive without Ruth for five minutes?

Omi tried to pretend it was Bo's puppylike devotion to Ruth that annoyed her, but if she had been the recipient of that devotion, she would have welcomed it. In truth, she didn't know if she was more irritated with Bo or Ruth. It felt like neither of them really cared about her except as a connection to the other. She swallowed her irritation, made her way down the hall, and knocked softly on the bathroom door. "Ruth, it's Omi. Are you okay?"

The door opened a crack and then wider as Ruth yanked Omi into the bathroom and quickly shut the door. "Omi, what took you so long?"

Omi glared at Ruth. "I had to finish my pretzel, do a

batch of dishes, and flirt with three boys. I couldn't just drop everything and come at your command."

Ruth sighed dramatically. "Okay, okay, I'm sorry if I was bossy."

Omi felt so irritated, she didn't even want to temper her honesty. "It's because you always think your life is more important than mine."

"That's not true, Omi. Nothing in my life is more important than you are." The mischievous grin on her lips made Omi doubt Ruth's sincerity. Why should Ruth care about what happened in Omi's life? Ruth's life *was* much more exciting. "I have something very important to do tonight, and I need your help. I need you to trade places and pretend to be me."

Omi groaned. Trade places? That was only the cause of more trouble. "*Nae, nae,* not for a million dollars."

"*Ach,* come on, Omi. It will be a funny joke."

"I'm not laughing," Omi said. Ruth, who didn't seem to be afraid of anything, including consequences, thought trading places was the funniest trick in the world. Like the time she didn't want to go to the dentist and begged Omi to go in her place. Or when Omi had done her own chores and all of Ruth's so Ruth could sneak off with her friends to a movie when she was only fourteen. They had both gotten in trouble for that one because Mamm had rightfully pointed out that it was a deception to go along with a deception, even if Omi hadn't uttered a false word.

"Come on, Omi. I need you to be brave. Can't you be brave for your own *schwester*?"

Omi folded her arms and squared her shoulders. "What you call brave, I call reckless."

"Nothing like that, Omi. I just need you to pretend to be me and let Bo drive you home."

Omi's heart pounded so hard, it felt like a prisoner

knocking on her rib cage begging to be set free. "Ruth, what are you thinking? He'll know it's me in a second."

"*Nae*, he won't. It will be dark, and you can tell him you're not feeling well. He won't even ask to come in the house."

"I won't do it. It's a lie, Ruth."

Ruth huffed out a breath. "You're such a stick in the mud. It's why all *die buwe* like me better than they like you. You never want to have any fun, and you never like it when other people are having fun behind your back."

For sure and certain, Ruth had tossed those words at Omi like she tossed her shoes on the rug after a hard day, but Omi felt the sting of them clear to her heart. Is that why *buwe* smiled when they talked about Ruth? Why Bo didn't give her a second glance? Why Ruth seemed wildly happy and Omi felt as if she'd been pushed into the shadows?

Ruth studied Omi's face and frowned. "*Ach*, Omi, I'm sorry. I didn't mean it like it sounded."

"*Jah*, you did."

Ruth cupped her hands around Omi's arms. "I love you, Omi, but you're so afraid of making a mistake, you can't even bring yourself to try."

Omi felt worse and worse. Ruth was right. Omi had never been one for taking risks or stepping one toe out of line, but why was that her problem? Ruth was just accusing her to get Omi to do what she wanted. She eyed Ruth resentfully. "What is so wrong with being cautious?"

"Nothing, nothing, you're right, of course," Ruth said, sounding as if she were agreeing to hurry the conversation along. "There's nothing wrong with being cautious and careful. I've always appreciated how sensible you are."

Omi waited patiently for the "but."

"But it's also important to have fun and be young and enjoy life before you get old."

"It sounds like you want to have all the fun and let me to take all the risk."

Ruth dropped her jaw in pretend indignation. "Of course not. Don't you think it will be fun to trick Bo and get away with it?"

Omi narrowed her eyes in suspicion. "What is it you want to do that doesn't include taking Bo along? Isn't he supposed to be the *bu* you love?"

"I like Bo very well, and he's going to make an excellent husband, but do you remember me telling you about Raymond Fisher and his cousin?"

"*Nae.*"

"*Ach, vell*, his cousin Elam has a car, and he wants to take me and Raymond and Lydia out to the back roads to show us how fast it goes. Doesn't that sound fun?"

It didn't sound fun at all. In fact, it sounded dangerous, but Omi wasn't about to mention the danger part, not after Ruth had accused her of being a stick in the mud. "It's not like you haven't ridden in a car before, Ruth."

"I know, but Elam is the handsomest *bu* I've ever seen, and that includes his cousin Raymond. His teeth are bright white, and he has a dimple that shows up on his cheek whenever he moves his mouth. I just . . . I just want to know how it would feel to sit by him and gaze at his dimple."

Omi suddenly felt quite offended on Bo's account. He would be deeply hurt if he ever found out that Ruth would rather go driving with Raymond's cousin than be with him. "But you and Bo are dating. You have a wonderful *gute bu* who adores you, and you don't even care."

"It's just this one time, Omi! I have a whole lifetime

to spend with Bo, but Elam is leaving for Cashton on Tuesday."

A crushing weight pressed on Omi's chest. Ruth didn't deserve the love of a *bu* like Bo Helmuth. She was acting like a selfish, spoiled child who had an abundance of toys and still wanted more toys. Omi frowned and pushed those thoughts away, ashamed of herself for thinking such things about her twin *schwester*. Ruth made every room brighter, every gathering more joyful, and every song more beautiful. Ruth deserved every *gute* thing. And that included Bo Helmuth.

Ruth grabbed Omi's hand. "Please do this one thing for me, and I'll never, ever ask you again." She drew Omi close and planted a kiss on her cheek. "Please, Omi. For me?"

A look of true longing pooled in Ruth's eyes. It was an emotion Omi couldn't resist. Maybe Ruth wouldn't love Omi as well if Omi didn't help her out. Maybe Ruth would be unsure of Omi's love if she refused. Maybe Ruth would believe she couldn't count on Omi in a crisis. And maybe, just maybe, Omi secretly contemplated the pleasure of sitting alone in the buggy with Bo for twenty whole minutes. But most of all, even if it was a selfish and *dumm* idea, it would make Ruth happy, and Omi valued Ruth's happiness much more than her own.

Omi expelled all the air from her lungs. "It's not going to work."

Ruth must have heard the resignation in Omi's voice. She bloomed into a smile and let out a little squeal. "For sure and certain it will work." She unsnapped the apron around her waist. "For one thing, we're going to trade dresses. That will make Bo think twice."

One corner of Omi's mouth twitched. "I guess that's a *gute* plan."

Ruth pulled a tissue from the box on the bathroom

counter. "You . . . or rather, I am going to have a fit of coughing that will last from the bathroom to the buggy. You . . . I mean, I, will have to cover my mouth the whole time. It's only polite."

"But how do I ask Bo to take me home if I have a tissue stuck to my mouth?"

Ruth didn't even bat an eye. "Anyone can talk through a tissue. Just speak loudly. When you get in the buggy, it will be too dark for him to see you clearly. Then you're home free. Just ask him to drop you off at the front steps because you don't want him to get sick if you're coming down with something contagious."

Omi drew her brows tightly together. "It's dishonest."

Ruth was still unconcerned. "What Bo doesn't know won't hurt him. Besides, you never have to say you're me. Then it's not a lie."

"It's akin to a lie."

"Tell the deacon later if you feel like you have to, but why would you when you haven't been baptized? I don't see it as anything more than a funny joke that we will all laugh about in twenty years."

Omi felt such a flurry of emotions, she doubted she would laugh about this *ever*. But they had already been in the bathroom way too long. She made up her mind, ignored the dizzy, light-headed feeling of doing something outrageous, and undid her apron.

# Chapter 3

Bo realized he'd been acting pathetic when Marilyn tapped him on the shoulder. "She's not going to come out any sooner with you standing guard at the bathroom door." She said it with a smile on her face, but Bo could tell she thought he was being a little foolish and a lot overeager.

"Is everything okay? Is she feeling well?"

Marilyn's expression was unreadable. "She's fine."

He nodded and quit talking because he didn't want to be overeager, but was it his fault that Ruth was everything he wanted in a *fraa* and more? Of course she was pretty, but beauty was just the icing on the cake, as Mammi Helmuth would say. *Ach, vell*, Mammi's icing tended to be so runny it sagged off any cake she made, or was so hard that a sharp knife was needed to cut the cake into slices. *Nae*, what Bo liked about Ruth was how fun and exciting everything seemed to be when she was near him. She got so excited about things that her enthusiasm rubbed off on everyone and everything, until the world seemed so much brighter and happier when she was around.

Bo turned his back on the bathroom door and made his way to the eats table where Lea Mischler was just putting out another heaping plate of steaming hot pretzels. "Right out of the oven," Lea said. "Get them while they're hot."

Bo thanked her and declined. He wanted his mouth to be completely empty when Ruth came out of the bathroom so he wouldn't have to talk to her while also trying to chew.

"You might as well take a few home yet," Lea said.

"For sure and certain." Bo wrapped two pretzels in a napkin and stuffed them into his coat pocket. He'd already put on his coat because he wanted to be ready to leave as soon as Ruth emerged from the bathroom.

*Die youngie* were starting to head for home, and there were still three plates full of pretzels on the table. Lea grinned sheepishly. "My *mamm* was worried there wouldn't be enough yet."

"My *mamm* is like that. She'd rather have too much food than not enough."

Lea nodded. "It's much worse to run out." She tilted her head to one side. "It wonders me if you can use pretzels in bread pudding."

Finally, Ruth came down the hall pressing a tissue over her mouth. She coughed softly two or three times as if she didn't want to disturb anyone, but when she'd finished coughing, the tissue stayed in place. She caught sight of Bo and smiled. Or at least he suspected she smiled. He couldn't see her mouth behind the tissue. "I'm not feeling well," she said, her voice muffled by the tissue. "Could you take me home?"

Bo frowned. *Wait a minute!* Was that Ruth or Omi? Ruth and Omi were identical twins, and they did look remarkably alike, but Omi's nose was a slightly different shape than Ruth's, and her eyes were a slightly deeper shade of blue. Ruth also had a single chicken pox scar on her forehead and Omi did not. This twin had no chicken pox scar and a light smattering of freckles across her cheekbones. What freckles Ruth had as a teenager had faded over the years, but Omi's freckles persisted even after her twentieth birthday. Most people didn't notice the freckles or even know that it was one way to tell the twins apart, but Bo knew. And the twin wearing Ruth's pastel pink dress was not Ruth.

Lea probably would have been able to tell the twins apart, even if they covered their mouths with hand-kerchiefs, but she was gazing at her three plates of pretzels as if wondering how to get rid of them. "Ruth, can you take some pretzels home?"

Bo expected Omi to correct Lea about who she was. Instead, she nodded and coughed more forcefully into her tissue. "Give them to Omi when she comes out of the bathroom."

Bo's frown cut itself into his face. Omi was pretending to be Ruth, and Ruth was hiding in the bathroom. He'd heard stories of twins trading places as a joke, but what were Ruth and Omi up to, and why did either of them believe they could fool him?

Lea looked up at Omi, but she must have been too distracted to look very hard. "Okay. I'll ask her. She told us we'd have enough, and we didn't believe her. Mamm made two extra batches."

Omi coughed again, giving her an excuse to hide her mouth with that tissue. "It's always better to have more than not enough." She turned her head in Bo's direction, but not so he could look at her straight on. "Can you take me home, please?"

She was doing her best to hide her identity. Bo had to admire her nerve, even though his confusion left him dizzy and his anger threatened to boil over like a pot of bubbling jelly on the stove. Should he scold her for deceiving him right there in front of everybody? Should he take her outside and lecture her on the front porch? Should he stay quiet, take Omi home, and let her think she'd tricked him? He wasn't sure, and even though he hated being made a fool of, he always regretted when he made a decision in the heat of anger.

Ruth would probably laugh or scoff if he got mad at her, but Omi was more sensitive, and she'd probably burst into tears at Bo's anger. Better to ignore the whole thing and confront Omi or Ruth or both of them later. Harsh words rarely made anything better.

Bo quickly retrieved his horse and hitched her up to the buggy while Omi climbed in. Bo got in the buggy and picked up the reins. Even though it was dark and there was less danger of her being discovered, Omi sat close to the far door and kept the tissue pressed to her mouth and nose. She was nervous, all right. She didn't know he'd already figured it out.

"*Denki* for taking me home," she said softly.

He clenched his teeth while trying to pretend he was none the wiser. "No need to thank me. It's my pleasure." It wasn't really his pleasure, but hopefully Derr Herr would forgive him for the lie. There were so many lies floating around in the air tonight, Bo doubted his would make any difference. He should probably keep his mouth shut so he wouldn't say something he regretted, but he was mad enough that he wanted to make her feel a little uncomfortable. He leaned toward her. She tried to press herself through the door of the buggy to the other side. "I'm worried about that cough," he said, putting a nauseating dose of concern in his voice. "Do you think you're getting the flu?"

"I'll be fine," she squeaked.

"I would hate it if you got sick, sweetheart." He smiled his most devoted smile, though she couldn't get the full effect in the dark. "I hope you're not too sick for a good-night kiss." Maybe it was beneath him, but Omi deserved to squirm a little. He had never kissed Ruth, but Omi didn't know that. What would she do? Her panic must be rising by the second.

She let out a little gasp. "Stay away from me." She must have thought better of her tone. She lowered it by several pitches. "Or I'll get you sick for sure and certain."

"I don't mind."

"I do."

They rode most of the rest of the way in silence, except for the occasional times when Omi remembered to cough. Bo spent the trip wondering why the twins had lied to him, growing more and more puzzled and more and more angry. He felt as if he were going to explode. If Ruth hadn't felt well, surely she wouldn't have hesitated to ask Bo to take her home. There was no need to lie about something like that, even if she was having some sort of female problem. Bo had two *schwesteren*. There wasn't much he didn't know—or at least he didn't know he didn't know. What was Ruth up to?

Bo hadn't thought much about it at the time, but he had seen Ruth and Lydia with their heads together right after the singing, whispering as if they were planning to rob a bank or steal a car. Bo remembered seeing Raymond Fisher sidle up to Ruth shortly after that, along with someone Bo didn't know, a lanky *bu* with brown hair that hung about his face in soft curls. Not only that, but he had the longest, darkest eyelashes Bo had ever seen on a *bu*. Did Ruth find him attractive, and had she persuaded Omi to trade places with her so she could spend some free time with "Curly"?

Bo ground his teeth together. His anger simmered as his confusion mounted. Confusion turned to a dull ache in the pit of his stomach. Didn't Ruth love him as much as he loved her?

"You're going to break a tooth."

The voice from the far side of the buggy startled him. He hadn't expected Omi to speak. She must have known that the less she said, the less chance of being discovered. She'd finally pulled the tissue from her face. She obviously felt it was safe, and it was. He could barely see her.

"Um, what?"

"You grind your teeth. One of these days, you're going to crack a tooth."

Bo trained his gaze on the road. If she didn't stop talking, he'd growl at her for sure and certain. "You don't need to worry about my teeth. I'm fine."

"You'll live longer if you have healthy teeth. The dentist told me. That's why I get my teeth cleaned once a year."

Bo bit his tongue until he couldn't resist any longer. "You hate the dentist."

He could almost hear her mouth snap shut. She raised the tissue to her face and coughed again.

She was quiet for another five minutes. "Bo?"

She'd startled him again. Why was she still talking when one slip of the tongue would risk her secret? Omi wasn't stupid. "What?"

"Why . . . why do you like me?"

Bo cocked an eyebrow. His temper was wearing thinner and thinner, and this night was getting stranger and stranger. He didn't want to answer that question. Right now, he was too mad at Ruth to remember why he liked her and too hurt to put his loss into words. This might be a hilarious joke to Ruth and Omi, but to him it was humiliating, even though he hadn't fallen for their trick. If they wanted to make fun of his feelings for Ruth, he wouldn't give them more fuel for their fire. "I don't want to talk about it."

"*Ach*," Omi said. "Okay." She turned away from him and stared out the window.

In a few minutes, they reached Ruth and Omi's house. Their *dat* always left the lanterns on the porch lit when Ruth and Omi came home after dark. The gesture said "I love you" as sure as snow fell in Wisconsin.

The minute Bo stopped the buggy, Omi jumped out as if her dress was on fire—or, more accurately, *Ruth*'s dress was on fire. Bo wasn't going to let her get away so easily. He jumped out and raced after her. Luckily, he caught up to her before she reached the porch. "Wait."

Omi stopped, though he could tell she did it reluctantly. She was on the verge of escape. "*Denki* for taking me home. I should go in and make myself a mustard plaster."

"*Jah*, a mustard plaster is the very thing," he said, taking her hand gently in his and caressing her knuckles with his thumb. She trembled at his touch, and he almost pulled away, suddenly feeling guilty for the trick he was about to play on both *schwesteren*. But his anger and his wounded pride got the better of him. He lowered his head so his mouth was mere inches from hers. "Can I kiss you?" he whispered. Would Ruth be mad when she found out? Amused? He didn't know, but he did know that he wanted her to have some sort of strong reaction, no matter what it was. She wasn't the only one who could toy with other people's emotions.

"You . . . you . . . but," Omi stuttered breathlessly, as if she'd just run a very long distance. "But I'm sick."

"I don't care. Please let me kiss you."

An uneasy emotion traveled across her face then disappeared. Sighing, she turned up her face expectantly and closed her eyes. "*Jah.* You may kiss me."

Guilt grabbed him around the throat and nearly choked him, but he'd already made his decision and he wouldn't back down now, no matter how ashamed he felt. He placed his hands on either side of her face, moving closer and closer until he felt her breath on his cheek. She smelled so *gute*, like citrus and coconut and warm skies. He drew back in surprise as his gut clenched and his heart raced. He wasn't supposed to have that kind of reaction to a girl who was playing a nasty trick on him, but there it was. He brought his lips down on hers and kissed her tenderly, despite the rage and the guilt and the longing all swimming together in his head. She snaked her arms around his neck and pulled him closer, and fireworks and rockets went off behind his eyes. He held his breath as yearning washed over him like a giant wave on the lake that capsized boats and leveled sandcastles.

When they separated, he felt giddy, as if every piece of himself had scattered to the wind like a bag of feathers. Omi looked just as *ferhoodled* as he felt. A light glowed behind her eyes, and an affectionate smile formed slowly on her lips.

For a few seconds, they stood staring at each other, caught somewhere between reality and their own private world. Bo thought he might be perfectly happy forever in this private world, but Omi suddenly lost her smile, as if the vacation was over and it was time to do the laundry. "Bo, I have something I need to tell you."

The way she said it, like she felt so horrible about it,

shook him out of his stupor. Her expression made him feel guilty, which in turn reminded him why he had been mad to begin with, which reminded him that he had just behaved very badly. To cover his pride and his shame, he turned his anger outward. "I already know," he snapped.

Her eyes widened. "Know what?"

He clenched his teeth until they made a scraping sound in his mouth. Just in time he remembered his resolve to let his anger cool. "*Guten owed*, Omi. Ruth knows where to find me, if she even wants to."

"She does. It was just a funny trick, nothing more."

Bo didn't want to hear about Ruth's feelings. He turned on his heels and marched to the buggy. "Not funny at all, Omi."

"You're going to break a tooth someday," Omi said weakly. "And I'm wonderful sorry."

He didn't turn around.

# Chapter 4

Omi paused in the hallway and listened to Emma Helmuth sing her *buplie*, Lindy, to sleep. Emma had a lilting, delicate voice that was perfect for quiet lullabies and singing babies to sleep. "*Sleep, my child, and peace attend thee, all through the night. Guardian angels God will lend thee, all through the night.*"

Omi flinched as a deep bass voice joined Emma's on a harmony part. Omi hadn't realized that Ben was in the *buplie*'s room with Emma. Ben's multiple sclerosis was thankfully in remission, but it was still an effort for him to walk and eat, and he tired easily. Emma and Ben lived in a small house right next door to his parents, and Ben helped his *dat* and *bruderen* farm the acreage behind the houses. Ben was fully aware that he couldn't pull his weight around the farm, but he didn't seem to spend his days feeling sorry for himself. Instead, he did what he could and graciously let people serve him when his strength gave out. It must have been hard for him, not being able to do more, but Omi admired him for not letting his pride get in the way of his family's well-being. It took a strong man to receive help he wished he didn't have to take.

Omi listened to the singing for a few more minutes then ambled downstairs to the kitchen to start the dishes. She'd put Mary, the three-year-old, to bed earlier, and now the house was still except for the sound of the rocking chair creaking back and forth on the floor above and the soft melody of Emma's lullaby wafting down the stairs.

Normally, Omi loved the fifteen minutes of quiet after *die kinner* had gone to sleep and Ben and Emma tidied things upstairs and spent some time together. But tonight, the quiet left too much room for unwelcome thoughts of Bo Helmuth, pretend coughing, and that shocking, inappropriate, *wunderbarr* kiss.

Omi pressed her fingers to her lips. They were still tingling almost twenty-four hours later. Should she feel guilty about how much she enjoyed that kiss? Had she betrayed Ruth's trust by letting Bo kiss her? She frowned. Bo had known it was her all along. Why had he kissed her? Was it to teach her a lesson? Make her feel guilty or foolish? She was bewildered and ashamed and confused. And wildly angry, though she had no right to be. Bo might have known she was Omi all along, but she had deceived him first.

*Ach!* Her feelings were a jumble of reds and pinks and blacks, browns, and purples. Ruth had sneaked into their room late last night, and Omi had pretended to be asleep because she didn't want to talk about Bo. Ruth didn't even know that Bo had figured out their secret, and Omi would never tell Ruth about the kiss. Was it because she was mad at Ruth for putting her in that awkward position or ashamed that she had let her *schwester*'s boyfriend kiss her?

Omi finished the dishes as quickly and quietly as possible so as not to disturb *die kinner* or the parents. She wiped the counters, took off her work apron, and slid into her coat, though it was warm enough outside now that she almost didn't need it. She dashed off a quick note to Emma, telling her that Mary had gone to the toilet without being told and that they were running low on diapers. Then she slipped out of the house as silently as possible so Emma and Ben could have their privacy. That must have been another hardship of Ben's disability. Emma and Ben were rarely alone in their own home.

Darkness was just beginning to settle over the sky when Omi shut the back door behind her and strolled down the driveway. Emma and Ben lived only a mile from Omi's house, and she usually walked.

Her heart sank when she looked up and saw Bo leaning against his buggy with his arms folded across his chest. Bo sometimes came to Ben and Emma's when Omi was there, but he rarely said more than a cheerful hello before going off to the workshop with Ben or starting on some repair in the house. He didn't know it, but Omi had always looked forward to seeing him. She enjoyed watching him out of the corner of her eye as they both worked, and she loved to hear his voice, even if he wasn't talking to her.

But tonight there was no one in the world she wanted to see less. She would have hurried through the dishes if she had thought for one minute that she'd run into Bo tonight. Surely he wanted to avoid her as much as she wanted to avoid him. She would say a friendly hello, walk right past him, and pretend she hadn't deceived him and they hadn't shared a stunning kiss.

Bo didn't smile, but he didn't frown either, so she had no idea what was on his mind. *Ach, vell*, she had a pretty *gute* idea what was on his mind. She just didn't know if he was angry, hurt, insulted, or amused. Lord willing, he wasn't of a mind to have a conversation with her.

"Omi, I need to talk to you." So much for her dearest hopes.

"I have to get home. It's almost full dark yet."

"I can drive you home."

She should have known he wouldn't take no for an answer. Bo had always been firm and purposeful when he wanted something done. She eyed him, dread and affection warring against each other in her brain. She should probably apologize to him for lying, but she didn't know where to begin, and if she said anything, she feared his thoughts would go right to the kiss, and she most certainly didn't want to talk about that. It had been the best thing that had happened to her so far in her short life, and she didn't want anyone to ruin it for her, especially not Bo.

Omi took a deep breath and steeled herself against whatever Bo had to say. "Okay then?"

He pinned her with a serious glare. "Why did you let me kiss you?"

Of all the things he could have said, Omi hadn't expected that. She searched for a believable excuse because she would never reveal the real reason in a million years. She may have been pretending to be Ruth, but she wasn't Ruth, and she had let him kiss her because she wanted to know what it would feel like to have Bo wrap those strong arms around her and cherish her, even for a minute. But she shouldn't have been so weak. With one kiss she had betrayed Ruth, deceived Bo, and embarrassed herself. No matter which way she studied it, Omi didn't come out looking very *gute*.

She had been quiet for too long. "I . . . I thought you'd get suspicious if I said *nae*."

He frowned and took a step forward. "That's not the reason."

She wanted to lift her chin and chastise him for calling

her a liar, but she'd proven last night that she *was* a liar, so she couldn't really get mad at him for accusing her. When painted into a corner, it was always best to answer a question with a question. "What do you think is the reason then?"

"You and Ruth must have had a *gute* laugh about it."

Her mouth fell open. "You think we traded places as a joke?"

"You said yourself it was just a joke. You wanted to make me look foolish."

She made a face to show him just what she thought of that accusation. "You know me better than that, Bo. I would never play such a mean trick."

Uncertainty traveled across his face. "Ruth would."

"Ruth wouldn't either," Omi insisted, though neither of them necessarily believed it. Ruth could be a little self-centered.

"It offends me that you think I'm so *dumm*."

"Would you stop putting words in my mouth," Omi said. "I don't think you're *dumm*. Why would you say that?"

"Because you thought I wouldn't be able to tell the difference between you and Ruth. You think I'm *dumm*." He glared at her, daring her to contradict him, or maybe hoping she would.

"I told Ruth you'd know it was me."

"Then she's the one who thinks I'm *dumm*?"

Omi growled softly. "Now you're just being contrary for contrariness' sake. Ruth was sure that trading dresses and putting a tissue over my mouth would be enough."

He shook his head. "That's just wishful thinking. You have more freckles than Ruth and your nose is a little different."

"Ruth broke hers three years ago."

"I know. And she has a chicken pox scar on her forehead."

Omi was impressed and a little bit breathless. He really had looked closely at both of them. "I have some chicken pox scars on my back." In horror, she tried to suck the words back, but they were too far gone. She shouldn't talk about scars that were hidden in private places. "Ruth said you'd never know because it was dark in the buggy. You figured it out in a matter of seconds. I don't think you're *dumm*."

He frowned. "Did you tell Ruth we kissed?"

"Of course not." Omi wanted to kick herself for speaking without thinking, because now Bo was going to ask . . .

"Why not?"

Because. Because even though Ruth had been the one to put Omi in an awkward position, she would be upset if she found out Omi had let Bo kiss her and even more upset that Omi didn't regret it. *Ach, vell,* Omi didn't regret the kiss, but she regretted that it wasn't really meant for her and that she had betrayed her *schwester* and deceived Bo. *Jah,* she regretted a lot of things post-kiss, and none of this could be spoken aloud to anyone.

She decided on the answer-a-question-with-a-question strategy. "Why did you kiss me when you knew I wasn't Ruth? It was mean."

"Why was it mean?" He knew that question trick too.

"Because . . . you never should have put me in that position. It made me uncomfortable."

He looked overly concerned. "The kiss made you uncomfortable?"

She shouldn't answer that, but her mouth sometimes ran away from her brain. "*Nae.* Not the kiss."

"You liked it?" One side of his mouth curled upward, but it didn't seem like he was teasing her.

Her face felt so hot, there was probably steam rising from beneath her *kapp.* "It doesn't matter if I liked it."

"I think it does."

Why was he being so difficult? And how was she to make sense of the smile that was slowly growing on his lips? "*Ach*," she huffed. "Fine. I was uncomfortable that I lied to you. I guess it was my own conscience scolding me yet."

"But you liked it?"

Why was he obsessing over the kiss? It was over and done and, to her great regret, would never happen again. "Of course I liked it. Who wouldn't have liked it?" *Ach*, she wanted to crawl into a hole and never come out after letting her mouth run away from her like that.

His smile bloomed like a lawn full of dandelions. "Really?"

She had to divert his attention before she died of embarrassment. "You never answered my question. Why did you kiss me when you knew I wasn't Ruth?"

Success! He folded his arms and gritted his teeth. "I was angry."

"It's a sin to be angry."

"It's a sin to lie."

She nodded, wondering if she could go press her cheek against the cool metal of the light pole across the road. Her face was on fire. "I agree, and I apologize."

For some reason, her apology disarmed him. He sighed in resignation. "I'm sorry too. I shouldn't have gotten mad at you. I was upset that you deceived me." He slumped his shoulders in defeat. "If Ruth doesn't want to be my girlfriend, she should have just told me, instead of hurting me worse by playing a trick."

Omi hated seeing him so low, but it was hard to defend what Ruth had done, or what Omi had done, for that matter. "For sure and certain, Ruth didn't set out to hurt your feelings. She and I are alike that way. Sometimes we just don't think things through very well."

Bo's expression softened. "That's not like you at all, Omi."

Omi lowered her eyes. "Oh."

"Ruth is high-spirited, to be sure. It's one of my favorite things about her. But she can get so caught up in the excitement that she doesn't care about people's feelings. Like you said, sometimes she doesn't think she's doing any harm. Other people are just obstacles to her having fun."

"That's not quite fair," Omi said, out of loyalty to her *schwester*.

"You're right. I mean, she's my girlfriend. I adore Ruth. We all say things we don't mean when we're angry. We also do things we regret when we're angry. Like kiss our girlfriend's *schwester*."

Omi felt the sting of his words clear to her toes. He regretted kissing her. If she didn't get angry, she'd burst into tears. "You should regret it. You knew I wasn't Ruth. Your deception was even worse than mine."

"It was not. I was hurting."

She glared at him. "How do you think I feel? You knew I wasn't Ruth, and you still kissed me. It wonders me why you did."

He hesitated, as if weighing his words carefully. "I kissed you to punish Ruth."

Omi swallowed past the lump in her throat. "It must have been quite unpleasant to kiss Ruth's *schwester* when you really wanted to kiss Ruth."

"I told you, I was angry."

"Oh, I see. Angry enough to kiss *anybody* if it would make Ruth cross."

He seemed less sure of himself now. "I guess so."

"It's too bad our pig didn't wander into the yard. That

would have irritated Ruth to no end. *Vell*, the joke's on you, because I didn't tell Ruth about kissing you, so unless you tell her yourself, she won't even know to be mad. She doesn't know that you know we traded places." She grimaced at the little catch in her voice, but maybe Bo hadn't noticed it. What did it matter if he had? She was just Ruth's *schwester*. Her feelings didn't matter to Bo Helmuth.

Bo fell silent and studied Omi's face as if he was seeing her for the first time. The expression was unnerving at best. Omi took a step back so he couldn't look as closely. "Last night, I realized that I was both angry and surprised that you two had traded places. I was angry at Ruth and surprised that sweet, guileless Omi Coblenz would set out to deceive me."

Omi's indignation melted. Her shame multiplied. "I'm not guileless or sweet. You found that out last night."

"I can see Ruth hatching the plan, but it wonders me why you agreed to it."

He was a hairbreadth away from the truth. She couldn't breathe. She took another step back. "Ruth is my *schwester*. I would rob a bank if she asked me to."

He narrowed his eyes and took a step forward. "I don't think you would. You have more sense and integrity than that." After having just moved toward her, he surprised her when he backed up to his buggy and propped his hand on the front wheel. Another long, uncomfortable silence followed. Could she just walk away? "Omi, do you . . . do you have feelings for me?"

The question knocked the wind right out of her. *Ach!* Had she been that obvious? Had Bo sensed the way she leaned into him when they kissed? Had her racing heart betrayed her? There must be a way to get out of this without incriminating honesty. *When painted into a corner, it was always best to answer a question with a question.* "Why would you ever in a million years think that?"

His voice softened. "Omi, I'm not trying to embarrass you. Do you have feelings for me?"

Okay, the question trick hadn't worked. She'd have to go on the attack. "Do I have feelings for you?"

He nodded, the unmistakable look of sympathy on his face.

That arrogant, proud, selfish *bu*! She wanted to smack him upside the head. *I don't want your pity, Bo Helmuth. I don't want anything from you but the sight of you walking away from me.* "For sure and certain I have feelings for you," she said, clipping her words so he would know exactly what she thought of his pity. "I'm feeling angry and frustrated and disgusted. I'm feeling the urge to push you into a mud puddle. You have a very high opinion of yourself to believe I have feelings for you."

*Vell.* That shut him up but good, probably because he was shocked that Omi would even consider pushing anyone into a mud puddle. He seemed almost disappointed that she hadn't fallen at his feet and declared her undying love. But she would never do that. Bo belonged to Ruth, and the sooner Omi accepted that, the better. "I'm sorry, Omi," he finally said.

Sorry for what? For kissing her? For loving Ruth? For not loving Omi? For unintentionally breaking her heart every day? "I'm sorry too," she said, not even pretending to be mad anymore. It just took too much energy. Nursing the ache in her chest was enough of a burden.

He flinched as if coming out of a deep sleep. "Let me take you home."

The sky was darker now, but Omi wasn't about to go anywhere with him. She stepped around his buggy and onto the road before turning back. "I won't be used as a go-between any more in this little game you and Ruth are playing with each other. If you want to know anything else, talk to Ruth."

*And leave me alone to wallow in what might have been.*

# Chapter 5

Milking the cow was usually a chore Bo enjoyed. He just had to point the cow's teats in the right direction, squeeze hard, and hum a tune to help the cow relax. The stream of milk gave a satisfying ping every time it hit the galvanized bucket, and the mundane nature of the task left his mind free to wander. He worked out a lot of problems in his head while milking cows. Many of the farmers in the area who owned more than two or three cows had invested in milking machines. They were cheap and efficient and easy to use, but Bo was usually more than happy to milk Mammi's cow by hand.

Today, unfortunately, milking the cow gave him too much time to linger over the kiss he and Omi had shared and to regret it all over again. The trouble was, he didn't know why he regretted it so badly. Was it because he'd kissed Omi instead of Ruth? Or because he had enjoyed it a little too much? Or, most troubling of all, what if Ruth found out he'd purposefully kissed Omi? Would she stop liking him? Would she want to break up?

Even though Ruth and Omi had deserved it, he was ashamed of himself for giving in to his anger and kissing

Omi. It smacked of petty revenge, and Bo wasn't usually so small-minded. His only excuse was that he was obsessed with Ruth, and his apprehension had been growing for weeks. What if Ruth didn't like him as much as he liked her? Sometimes he sensed that she grew bored with their conversations or that her mind was somewhere else when they were together. He had hoped he was imagining things, but when Omi had taken Ruth's place at the gathering, all his worst fears seemed to be coming true.

At the same time, he couldn't grasp why he had enjoyed that kiss so much. He was in love with Ruth, not Omi, and the pleasure he took in the kiss felt like disloyalty to Ruth. Bo's bottom lip twitched in amusement. Omi said she liked the kiss. It was an unguarded moment of honesty that he found endearing and unnerving at the same time. He had felt the same way. Who knew a simple kiss with the wrong girl could bring him to his knees and shoot him into the sky at the same time?

Ping, ping, ping went the milk into the bucket.

He was *froh* that Omi didn't seem to have feelings for him. The way she'd kissed him back made him worry that maybe Omi had a crush on him, but she seemed pretty adamant the other night that all she felt for him was disapproval. He supposed he deserved that.

Bo finished milking and sent the cow out to the small, gated area behind the barn. He and some of the other cousins and siblings took turns milking the cow every day for Mammi and Dawdi. Dawdi insisted on milking the cow in the mornings, but one of the grandchildren milked for their grandparents every afternoon. Bo's day was Tuesday. He carried the full bucket of milk to the house and knocked on the door.

"*Cum reu*," Mammi called from inside.

Bo opened the door and stopped in his tracks. Mammi and Dawdi were perched side by side on two kitchen chairs that had been pulled away from the table. They sat with arms outstretched in front of them and palms facing inward. "Did I interrupt something?" Should he set the milk inside the door and run away as fast as he could?

"*Hallo*, Bo," Mammi said between shallow breaths. "Give us just a second. We must do our Sun Salutation." She and Dawdi lifted their arms until they were directly over their heads then brought their palms together and lowered their hands level with their chests as if they were getting ready to pray. They both inhaled loudly, opened their arms wide, then dropped them to their sides while exhaling even more loudly. Mammi grinned at Bo. "Felty thinks we should try a new hobby, so we're doing sitting yoga. It's supposed to be good for your circulation, and"— she gave Dawdi a pointed look—"it keeps you busy so you won't be tempted to meddle in other people's lives."

"Sitting yoga," Bo said. "I've never heard of it, but it sounds like a fun new hobby."

Mammi looked over her right shoulder and hooked her elbow behind the back of her chair. "It's not that fun. I'd rather meddle, but your *dawdi* suggested it, and I didn't want to disappoint him."

Dawdi mirrored Mammi's movements. "I appreciate that, Annie-banannie. This is almost as fun as the license plate game."

They both turned forward and placed their hands in their laps. "This is called Tall Mountain," Mammi said. "It makes you feel like you're out in nature."

Bo poured the milk through a strainer and into two large white pitchers on the counter while Mammi and Dawdi lifted their arms into a T shape and rocked from side to side.

"This is Seated Half Moon pose," Mammi said. "You see, it's all about nature."

Bo smiled. At least Mammi and Dawdi were thinking about the great outdoors, even if they weren't actually getting there. He finished with the milk and rinsed out the bucket. After that, he wasn't sure what to do. Mammi usually invited him in for a cookie and a glass of newly milked milk. The cookies were never very *gute* and the milk was warm, but it was a tradition and a *gute* opportunity to check up on Mammi and Dawdi. "*Ach*, *vell*, I guess I'll be going now."

Mammi leaped from her chair as if she'd been poked by a pin. "*Ach*, *nae*, Bo. We can do sitting yoga anytime."

"Except when we're standing," Dawdi said.

Mammi pushed her yoga chair back under the table. "*Cum*, Bo. Sit down and have some milk and cookies. I made my famous BM cookies. I know how you like them."

Bo forced his most delighted smile onto his face. "Sounds *appeditlich*, Mammi." Mammi's BM cookies tasted like sweetened sawdust, so it wasn't too hard to gag them down, but they were famous—or infamous—for what they did to your intestines. BM stood for "bowel movement," and Mammi's BM cookies were named for their efficiency. Bo couldn't eat more than one, or he got in big trouble. He'd learned that lesson the hard way.

Mammi set three glasses and three small plates on the table along with one of the pitchers of lukewarm milk and a heaping plate of cookies that looked like miniature cow pies.

Dawdi picked up a cookie and took a bite. "How are things going on the farm? Your *dat* says you want to plant soybeans this year."

"*Jah*. Soybeans and feed corn."

"You can never go wrong with feed corn," Dawdi said.

Mammi poured everyone some milk. "There's not much to say about soybeans, is there?" Mammi found farm talk very dull.

"There's a hundred things to say about soybeans, Annie."

Mammi ignored Dawdi, sat down, and picked up her glass, her eyes twinkling with some grandmotherly secret. "Who wants to talk about soybeans when we can talk about that adorable Coblenz girl Bo is dating?" She leaned forward. "It wonders me if there isn't some trouble brewing."

Bo nearly choked on the one bite of cookie he'd taken. What did Mammi know? Had Omi and Ruth been gossiping? "Trouble?"

Mammi studied his face, and the wrinkles around her eyes bunched together. "*Ach.* I sensed it weeks ago. What has happened?"

Bo tried to lose whatever expression had given him away. "Have you heard something?"

"*Nae*, but my toe never lies. It started aching, and I said, 'Felty, Bo needs our help.'"

Bo sighed. He usually kept things to himself. Why burden anyone with his own problems? "It's really nothing, Mammi."

Mammi didn't seem offended. "*Ach*, Bo, your feelings are wonderful important to us. Let us help you."

"Let's do some more yoga poses," Dawdi interjected.

"Felty, how can you think of yoga at a time like this?"

"A time like what?"

"A time when Bo desperately needs our help." She turned to Bo and gave him her you-can-tell-your-*mammi*-anything smile. "Now, Bo, your *dawdi* and I have gained a little bit of wisdom in our more than eighty years on the Earth. A hundred and seventy-two if you add our years together. That's a very long time. Aside from your *mamm* and *dat*, we love you more than any two people in the world love you. It couldn't hurt to get our advice."

Dawdi raised his hand. "I would like to stay out of it."

Mammi nodded. "Okay, then. You will only get eighty-five years of experience instead of a hundred-and-seventy-two. But that's still quite a bit."

"You were always so *gute* at math, Annie-banannie."

"*Denki*, Felty. Addition is one of my talents." Mammi took another bite of cookie and smiled at Bo. "Felty and I are very *gute* at keeping secrets."

Dawdi nodded. "We were the only ones who knew your cousin Cassie was thinking of jumping the fence before she did it."

"We knew that Mary Anne had moved out of her house before Jethro did," Mammi said. "And Felty kept the secret that Ben had MS for weeks before Ben got up the courage to tell Emma."

Bo exhaled a deep breath. It looked like he wasn't going to be able to dodge Mammi's curiosity. "I think I'm in love with Ruth."

He hadn't expected this news to take Mammi and Dawdi by surprise. It didn't. Mammi took a sip of milk. "Don't rush into anything. Be certain before you get engaged."

"Now, Annie-banannie, don't make the boy doubt himself."

That was exactly what Bo was doing. "Sometimes I think Ruth doesn't like me as much as I like her, and I get nervous she's going to find someone else."

"I see." Mammi was nice that way. She tried not to interrupt, but she also wanted to make sure you knew she was still listening.

"And then . . . well, last week something happened that

made me think she wants to break up with me, and I'm even more worried."

Mammi leaned in, her eyes wide, her lips tightly pressed together.

"I always take Ruth home from gatherings, but last week at the gathering she hid in the bathroom."

"That's not a *gute* hiding place," Mammi said. "It's the first place people look."

"Omi went in the bathroom to fetch Ruth, but when she came out, she was wearing Ruth's dress and pretending to be Ruth. She didn't think I could tell the difference. I didn't want to say anything while all those people were watching at the gathering, so I just took her home."

Mammi lifted an eyebrow. "You took Ruth home?"

"*Nae*, I took Omi home, but she was pretending to be Ruth, so Ruth thought that *I* thought I was taking Ruth home."

"*Ach, du lieva.*" Mammi pressed three fingers to her forehead. "So Omi pretended to be Ruth, and you took Ruth home, but she was really Omi. What happened to Ruth?"

Bo clenched his teeth. "That's what I want to know."

Dawdi propped his chin in his hand. "You think Ruth has another *bu* on the side?"

"I don't know, but I do know that she didn't want to go home with me. I just . . . I just like her so much, and she tricked me. You don't do that to someone you love."

Mammi seemed more and more confused. "Does Ruth know that you know it was Omi and not Ruth?"

Bo shook his head. "I'm afraid if I confront her, she'll get defensive and break up with me."

Dawdi tapped his palm on the table. "You'll never have a *gute* relationship without honesty, and honesty goes both ways. You've got to tell her that you know she and Omi traded places, and if she really cares for you, she will be eager to explain herself. There is no love without trust."

Mammi's smile lit up the whole room. "Felty, I'm *froh* you have decided not to stay out of it." She reached over and wrapped her fingers around Dawdi's hand. "Felty is right, Bo. Trust is the secret to a long marriage. And raisins. Trust and raisins are the secret to a long and happy marriage."

Bo winced. "There's more."

"More?" Mammi beamed. "I love it when there's more. Like a second helping of pie."

"I was angry that night, knowing Ruth had tried to trick me."

"Understandably so," Dawdi said.

"I guess I wasn't thinking straight, but I wanted to make Omi regret what she'd done, so I kissed her, even though I knew she wasn't Ruth."

Mammi deflated like a balloon. "Second helpings can give you a stomachache." She rubbed that spot on her forehead again. "So let me get this straight."

"I don't think that's possible, Banannie."

Mammi's brows inched together in concentration. "Omi pretended to be Ruth, but you weren't fooled. You were mad, so you kissed Omi. She thought you meant to kiss Ruth, but you actually meant to kiss Omi pretending to be Ruth."

Bo thought about that for a minute. "*Jah*, Mammi. That's about right."

Mammi leaned even closer. "So, what did you think?"

"About what?"

Her eyes sparkled with excitement. "About the kiss. Was it a *gute* kiss, or would it have been better if Ruth had been the one you kissed instead of Omi pretending to be Ruth?"

Bo did not want to wade into those waters. He was confused enough as it was. "It doesn't matter. I've made a mess of things."

Dawdi stroked his beard. "It seems to me the mess is Ruth's."

"Ruth is a very sweet girl," Mammi said, her eyes aglow with something that looked suspiciously like excitement. "She's a little self-centered, but life cures everyone of that. Omi is a *gute* girl too. Sometimes she brings me day-old from the bakery, and then she stays and sweeps my floor. But she's not flashy like Ruth."

Dawdi cocked an eyebrow. "Flashy? That's a fancy word."

Mammi turned to Bo. "Is that why you like Ruth? Because she's flashy?"

"I wouldn't say she's flashy, though she does tend to attract attention. She's just full of life and happiness. She acts like every day is the most special and exciting day of her life. I like how I feel when I'm with her."

"I know what you mean," Dawdi said. "That is how Annie makes me feel."

Mammi giggled like a teenager. "*Ach*, Felty, you are such a tease." She grew slightly more serious and looked at Bo. "It seems Ruth doesn't care about anyone's feelings but her own."

"That's not true," Bo protested half-heartedly. He wanted Ruth to care about his feelings as much as he cared about hers, but maybe she didn't care at all. "Most of the time, I'm pretty sure I'm not *gute* enough for her. She's so *wunderbarr*, and I'm just plain and boring."

Dawdi seemed surprised. "That's not true. My grandchildren are *gute* enough for anybody, even Ruth Coblenz, and don't you forget it."

Bo wasn't about to argue with Dawdi. It didn't matter

what Dawdi thought, or what Bo thought for that matter. It only mattered what Ruth thought. "I . . . I think she cares for me. We've been seeing each other for four months."

"Of course she cares for you," Dawdi said, just as half-heartedly.

Bo wasn't fooled. Dawdi didn't believe any such thing. He was looking at Bo as if Bo were a homeless, hungry puppy caught in a rainstorm.

Mammi gazed at Bo in concern. "For sure and certain Ruth is a pretty girl, just like her *schwester* Omi. Omi makes her cinnamon rolls with raisins. I like her a lot." She stood and marched into the great room, where she opened a drawer in the end table and pulled out two cherry-red, fuzzy pot holders. She brought them back to the table and set them in front of Bo. "It wonders me if I shouldn't do a little spying."

"Spying?"

"*Jah.*" Mammi sat and tapped her finger to her chin. "I'll do some snooping around to see if I can find out what Ruth was doing the night she traded places with Omi."

"I don't want anybody to know, Mammi."

Mammi looked deeply offended. "Of course not. I won't tell a soul about any of this, but it's amazing what you can hear when people think you aren't listening. They always underestimate us old *fraaen.*"

"I don't think anybody would ever underestimate you, Annie-banannie," Dawdi said.

"*Denki*, Felty, but you love me, so you're not exactly unbiased." She pointed to the fuzzy pot holders. "In the meantime, take these pot holders. They're sure to make any girl fall in love with you."

One side of Bo's mouth curled upward involuntarily. "How do they work? Do I need to wear them?"

Mammi grinned as if Bo was the wittiest *bu* in the

whole world. "You don't wear them. You give them to the girl you love, and she'll fall in love with you."

Bo was sure pot holders didn't work that way, but it wouldn't hurt to do as Mammi suggested. Who didn't appreciate a set of cherry-red pot holders? If Ruth didn't want them, she could pass them on to Omi. For sure and certain Omi could use them at the bakery.

Without warning, Mammi stood and quickly cleared the cookies and milk from the table. "I don't mean to rush you off, Bo, but I've got to get to the bakery to see what I can find out. And buy a cinnamon roll. Nobody makes them like Omi." She gave Dawdi a pointed look. "How could I even think of starting a new hobby when Bo needs me so badly? You'll have to do the Tree Pose by yourself."

Dawdi shook his head. "It won't be the same without you, Annie. I'll just wait in the Chopped-Down-Tree position until you get back."

# Chapter 6

Omi breathed in the *wunderbarr* smell of fresh air and newly cut wood and smiled. What a gloriously beautiful day for a barn raising. The skies were clear, and the temperature hovered just below sixty degrees. Much nicer than putting up a barn in July or August, and the plowing season hadn't begun, so there were plenty of men who wanted to help.

Ruth, Omi, and Marilyn set up one of the serving tables and covered it with white butcher paper. The men and *buwe* had been hard at work since eight this morning, and more than a dozen *fraaen* and girls were busily preparing lunch for fifty. Omi had brought four dozen cinnamon rolls plus four loaves of bread. Ruth had made a whole quart of church spread and cored and cut about fifty apples.

Omi had always loved watching a barn go up in a day, but she tried not to stare in that direction because Bo was everywhere she looked. He climbed ladders and nailed planks and used his power screwdriver a hundred times. He was strong and capable and breathtakingly handsome, and he had no interest in Omi whatsoever. Why in the world couldn't she forget him and find someone less *wunderbarr*, less considerate, and less obsessed with her *schwester*?

Even though Bo had made it clear how mad he was at both the *schwesteren* for playing that trick on him, he had been to their house to visit Ruth twice since then, and he'd acted as if none of it had happened. Was he waiting for a *gute* time to confront Ruth, or was he reluctant to talk to her about it for fear it would hurt their relationship? He seemed to have no trouble telling Omi exactly how he felt. Maybe he was less willing to make trouble with Ruth. Or maybe he had forgiven and forgotten? Omi told herself she didn't care. If Bo was too afraid of Ruth to talk to her about it, then he deserved what he got, which was a whole barrel full of insecurity and distrust.

"Let's put two of everything on the tables so the men can go down both sides," Rebecca Bontreger said, smoothing her hand along the clean, white butcher paper.

"*Gute* idea," Ruth said, glancing toward the road that ran in front of the Bontregers' house. She'd been doing that for twenty minutes, and Omi suspected she was looking for someone. It wasn't Bo, because Bo was in the other direction, and Ruth didn't seem to care about looking at him.

Omi would just have to do the looking for her.

Marilyn helped Omi set out paper plates and napkins while Ruth worked her way up the other end of the table with two plates of cinnamon rolls and two bowls of sliced apples. Marilyn had not stopped smiling since the start of the barn raising. Her boyfriend, Tyler, from Pennsylvania, was planning to meet her here in an hour. He was coming to Wisconsin specifically to spend time with her, and she looked positively giddy. Naturally, Omi was exceedingly happy for her. There was nothing so beautiful as a girl in love, unless the girl was Ruth. Omi found Ruth's gushing as annoying as fingernails on a chalkboard.

Marilyn glanced toward the Bontregers' apple tree. "*Ach*, Omi, look who Danny Mischler is flirting with. I thought he was interested in you."

Omi didn't really care about Danny Mischler, but she humored Marilyn by peering in that direction. Danny leaned against the apple tree with his arms folded while Sadie King seemed to be talking his ear off. "I'm not interested in Danny," Omi said, her lips twitching upward. "But it looks like Sadie is."

"Omi, how do you expect to find a husband if you don't at least give *die buwe* a little encouragement?" Marilyn thought getting a *bu* was easy. It was love at first sight for her and Tyler.

"Ruth will have to get married first," Omi said. "I'm everybody's second choice."

Ruth huffed her disapproval. "*Ach*, Omi, I've never heard anything so silly in my life. Besides, *die buwe* know I'm spoken for. You can take your pick."

What would Ruth say if she knew that Omi's first pick was Bo Helmuth? How would Ruth react if she knew Bo and Omi had kissed? "Are you saying you'll gladly give me your leftovers?"

Ruth giggled. "Okay, you're right. It doesn't sound so romantic when you say it like that."

Marilyn went to the house to find some paper towels. Omi opened two big bags of potato chips and set them next to the apples. "Do you think we should put these chips in a bowl? They'd probably be easier to get to."

Ruth didn't answer. She was watching the road. A faded red sedan pulled off the pavement and stopped.

Ruth caught her breath. "There he is! *Ach*, Omi, he said he'd come."

Omi narrowed her eyes. "Ruth," she said, with a tinge of warning in her voice.

Ruth's smile was like the sunshine breaking through the clouds. "He's so fun, and he doesn't mind driving all the way up here to see me. He said we could go driving around Bonduel and maybe even stop at the Walmart in Shawano."

"Ruth," Omi said again, more urgently this time. "You're here to help with the barn-raising supper. You can't just leave. Besides, you'll hurt Bo's feelings."

"*Ach*, Omi, Bo won't care. He won't even notice."

"Of course he'll care."

"We're not married yet, and there's nothing wrong with having a little fun."

Omi gritted her teeth, even though she'd cautioned Bo against doing such a thing. "He's your boyfriend. Don't you care how he feels?"

Ruth smoothed down the hair at the base of her neck. "Come on, Omi. You're making a mountain out of a molehill. Bo won't care, and if he does, well then, he shouldn't. He's not in charge of my life. I'll only be gone for a few hours."

Omi started grasping at straws. She motioned toward the table. "We're going to need your help. We have to feed fifty men."

Ruth was too distracted and determined to give heed to any scolding Omi might give her. "They're not babies. They can feed themselves. We've already put out all the food, and there are several *fraaen* with nothing to do. You won't even miss me."

"Bo will miss you."

Ruth was already halfway to Elam's car. She glanced at

Omi. "I'll be back soon." Grinning like a cat, she turned and ran the rest of the way, as if she couldn't get away fast enough.

Omi's heart sank. She loved her *schwester*, but sometimes Ruth was blind and selfish. Unfortunately, Bo was blind too. Blind and devoted.

With Rebecca Bontreger's help, Omi and Marilyn finished setting the food on the table. They put lunch meat on plates with mayonnaise and mustard so the men could make their own sandwiches. There were two serving tables, each with more or less the same things on them. Rebecca assigned Omi to keep watch over the first table and refill plates when they ran low.

At exactly twelve thirty, the men stopped what they were doing and congregated around the tables. The bishop led them in prayer, and they lined up to eat. Omi had secretly kept her eye on Bo the whole time, so she saw him approaching her even before he made himself a plate of food.

"*Hallo*, Omi," he said. His smile wasn't as wide as usual, probably because things couldn't be the same between them since that kiss. Omi never wanted to go back to before Bo had kissed her. It had been the best day of her life, but the memory was bittersweet, because Bo loved Ruth, and he would never love Omi and certainly never kiss her again.

"*Hallo*, Bo. You sure are working hard on that barn."

"We're ready to start on the roof after lunch." He looked toward the house. "Where's Ruth? I thought I saw her earlier, but I can't find her."

For sure and certain, Omi wasn't going to lie for Ruth. But she didn't want to hurt Bo's feelings either. "She left." Short and true, while not telling Bo much of anything.

Bo's expression clouded over. "I see." He watched her

for a few seconds, probably wondering if she would say more about Ruth, but Omi couldn't say much without getting righteously indignant, so she closed her mouth and smiled as if she wasn't annoyed with her *schwester*. Bo finally gave up waiting for more of an explanation and cleared his throat. "*Ach, vell, denki*, Omi. I should eat so I don't delay everybody else."

Omi nodded and watched him walk away, dejection oozing from his skin like sweat. Should she have told him about Ruth and Elam? Was the truth more painful than not knowing? She drew her brows together and bit her bottom lip. She had told Bo she wouldn't be the go-between for him and Ruth, but here she was, trying to protect Bo's feelings and save Ruth's relationship. Neither was her job. This was going to stop now.

After everyone finished eating, Omi didn't even help clean up. She had to say what she had to say, and she had to say it now before her anger cooled and she lost her nerve. Bo was near the tall stack of wood, about to get an armful of two-by-fours to use on the roof. "Bo," Omi said, adding a sharp edge to her voice so he knew she was serious—so he knew that she wouldn't carry his heartache or spare his feelings. He was Ruth's boyfriend, and Omi wasn't going to care more about Ruth's relationship with Bo than Ruth did.

Bo turned and frowned at her, as if it was Omi's fault that Ruth had left the barn raising. "Omi?" He was just as abrupt and even more irritated.

"I need to tell you something."

He glanced behind him. "I've got to get on the roof. Andy Lapp thinks he's forty years younger than he is, and if I don't climb up there, he'll do it."

Omi tried not to be angry or hurt that Bo couldn't be bothered talking to her. To him, she was just another girl in the *gmayna* who happened to be related to his girlfriend. "It won't take long."

Bo propped his hands on his hips. "Okay. What do you want to say?"

"You and Ruth can have whatever strange relationship you want, but I'm not going to get in the middle of it anymore."

His frown lines etched deeper into his face. "What do you mean we have a strange relationship?"

She took a step back. "Maybe that's not the right word. What matters is that I'm not going to get involved with it."

He stepped forward, moving like a cat stalking its prey, graceful and deadly. "Go on. I want to hear why you think we have a strange relationship."

"I didn't mean it like that."

He looked ready to pounce. "I think you did."

Fine. If he wanted the truth, he was going to get it. "Your girlfriend played a very mean trick on you, and you act like you're the one who should apologize. She goes off with other boys, and you mope around like it's your fault."

The catlike confidence wavered, then shattered. His expression wilted. His shoulders slumped. "She goes off with other boys?"

"I'm not going to feel guilty about Ruth's behavior anymore. You can do what you want, but I wash my hands of the whole thing. Raymond Fisher's cousin from Cashton has a car, and I suppose he's very handsome. The night of the gathering, he invited Ruth to go for a ride. That's why she asked me to trade places. She didn't want to tell you."

Bo shifted his feet. "Okay?"

Omi pretended not to notice how his voice cracked, reminding herself that she'd done nothing wrong. This wasn't her guilt to carry. "Elam came again today, and he took Ruth to Walmart. She said you wouldn't mind."

Bo swiped his hand across his mouth. "Did she?"

Omi had resolved to stop caring about Bo's feelings, but she wasn't like Ruth, and she hated to see him so upset. "I'm . . . I'm sorry, Bo. I don't approve of how Ruth treats you, but it's not my fault, and I can't carry the responsibility for it anymore."

"I know." He looked down at his hands, big, strong, worker's hands layered with calluses. "Do you think she wants to break up?"

It irritated Omi that he would ask such a thing. Bo should have broken up with Ruth after she and Omi pulled that trading-places trick. Why hadn't he? Did he really love Ruth that much and respect himself that little? As she'd told Bo, it was a strange relationship. "I don't know if she wants to break up."

"You're her *schwester*. I want to know what you think."

Omi couldn't swallow. "She . . . Ruth is excited about Elam because he has a car, but she says she wants to marry you."

He smiled doubtfully. "Really? She told you that?"

Omi found it impossible to utter a word. She nodded instead.

"Ruth likes cars, for sure and certain." His smile grew like a weed. "She should have explained it to me. I would have understood." Bo could tell himself that if it made him feel better, but Omi didn't believe it for a second.

Omi eyed him in puzzlement. "Why do you like my *schwester*?" She winced. It sounded like an accusation.

He seemed surprised by the question and maybe a little defensive. "Ruth is fun to be around. There's always excitement when I'm with Ruth—it's electric. She's enthusiastic and energetic and always laughing, always ready for a *gute* time."

Omi swallowed hard. She'd asked for it, even though

his answer felt like a shard of glass in her heart. Ruth was all the things Omi was not. All the things Bo wanted in a *fraa*. "*Jah*. I . . . mean, of course you like her. She's fun." *And I'm not.*

Bo must not have liked what he saw on her face. "There's nothing wrong with having fun, Omi. After my *bruder* Ben was diagnosed with MS, I promised myself I would never pass up an opportunity to enjoy life before I die. Ruth is the kind of person I want to be. That's why I like being around her."

"But she tricked you." Omi felt disloyal saying it, but Bo was being willfully stupid.

"You tricked me too," Bo said.

"I'm not your girlfriend."

"That's no excuse."

Omi lowered her eyes. Bo would give Ruth the benefit of the doubt where he wouldn't even budge with Omi. She should just quit talking. Ruth was her favorite, dearest *schwester*, and here Omi was, trying to convince Bo that Ruth didn't deserve him. But Omi deserved him even less. She was a wicked girl, and she suddenly felt very ashamed of herself.

Bo sighed. "Ruth and I just need to be honest with each other. I've got to tell her about the kiss."

Omi felt as if she was choking. "There's no *gute* reason to tell her."

Bo squared his shoulders. "There is no love without trust."

"There will be no love at all if Ruth finds out you knew it was me."

"She'll understand. We just need to be honest with each other."

Omi couldn't argue with that, even though she wanted to. When she found out, Ruth would be annoyed with

Omi, not Bo. Bo had behaved badly, but so had Omi. Bo would be easier to forgive. How dare he throw her under the bus? as the *Englisch* would say.

Bo picked up a stack of two-by-fours and hoisted them onto his shoulder, as cheerful as she'd seen him for a month. He felt better about everything. Omi felt worse. She took a few steps toward him to tell him what she thought about his newfound integrity, when Bo turned suddenly, swinging the two-by-fours around as he pivoted. She was too close, and the end of one of the two-by-fours conked her hard in the forehead and sent her sprawling backward into the dirt.

"*Ach*, Omi! Are you okay?"

# Chapter 7

Omi opened her eyes. Four people, including Bo, hovered over her like vultures waiting for something to die. "Are you okay?" Bo said again, his face twisted with concern. "I'm so sorry."

Omi groaned. The skin from her hairline to her eye socket felt as if it was on fire. She grabbed the closest thing to anchor herself on, which happened to be Bo's knee, and tried to pull herself up. Bo shoved her back to the dirt, and before she could slap his hand away, the world started spinning. "*Ach, du lieva.* I think you gave me a concussion."

"He gave you more than that," said Wayne Hostetler, who was kneeling to Bo's right. "It's going to be quite a scar."

Omi tried to sit up again, but Bo was determined to keep her down. The urge to smack him was almost overpowering. "You gave me a scar?"

"I'm sorry, Omi. You came at me at just the wrong moment."

"I came at you? You make it sound like I was on the attack."

He tilted his head to one side. "Were you?"

She tried to touch her forehead, but Bo grabbed her wrist. He was really starting to make her mad. *Ach*, *vell*, she was already mad at him and his blind devotion to Ruth, but now she was even madder.

"Don't, Omi."

"Let go." She yanked hard enough that he released her, maybe out of fear for his life.

"Don't touch it, Omi. You're bleeding. Mary is bringing some napkins."

Omi did as she was told, though she would rather eat a worm than agree with Bo Helmuth about anything. She could tell there was more than a little blood. It trickled down both sides of her forehead and into her hair, and another dribble was slowly making its way toward her eyebrow. She'd attracted a crowd of eight or nine men who should have been working on the barn, plus Sadie King and Marilyn, who both looked as if they might faint.

Rebecca was soon by her side with a fluffy white towel. She laid it gently on Omi's forehead, and Omi winced. "*Cum*," Rebecca said, holding out a hand. "Can you sit up?"

"*Jah.*"

Bo took Omi's other hand, and he and Rebecca slowly pulled Omi to a sitting position. Omi leaned forward and pressed the towel to her head as the blood seemed to flow with renewed vigor. A trickle escaped the towel and dripped from the bridge of her nose onto her apron. "How do you feel?" Rebecca said.

"Like I need to wash my hair."

Marilyn grimaced. "*Ach*, Omi, he got you but *gute*."

Wayne was never without an opinion. "You need to go to the hospital for stitches."

Omi wasn't going to agree to that until she saw for

herself how bad the damage was. She pulled the towel away from her forehead. "How deep is it?"

Marilyn bit her bottom lip. "Wonderful deep."

Bo leaned in for a closer look and frowned. "It looks to be about three inches long. I can't tell how deep. There's too much blood."

Omi returned the towel to her forehead and closed her eyes. Her entire head throbbed with every heartbeat. Should she go to the hospital or home? Hospitals were expensive. Dat would not be happy, but if she went home without Ruth, Mamm would be mad. "I don't want to go to the hospital."

"You're in no condition to make that decision," Wayne said.

Omi bit her tongue and reminded herself that no good would come of being rude to Wayne.

"I've already called a driver," said someone behind Omi. She wasn't sure who it was, but she sounded like someone sensible and calm.

Omi turned the towel over to the clean side and pressed it against her forehead. "I guess I can decide when I get to the car." Hospitals were expensive, but going to a hospital was probably better than dying.

"I'll go with you," Marilyn said.

Omi shook her head as best she could while it was buried in a towel. "*Nae*, Marilyn. Tyler will be here soon. You don't want to miss him."

Marilyn pressed her lips together. "Are you sure?"

Bo brushed his hand down Omi's arm, making her heart race faster than it already was. She growled to herself. Couldn't she stay mad at him for more than two minutes? "I'll go. I'm the one who clocked her with a two-by-four. I want to make sure she's okay."

Wayne nodded. "It was your fault. You should be ashamed of yourself."

Wayne had a special talent of always making you feel worse about everything. It all just seemed so funny all of a sudden. A giggle escaped Omi's lips. And then another. And then she couldn't stop.

"She's delirious," Wayne said.

Omi tried to communicate between fits of laughter. "I'm . . . o . . . kay . . . really."

Marilyn smoothed her hand up and down Omi's arm. "Really, Omi. I'll come if you need me."

Omi inclined her head toward Bo. "I'll be okay." Even though being alone with Bo would be as unnerving as getting hit in the head with a two-by-four.

Rebecca took her hand. "The car is here. Can you stand up?"

"I think so."

With Rebecca on one side and Bo on the other, Omi pushed herself to her feet. She managed to stand up only to have another dizzy spell. Bo didn't hesitate when she slumped against his chest. He swept her into his arms and headed toward the road where the car was waiting. Omi wedged her towel in the space between Bo's chin and his collarbone, propped her forehead against the towel, then wrapped her arms around his neck. His hold was firm and solid, and she had no fear whatsoever of being dropped. She closed her eyes to better enjoy his earthy scent and the sound of his slow, rhythmic breathing.

"You smell *gute*," she said, then immediately regretted it. She really should stop thinking out loud, especially with her *schwester*'s boyfriend.

There was a slight pause in his stride. "So do you."

He thought she smelled *gute*? That couldn't be true. She

mostly smelled like blood. "I'm sorry, but I got blood on your shirt."

"I'm sorry, but it's my fault you're bleeding."

Cradled in his arms like this, Omi found it hard to be cross with Bo for anything. "I guess it will be easier to tell me and Ruth apart now."

Another stutter in his step. "I never had a problem."

Now they were right back to where all their troubles had started. Omi chided herself for bringing it up. "I'm going to be the ugly *schwester* from now on."

"You won't, Omi. If anything, you'll have a scar that will make your face even more interesting and an exciting story to tell your grandchildren."

"Not that exciting. I wasn't smart enough to get out of the way."

Bo chuckled. "And I wasn't watchful enough to be careful where I was swinging my boards."

"It takes a lot of muscles to swing boards around like that."

"What *gute* is muscle if you use it unwisely?" He slowed his steps. "We're here. Can you climb in the car on your own or do you need help?"

Omi lifted her head. Patricia Coombs stood by her car looking at her phone. Patricia often drove the Amish to doctor's appointments and the store. She was a sweet woman who said she liked driving the Amish around because she got to hear all the gossip. She looked up from her phone, and her eyes nearly popped out of her head. "For goodness' sake, Nebo, what happened?" She looked at Omi apologetically. "I'm sorry, but which twin are you?"

"I'm Omi."

"It looks like we need to get to the hospital as quickly as possible."

Omi's head was throbbing, and she felt like leftover oatmeal in a bowl, but the thought of big hospital bills made her hesitate. "Maybe you should just take me home." Mamm would be mad about Ruth, but Dat would be happy he didn't have to pay the bill.

"We should go to the hospital," Bo said.

Patricia raised her hands and backed away. "I'm going to let the two of you decide that." She opened the back car door, and Omi grabbed the door as Bo set her on her feet. A single drop of blood dripped from her forehead and onto the back seat as she ducked her head and slid into Patricia's car. "It's almost stopped bleeding," Omi said. "It's not that bad."

Bo didn't argue, but he didn't act as if he agreed with her. He handed her the towel, already soaked in blood, and she pressed the cleaner side to her forehead. It wasn't much cleaner, but at least she wouldn't bleed all over Patricia's carpet. Bo went around to the other door and slid in the back seat beside her.

"Buckle up," Patricia said.

Bo reached over Omi, grabbed her seat belt, and buckled it for her. She didn't know whether to be offended or touched. "Don't look in the mirror," he said.

"Why not?"

"Just don't."

Well, now of course she had to look. She lowered the towel and leaned to her left so she could get a better look in the rearview mirror. Bo slid to his right and halted her progress, buckling himself into the seat belt in the middle. "Scoot, Bo. I want to see."

"I told you not to look."

Frowning made her whole head hurt. "It's *my* forehead."

Concern was the only expression on his face. At least he wasn't being bossy for bossiness' sake. "I know, but to be honest, it looks very bad, and I don't want you to go into shock." He leaned even farther to his right, reached out, and tucked an errant lock of Omi's hair behind her ear. It was stiff with blood, so it just sprung back to sit on her cheek.

The small gesture threw her further off balance. Why did he have to do that? Clearing her throat, she concentrated on being mad at him—for about twenty things. "Scoot over, Bo."

He scrubbed his hand down the side of his face. "*Ach*, Omi, it looks wonderful bad. I feel terrible about it."

She finally understood why he didn't want her to see herself in the mirror. "Bo, this was not your fault. You were turning to go, and I wanted to argue with you."

"I shouldn't have turned so quickly."

Her lips twitched upward. "You just wanted to get away."

His expression relaxed. "Maybe I did."

"At least you admit it."

"I'm supposed to watch out for women and girls, and I hurt you instead."

She pressed the towel to her forehead. "That's the thanks I get for feeding you a very delicious lunch."

They got to a stop sign, and Patricia glanced behind her. "Where are we going?" She eyed Omi and winced. "I would recommend a hospital."

"They'll charge me an arm and a leg."

"And a forehead," Bo said, trying to be funny, failing miserably.

Patricia pointed down the road. "That will take you to

the Shawano hospital. The other way will take you home. I'm not going to force you one way or the other, but it looks serious, Omi."

"I hate hospitals."

Patricia turned her body to look squarely into Omi's face. "Everybody does."

"I need to see it before I make a decision."

Bo exhaled a deep breath. "*Ach,* okay. Much as I hate to admit it, you're right." He unbuckled himself and scooted to his left.

Omi also got unbuckled and slid to the center of the back seat where she could see herself in the rearview mirror. She tilted her head to get a better look and gasped when she saw a hideous face staring back at her. Even though she could only see about a third of her face in Patricia's rearview mirror, she got an eyeful. The gash on her forehead looked to be at least three inches long. It was oozing blood, angry red, plus various shades of yellow, black, and purple. A bump the size of a chicken egg bulged from her forehead, giving her face a distorted shape. Dried blood caked her forehead and matted her hair, and the front of her *kapp* was also spotted red. Bo had been right. She did not want to see it.

Unable to catch her breath, she grabbed Bo's wrist to steady herself. He immediately wrapped his arms around her and pulled her firmly against his chest. "It's okay, Omi. It's okay. You're going to be okay. I'm sorry. I didn't want you to see."

Tears blurred her vision. "I'm a monster."

"Not a monster. You just look like someone who's had a bad day."

"A very bad day." Omi sniffed back the tears, but sniffing hurt her whole face, so she quit.

Bo seemed torn between annoyance and concern. "I'm so sorry, Omi. Your head has stopped bleeding, mostly, so what if we go visit my *mammi*? She has thirteen children and over a hundred grandchildren. She's seen plenty of bruises and broken bones. She could look at your head and tell us if she thinks you need to go to a hospital."

Omi adored Anna Helmuth. She was feisty and sweet, and she loved Omi's cinnamon rolls with raisins. And Anna never had trouble telling Ruth and Omi apart.

"She's just up the road," Patricia said. "Not too far out of the way from the hospital."

Bo was right. Omi would feel better if they got Anna's opinion. She had years of mothering experience. "Okay."

Bo smiled. "*Gute*. Mammi will know what to do."

It only took five minutes to get to Anna Helmuth's house, and as Patricia pulled to the top of Huckleberry Hill, they saw Anna and Felty standing in their yard, each with a canvas bag slung over their shoulders, peering through binoculars.

Anna trained her binoculars on Patricia's car as it came up the hill and waved enthusiastically with the binoculars still up to her face. She kept watching through the binoculars as Bo got out of the car and came around to Omi's side to open her door.

"Felty, look. It's one of our favorite grandsons."

Bo opened Omi's door, took her hand, and pulled her gently to her feet. "Do you need me to carry you?"

She must have looked helpless indeed. "*Nae*. I think I will be okay."

He didn't lift her off her feet, thankfully, but he did put his arm around her waist as a support in case she needed to faint. He had no idea that she was more likely to faint from the feel of his arm around her than her severe head injury.

Anna, still looking through the binoculars, shuffled closer to Omi and let out a little squeak. She lowered her binoculars and studied Omi's face with a look of deep distress. "Oh, dear, Omi, what has happened? Didn't Bo give you my pot holders?"

Omi glanced at Bo. "What about pot holders?"

Anna motioned toward the house, her binoculars swinging back and forth from a string around her neck. "We can talk about that later. *Cum reu*. Let's get you cleaned up."

Felty had his binoculars trained on a large maple tree on the far side of the house, and he hadn't even turned around when they had come up the hill. "Felty!" Anna called. "The bird-watching will have to wait. Omi needs our help." She glanced at Bo. "We're bird-watching, though I keep telling Felty I don't need any new hobbies. Bird-watching is even more boring than sitting yoga, and I haven't seen one bird. I would like to see a killdeer. They pretend to be injured to distract you from their nest. It's quite brave."

Felty finally lowered his binoculars. The second he caught sight of Omi, he stuffed his binoculars into his canvas bag and came running. Omi winced. Felty was in his eighties. Lord willing, he wouldn't trip and fall. But Felty didn't move like an elderly man, so if he wanted to run, Omi would try not to worry. "*Ach, du lieva*, Omi. It looks like you've had an accident. Come in the house, and Anna can help you get cleaned up."

Patricia got out of the car. "Hello, Anna. How are you?"

"Wonderful *gute*, except I haven't seen a killdeer yet. Or a sparrow."

Felty grunted and pointed to the nearest tree. "*Ach*, Annie, there's three sparrows sitting on that branch."

Anna's face lit up. "You have such a *gute* eye, dear."

Bo tightened his arm around Omi's waist. "Mammi, you've seen your share of cuts and bruises. Patricia and I think Omi should go to the hospital for stitches. What do you think?"

Anna's lips formed into an O. "*Ach, vell,* I have seen plenty of blood in my day. Your own *dat* fell out of the haymow and had to get seventeen stitches and a tetanus shot. Felty got stabbed in the heart during the war. He's seen a lot of blood too, most of it his own."

Felty shook his head at Anna, no doubt to communicate that today wasn't a *gute* day to tell that story.

Anna stretched an awkward smile across her face. "But enough about Felty. Let me have a look." She sidled closer to Omi and examined her head. "*Ach*, that looks sore, but I don't know if I'm the best person to ask. I never liked taking *die kinner* to a doctor, and Felty always thought we should. We had more than one argument about that."

"It never hurts to go to the doctor," Felty protested.

Anna's wrinkles bunched together on her forehead. "Patricia, can I use your phone?"

"Sure."

Omi frowned. "You're not going to call an ambulance, are you?"

Anna stared at Patricia's phone. "*Nae*, but Bo's cousin Cassie is married to a doctor. They live in Chicago. He works at the hospital, and Cassie runs a museum. Let's call him. I have his private number, and he always answers for family when he's not busy." She kept staring at the phone. "Bo, you're going to have to do this for me. We need to face call."

"You mean FaceTime?"

"*Jah*. The one where you can see each other."

Keeping his arm around Omi, Bo took the phone from Anna. "What's the number?"

Anna had the number memorized. Bo punched it in. The phone hummed, and a face appeared on the phone screen. It was a grinning, handsome *Englischer* with a stethoscope draped around his neck. "Nebo Helmuth, *vie gehts?*" he said, as if getting a call from his wife's cousin was the best thing that had happened to him all day.

Anna grinned at Omi. "His accent is atrocious," she whispered, "but he tries very hard."

Omi leaned closer so she could see the screen. Not only could she see Zach, but Bo's face also showed in the bottom corner. "I'm sorry to bother you, Zach, but my friend Omi has been hit in the head, and she doesn't want to go to the hospital."

Zach raised his eyebrows. "Do you think she has a concussion?"

Bo gazed at Omi for longer than he needed to. Omi might have held her breath. "I don't know about a concussion, but I think she needs stitches."

"Show me," Zach said.

Bo pointed the phone toward Omi. She didn't know whether to smile or keep a straight face. Which one would make it less likely that Zach would recommend stitches?

Zach squinted into the phone, seemingly unruffled by the grizzly gash on Omi's forehead and the dried blood smeared across her face.

Anna wrapped her hand around Bo's and turned the phone so Zach could see her. He exploded into a smile. "Mammi Helmuth! *Guter nammidaag.*"

Anna glanced at Omi and grinned. Zach's accent was

indeed atrocious. "I'm doing *gute*, Dr. Reynolds," Anna said, "and your *Deitsch* is coming along."

"You think so? Cassie teaches me a new phrase every day, but she says I'm not good at the accent."

Anna's mouth dropped open as if she couldn't believe it. "Why would she say such a thing? You've got a rare talent. Keep trying. That's the important thing."

Felty gazed over his glasses at Anna. "Annie-banannie, I think we'd better let the doctor look at Omi."

Anna let go of Bo's hand. "*Ach*, of course. Zach and I can chat anytime. Omi needs immediate attention. And a bath. And some Neosporin."

Bo turned the phone so Zach could see Omi again. "Could you turn your head a little to the right?" Omi did as she was told, then held as still as possible so the doctor could take a *gute* look. "Well, Omi, I can't tell how deep it is, but on the forehead, you're not that far from bone. If it were me, I'd go to the emergency room and ask for a plastic surgeon. That's the best way to ensure you don't get a bad scar."

Bo and Patricia nodded. Anna beamed as if Dr. Reynolds was her own son.

Omi didn't like the sound of stitches. People who had to get stitches were left with nasty scars. "Am I going to be ugly for the rest of my life?"

Zach gave her a reassuring smile, one he'd probably used on hundreds of patients. "If you weren't ugly before, you won't be ugly now."

"She's wonderful pretty," Bo said.

Omi's gaze flicked in Bo's direction, and her pulse skipped three beats until she realized that Bo only thought she was pretty because she looked like Ruth. "I don't want to be vain, but will I look different?"

Zach acted as if he was trying not to smile. "Nebo seems to like the way you look, no matter what, but the cut is pretty straightforward. If you get a plastic surgeon, you'll be much happier with the results." He pulled a pen from the pocket of his white coat. "In fact, I have a doctor friend who practices in Shawano. She's a plastic surgeon. I'll call her and see if she can meet you at the hospital. Or better yet, if she could stitch you up at her office, you wouldn't have to pay for the emergency room."

Even better. Dat might not have a heart attack when they got the bill. Omi looked up at Bo. "Okay. Take me to the doctor."

"I'll call my friend right now and text you the address," Zach said.

Omi leaned into the phone screen. "Thank you very much, Dr. Zach. You are very nice, and I'm glad Bo has a cousin-in-law like you."

Zach nodded. "Bo is a really great guy. I highly recommend him." He frowned and cleared his throat. "But no pressure. I'm not into pressuring anybody."

Bo curled his lips, shook his head, and pressed the End button. He handed the phone to Patricia and gave Omi's arm a squeeze. He didn't mean anything by it, but Omi's heart couldn't tell. It pounded against her chest. "Let's go. You're looking paler and paler. I don't want you to faint before we get there."

"I don't want to faint before or after we get there," Omi said.

Bo chuckled. "I agree."

Anna fingered her binoculars. "Do you want to come in for a snack before you go see the doctor? You shouldn't get stitches on an empty stomach."

"*Denki*, Mammi," Bo said, "but Omi isn't feeling well. I want to get her to the doctor as soon as possible."

Anna patted Bo's hand. "*Ach*, you're so kind and sensitive. He's a real catch. Don't you think, Omi?"

Of course Omi thought so, but she couldn't say that about a *bu* who was in love with her *schwester*.

After this, he'd be more in love with Ruth than ever, because Omi was going to have a hideous scar, and she'd scare away small children and all possible husbands.

# Chapter 8

Bo was so tired he could barely lift his arms, but he took extra time brushing down his using horses because they were even more spent than he was. They'd worked a *gute* hard morning plowing the fields, not misbehaving once, responding to his every command with precision and caution. They deserved a *gute* rubdown and a bushel of apples.

Brushing horses was like milking cows. The rhythmic, constant movement freed his mind to think about Omi and barn raisings and scars. His heart skipped three beats anticipating seeing Omi today. Dr. Patel would be taking out Omi's stitches, and Omi had invited Bo to go with her. *We've come this far together*, she had said. Her smile had about knocked him over.

It was nice to have a doctor in the family, because Zach's help and advice had been invaluable. Zach's plastic surgeon friend, Dr. Patel, had kindly squeezed Omi into her schedule and had cleaned Omi up, numbed her forehead, and given her ten stitches right there in her office. Omi had been very brave, and the doctor and nurses had laughed when Omi told the story of how she'd gotten the gash on her forehead, taking all the blame and making Bo seem like the victim. That was quite a feat since the whole incident had been Bo's fault.

By the time Bo and Omi had left the office, Omi and Dr. Patel had become *gute* friends. Omi was cheerful to a fault and treated everyone with consideration and kindness. She wasn't flashy and exciting like Ruth, but she had her own quiet way of making people feel glad to be around her. Bo was almost astonished that he hadn't noticed it before.

After the doctor, Patricia had taken them out for an early dinner at Longhorn Saloon, where they both ate as if they hadn't seen food for days. They'd talked, and at one point, Bo had laughed so hard, soda came out of his nose. It was a painful, comical experience. Bo drew his brows together. By the time they'd returned to Omi's house, Ruth was there, and Bo had no idea what to say to her. So he'd helped Omi to the door and left, needing more time to decide what to do about Ruth. And Omi.

Bo smiled to himself. Omi really was something special.

And she didn't even know it.

But Bo knew. Something had stirred inside him when he lifted Omi into his arms and carried her to Patricia's car. She smelled faintly of roses, and his heart had done a double-time jig when she'd wrapped her arms around him and buried her face in the crook of his neck. *Ach, vell,* there had been a blood-soaked towel between them, but he'd still felt the electricity of it down to his toes. And then, suddenly after that, all he wanted to do was to be close enough to touch her. Fortunately, she had been a little wobbly on her feet, and that had given him all the excuse he needed to keep her close. It was all so strange. Ruth had completely slipped his mind.

Bo pressed his lips together, wondering if he should feel guilty for hardly thinking about Ruth all day. All week, for that matter. Didn't he love her?

He filled the bucket with oats and his special vitamin mix and shut the stall door. Of course he still loved Ruth, but he and Omi had been through so much together the past few days that it was only natural Omi would be on his mind.

Anyway, Bo thought about Ruth a lot. He had just been to see her two days ago. They'd gone for a walk, and Ruth had talked on and on about the time she and Lydia had gone swimming, and she'd cut her foot on something sharp on the lake bed and had a scar that was much worse than Omi's. Bo had again avoided the subject of Elam and his car and kissing Omi and the barn raising. His resolve to tell the truth seemed to upset Omi, so he had held his tongue. He would eventually tell Ruth everything, but maybe not until Omi was fully recovered, and that might not be for months.

He pulled his watch out of his pocket. He needed to clean up. Patricia and Omi would be here in twenty minutes. His lips twitched upward. Would Omi be wearing the blue dress or the purple? It didn't really matter. She looked pretty in both. What should he wear? Would Omi prefer his blue shirt or the cream one?

Patricia pulled in front of his house at 3:00 P.M. sharp with Omi sitting in the front seat. Bo climbed in the back, disappointed that Omi wasn't sitting next to him, but when Omi looked back and smiled, he realized that sitting in the back would give him the perfect view of Omi's face. He could stare at Omi all the way to the doctor without her thinking he was weird.

"Are you excited to get your stitches out?" he said.

Omi fingered the white gauze taped to her forehead. "I'm not sure. At least with the gauze in place, I can pretend I don't have a scar."

Patricia turned onto the road into Shawano. "Dr. Patel said it would fade in a few months. Most people won't even notice it."

"You'll still be as pretty as ever," Bo said.

This seemed to make Omi sad. "I'll never be as pretty as Ruth."

Patricia glanced at Omi. "Each of you is pretty in your own way."

Omi looked down at her hands. "*Jah*. I'm sure we are," she said, leaving no doubt she didn't believe it.

What was wrong with Omi? She was usually so cheerful. "I don't think taking the stitches out is going to hurt at all," he said.

Patricia nodded. "Not at all. When the doctor took out my C-section stitches, he cut one thread and the whole thing just pulled right out. And that was much longer and deeper than your scar."

Omi made a valiant attempt to smile. "I'm not worried. Dr. Patel is very gentle."

Bo didn't like seeing Omi so unhappy. "I've never had stitches, but I almost sliced my finger off once."

"Really?"

He leaned forward and showed Omi the chunky scar that curved halfway around his middle finger. "I was fourteen."

Omi grabbed his hand and pulled it toward her. "*Ach*, that looks awful."

Bo nodded. "My *mamm* cleaned it off, and my *dat* glued the skin back together with superglue."

"Superglue?" Omi's mouth fell open in mock indignation. "You mean we could have used superglue on my forehead?"

Bo grinned. "I didn't tell you because I didn't want you to think that was an option."

Omi reached back and cuffed him on the shoulder then gave him the smile he'd been waiting for. "We went to all that trouble when there's a tube of superglue sitting in the junk drawer at home."

Patricia laughed. "You made the right choice with the stitches. Just look at Bo's scar. It's hideous."

Bo smiled wryly. "Thanks, Patricia. You make me feel so good about myself."

Patricia waited for them outside while they saw the doctor. Ten minutes later, Omi's stitches were out, and Dr. Patel had given her a sample of therapy cream to minimize the scarring, but it didn't look bad at all, and Omi seemed relieved. Right before Bo and Omi left, Omi got Dr. Patel's address so they could exchange birthday and Christmas cards.

They got back in the car, and this time, Omi sat in the back with Bo. She didn't explain why, and Bo didn't ask. He was just happy to have her close.

"Okay," Patricia said, backing her car out of the parking space. "Where to now?"

Bo glanced at Omi. "Do you mind if we go to my *mammi*'s house? She is very anxious to see your head, and I told her I'd try to bring you by."

Omi glowed like a propane lantern. "I'd love to see Anna. She's the one who suggested we call Dr. Zach. I need to thank her."

Bo cleared his throat. "She also wants you to stay for dinner."

Omi didn't even hesitate, even though Mammi's cooking was famous for being very bad. "I'd love to. Anna and I are both great fans of raisins."

"Do you want to come too, Patricia?"

Patricia glanced at them in the rearview mirror. "No, thanks. I hate raisins, and Brent shouldn't be allowed to fix his own dinner."

Patricia dropped them off at the top of Huckleberry Hill, and Bo couldn't resist grabbing Omi's hand and helping her out of the car. She *was* still recovering from an injury. He needed to watch out for her. Her hand felt so *gute* that he kept hold of it all the way up to Mammi and Dawdi's front door. He knocked, and Omi blushed and pulled her hand from his. Bo's face got warm, and he folded his arms and became very interested in the metalwork on Mammi's porch swing.

"*Cum reu*," Mammi called from inside.

Bo opened the door and ushered Omi into the room. Mammi and Dawdi were sitting with their backs to the door each with an easel and painting canvas in front of them. Mammi turned and smiled, a paintbrush in one hand and a smudge of yellow paint on her cheek. "*Ach*, Omi, did you get your stitches out?"

"I did." Dr. Patel had applied a large bandage to Omi's forehead. She peeled the bandage away and bent over so Mammi could get a *gute* look.

Mammi spread out her hands in delight and managed to smear red paint on Dawdi's sleeve. Neither of them noticed. "*Ach*, it looks *wunderbarr*. I can hardly see it."

That wasn't completely true, because Omi's scar was plenty visible, even to eighty-five-year-old eyes. But the doctor said it would fade over time, and it didn't look bad as it was. But Omi smiled with her whole face, so Mammi could say whatever she wanted.

Dawdi set his paintbrush on the lip of the easel. "They did a *gute* job."

"I think they did too," Omi said. "And Dr. Patel said I could come in anytime if I'm worried about it."

"What are you doing, Mammi?" Bo asked, even though it was plain that she and Dawdi were painting pictures.

Mammi pointed to a book on the kitchen table. The cover had a photo of a smiling man with wild hair and a paintbrush in his hand. "We're trying a new hobby. It's supposed to be relaxing, but I can't relax because my banana looks like a hot dog."

"I think your banana looks very nice," Dawdi said.

One of the kitchen chairs had been pulled out from the table, and a blue plate rested atop it. A banana and an apple sat on the plate, along with a sprig of parsley.

Dawdi had painted something that looked very much like a red apple sitting on a blue plate. Mammi's painting was a little harder to make sense of. She had indeed attempted to paint a banana, but it didn't look anything like a banana except that it was yellow. It didn't really look like a hot dog either, but Bo wasn't about to mention it. It looked like she'd tried to give the banana some brown lines, but she'd only managed to make it look like a yellow blob with one eyebrow and three noses.

Mammi studied her banana. "It's called a still life because nothing moves. It's supposed to be easier to paint that way."

"That looks fun," Omi said.

Mammi sighed. "I'm not sure how fun. My banana looks depressed, and I haven't even started on my apple."

Bo pointed to the chair. "You could work on painting the plate. That doesn't look too hard."

Mammi's expression fell. "I've already done the plate."

Oops. Bo hadn't even noticed the small blue circle at the bottom of Mammi's painting that was half the size of the Banana Man. "*Ach, jah*, I see it now. It's a very nice plate."

"I think it's *wunderbarr*," Omi said. "It takes courage to try new things."

Mammi tossed her paintbrush in the glass of water at her feet. "No need to sugarcoat it. The book is called *The Joy of Painting*, but all I'm feeling is the deep disappointment of broken dreams."

"I like your banana," Dawdi said.

Mammi seemed determined not to believe him. "Let's face it, Felty. I can't be *gute* at everything."

Dawdi leaned over and took Mammi's hand. "You're *gute* at everything that counts."

"What a sweet thing to say, dear." Mammi turned and looked at the clock on the wall. It had pictures of twelve different kinds of birds. One for each hour. "*Ach*, I've lost track of the time. I haven't even started dinner, and I was going to make oysters with cream sauce and raisins." She winked at Omi. "I know how much you like raisins."

Omi did like raisins, but Bo was pretty sure that nobody liked oysters.

"Why don't you let me make dinner, Anna? I don't mind cooking." Omi was so thoughtful. Bo loved that about her. He also loved that if Omi made dinner, it would taste *gute*. "That way, you can finish your painting."

Mammi gazed sadly at her Banana Man. "It's already finished, I'm afraid."

"That's not true. It's going to be very pretty when you're done." When Omi said it like that, with all that kindness and encouragement in her voice, even Bo sort of believed it.

Mammi wrinkled her forehead in concern. "Do you know how to steam oysters?"

Omi hesitated, and Bo didn't know if it would be better if she knew how to steam oysters or didn't. "What if you saved the oysters for another day, and I'll make something else. I'm *gute* at breakfast foods. I could make breakfast for dinner."

Mammi clapped her hands then frowned and laced her fingers together as if ashamed she had clapped prematurely. "I love breakfast for dinner, but I hate to ask you to cook. You just got your stitches out. I should be the one cooking for you."

Omi pressed her hand to the bandage at her forehead. "It didn't hurt at all when she took out the stitches, and my headache went away two days ago. I feel right as rain." She took off her jacket and black bonnet and hung them on the hook by the front door. "Do you have eggs?"

Mammi's smile was radiant. "Do I have eggs? I have seven chickens and four dozen eggs sitting in my refrigerator. *Ach*, *vell*, the chickens aren't in the refrigerator, but the eggs are. Please use all the eggs you can. And the raisins are in the cupboard above the knives in case you need them."

Omi tapped her finger to her chin. "Hmm. There are so many *wunderbarr* breakfast foods. What should I make?" She glanced at Bo. "What do you like?"

Bo was just happy that Omi wouldn't be making oysters. "I like everything."

"Do you have apples, Anna?"

Mammi pointed to the apple on the blue plate. "You could use that one, but I don't think I can paint it from memory."

"No need to use our apple," Dawdi said. "We have five or six apples in the fridge."

Omi opened the fridge and stuck her head in. "You have nine apples. That will be plenty, and we won't have to use your model apple."

Bo loved apples. He thought he might die of anticipation. "Are you going to make apple pie?"

Omi smiled. "I do love apple pie, but this is breakfast, so we're having German apple pancakes. And you're going to help me. How are you at peeling and coring apples?"

He laughed and held up his hand to remind her of the scar on his finger. "I have a bad history with knives in general."

She waved away his concern. "You'll be fine. I bet your *mammi* has superglue."

Mammi nodded. "Three kinds."

"I guess I can help." Bo feigned dejection and dragged his feet into the kitchen, but nothing made him happier than the thought of being near Omi and helping her cook. Was it bad that he wanted to spend time with Omi when her *schwester* was his girlfriend?

Omi found one of Mammi's aprons in a drawer and put it on. It was a deep royal blue, exactly the color of her eyes. Bo closed his mouth so he wouldn't drool. "Do you have maple syrup, Anna?" Omi asked.

Mammi clapped her hands again. "Do I have maple syrup! We got almost ten gallons from our trees this year."

Omi giggled. "That should be enough."

Mammi seemed as enthusiastic about dinner as Bo was. "We also have goat cheese from Titus and Katie Rose." Bo's *bruder* Titus had found his life's work in keeping goats and his life's love in his *fraa*, Katie Rose. There couldn't have been a more perfect match. Mammi had been responsible for bringing them together. She might not be a *gute* painter, but she was wonderful *gute* at making matches for her grandchildren. "In case you want to make something with goat cheese."

"I'll keep that in mind," Omi said.

With renewed cheer, Mammi picked up her paintbrush. "I think this still life would look better with Sparky sitting on the plate next to the banana."

Mammi's white fluffy dog, Sparky, perked up her ears and lifted her head from the rug where she'd been dozing.

Mammi puckered her lips and made a kissing sound. "*Cum* here, Sparky. I need you to model for me."

It looked as if Sparky raised her eyebrows, but Bo couldn't be sure because he didn't know if dogs had eyebrows. She stood up, seemed to think better of it, rolled onto her side, and stretched her legs in every direction. Then she stood up again, sneezed, and waddled down the hall in the opposite direction of Mammi and her canvas.

"*Ach*," Mammi said. "Sparky doesn't like being the center of attention. I suppose I'll have to settle for painting the apple." She caught her breath and set her paintbrush on the lip of the easel. "I'm going to paint one of my pot holders. That way, I can combine two hobbies into one. It will save time."

Dawdi brushed a smear of yellow across his banana. "Annie-banannie, the point isn't to save time. The point is to enjoy the time you spend."

Mammi scrunched her lips together and gazed at her Banana Man. "I'm way past enjoyment, Felty. I've reached the utter frustration stage."

Omi grinned at Bo, and her expression would have knocked the hat off his head had he not just taken it off. She retrieved the apples from the fridge and set them on the counter next to the sink then handed Bo a vegetable peeler. "Can you use one of these?"

Bo grimaced. "I'm not very *gute* at it. I've been known to peel the skin off my knuckles."

Mammi dabbed at her canvas with a glob of red paint. "I have three kinds of superglue just in case."

Omi scrunched her lips together. "I'd rather you not hurt yourself. How are you at cracking eggs?"

"Useless."

"*Ach, vell*, at least you can't get injured cracking eggs."

He shook his head. "I could. What if I hit one too hard and part of the shell bounces up and lodges in my eye?"

She laughed. Omi was quieter and more reserved than Ruth, but she laughed like she meant it. Bo loved the sound of it. "We'll just have to risk it."

"I have goggles," Mammi said.

Omi glanced at Bo, amusement flashing in her eyes. "Would you like your *mammi*'s goggles to crack your eggs?"

He pretended to think about it. "I would, but I'm afraid you'd make fun of me for the rest of my life."

"Okay, no goggles." Omi pulled a bowl of eggs from the fridge. "Here are your eggs. Try not to get any shells in my German apple pancakes."

Bo nodded in mock seriousness. "I'll do my best."

Bo carefully cracked eggs while Omi peeled apples as if it was what she did for a living. He cracked three eggs before he could do it without losing pieces of shell in the bowl. Omi didn't scold him or even seem to mind. She simply used her fingers to pull out each shell fragment, and all was well with the eggs.

Once the apples were peeled and cored, Omi fried them in a skillet with a whole cube of butter and some cinnamon. The smell was heavenly, and Bo's stomach growled. "These are going to be *appeditlich* pancakes."

Omi blushed. "I hope so. I'm just making the recipe from memory."

"That's what I do," Mammi interjected. "The best cooks make things by feel. I read that in a magazine once."

Omi measured milk, sugar, and flour and poured them into the bowl with the eggs. Bo loved watching her graceful hands move from one task to the next, almost as if she was making music that he could actually see. She pulled a whisk from one of the drawers and showed it to Bo. "Do you know how to whisk?"

"Nope."

She set the whisk in the bowl. "Just stir briskly. You'll know you're doing it right because it makes a delightful sound."

He raised his eyebrows. "A delightful sound? You're scaring me."

Omi smiled wryly. "I believe in you, Bo."

It turned out that whisking wasn't hard, though there was a skill to it, because Bo did it for a full minute without getting that "delightful sound." Just to prove to him that there was a "sound," Omi took a whisk to the egg mixture. As soon as she started whisking, Bo heard it. More music in the form of eggs bubbling and the whisk hitting against the metal bowl. "You're amazing," Bo said.

Omi blushed again—for no reason Bo could see—and whisked even more vigorously. "Will you butter the pie tins?"

He stretched his lips over his teeth. "I'm sorry, Omi, but it's like you're speaking a foreign language. I know how to butter bread, but I'm not sure how to butter pie tins."

Again, she gave him that amused, affectionate expression. "You definitely need to spend more time in the kitchen."

"I'd drive my *mamm* crazy."

"I can see that." Grinning, Omi took more butter out of the fridge, unwrapped it partway, and rubbed the open end around and around the pie tins until they had a thin coat of butter. She poured the apples into the tins and poured the egg mixture over the apples. "Now we bake it." Bo opened the hot oven for her, and she set both pie tins on the top shelf. She stood up straight and brushed her hands together. "Okay. Let's set the table. Do you know how to set the table, Bo?" she teased.

"I think I can figure that one out."

Omi pulled four plates from the cupboard and handed them to Bo. Their hands brushed, and Bo felt a zing of pleasure. Could he get her to hand him the silverware and the napkins too?

They made short work of the table, and Bo got to touch Omi's hand two more times. The contact made his heart race. What was wrong with him? He loved Ruth, not Omi. Why was he having this reaction?

While the apple pancakes baked, Omi decided to scramble some eggs with goat cheese and onions. She let Bo crack the eggs again and whisk them. He did much better the second time. Then he just leaned against the counter and told Omi funny stories about Titus and his goats as she scrambled the eggs, warmed the syrup, and pulled the German apple pancakes from the oven. She was a wonder.

She set the two piping hot pie tins on the table. "Dinner is ready."

Anna turned around. "*Ach, du lieva*, that was fast. I completely lost track of time trying to capture the essence of my pot holders on canvas." She had definitely captured something on canvas. Three red blobs had joined Banana Man in her painting. The lighter one looked like it was meant to be the apple because it had a stem. The two darker red ones were probably the pot holders. There was also what looked like a cotton ball with eyes. She'd decided to paint Sparky after all.

"That looks very nice, Mammi."

Mammi chewed on the end of her paintbrush. "*Denki*, Bo."

Dawdi nodded. "Adding the pot holders was a stroke of genius."

Bo didn't even know what that meant, but Mammi seemed to be pleased about it. Her smile stretched from ear to ear. "They do look nice. Then I decided to paint my grandfather because he loved apples. He had an apple tree in his backyard."

That white blob with eyes was not Sparky but Bo's great-great-grandfather. *Ach*, *vell*, it wasn't Bo's fault he hadn't recognized him. He had never seen a photo.

The four of them sat down at the table and said silent grace. Then Omi served slices of German apple pancakes to everyone. They each helped themselves to the eggs and syrup. "You just pour the syrup over the apple pancake like you would a regular pancake," Omi said. "It makes them extra sweet."

Bo took a bite, and his tongue shouted for joy. The tartness of the apples blended perfectly with the sweetness of the syrup, and Bo had never tasted a better pancake. The scrambled eggs were also delicious, with just the right amount of goat cheese to give them some tang but not overpower the flavor. Bo couldn't imagine that Ruth knew how to cook like this. *Did* Ruth know how to cook like this? He pressed his lips together. He shouldn't care how *gute* or bad Ruth was in the kitchen. He shouldn't love anyone just for their cooking. He adored Mammi, and she couldn't boil water without burning it. Still, he could appreciate a *gute* meal and the pretty girl who had prepared it.

"This is *wunderbarr*, Omi," Bo said. "I really can't say enough *gute* things about it."

The corners of Omi's mouth curled upward shyly. "I'm *froh* you like it."

"I love it," Mammi said. "Even though you didn't use raisins."

"It's wonderful *gute*," Dawdi said. "Who knew you could do so much with apples?"

Mammi nodded. "So true. You can bake with them, feed them to the horses, and put them in your paintings." Mammi put down her fork and leaned toward Omi. "So, Omi, why don't you tell us about this Elam fellow your *schwester* is dating? They say he has a car."

Bo nearly inhaled his eggs.

Omi coughed violently. She'd probably inhaled her eggs too. "Umm. I'm sorry, what was your question?" Omi was just stalling. She'd heard Mammi's question well enough. She hadn't choked for no reason.

Mammi didn't seem to notice the distress at the table. "It wonders me if Ruth and Elam will get married. I'd hate to see her living in Cashton. It's so far away."

Omi turned redder than one of Mammi's pot holders. Bo's face had to be at least as red as hers. "*Ach*, Ruth is dating Bo, not Elam," Omi said.

Mammi's gaze flicked from Bo to Omi and back again. "I'm confused. I know for a fact that Ruth likes Elam and his car. I thought they were dating yet."

Omi looked at Bo as if he'd betrayed her. "Who . . . where did you hear that?"

"I've seen them driving through town. That car is so noisy, it would wake every napping *buplie* within a mile. Some people don't have any consideration for other people's feelings."

Bo nearly sighed in relief. Mammi hadn't revealed that

he was the one who'd first told her about Elam. She truly was a *gute* spy. "I gave Hannah Fisher a pot holder, and she told me Elam is her nephew and he has a car and he comes up here at least once a week to see Ruth."

Once a week? Bo thought he might be sick. Ruth had yet to tell Bo about Elam, but he could only blame himself. He had yet to ask. Was she really seeing Elam once a week? That was more than she saw Bo.

Omi didn't seem mad anymore. She riveted her gaze to Bo's face. "She . . . I . . . you should ask Ruth. It's her story to tell, not mine."

Mammi turned to Bo, the lines of her forehead piling on top of themselves. "Did you know about this?"

Now it was his turn to feel betrayed. He eyed Omi resentfully. "I didn't know they see each other every week."

Omi slumped in her chair. "I told you I wouldn't be your go-between."

Mammi pointed her fork at Bo. "I would think after how Ruth has treated you that you would drop her like a hot potato. Don't you agree, Omi?"

Omi looked positively miserable. "It's not my place to say."

Bo didn't know how to defend himself. He wanted to proclaim his love for Ruth, to insist that he loved Ruth enough to forgive her. But he hadn't been honest with Ruth, and maybe he hadn't been honest with himself, because he was beginning to wonder if he really loved Ruth as much as he once thought he did. Ruth was pretty and exciting and desirable, but Omi was steady and kind and honest. And she made *gute* German apple pancakes. "Ruth doesn't mean to treat me badly," Bo mumbled. "She likes to have fun."

Mammi patted Bo's arm. "It's all right, Bo. I'm not cross

with you. I just hate to see any of my grandchildren so unhappy."

"I'm . . . I'm not unhappy. I'm . . ." Bo seriously couldn't think of one word to describe how he felt. Confused? Angry? Hurt? Unnaturally interested in his girlfriend's *schwester*?

Everyone at the table gazed at him curiously. Omi's curiosity seemed intensely painful. Mammi was puzzled, and Dawdi looked amused.

"You're what, dear?" Mammi prompted.

"I don't know if Ruth likes me anymore."

Mammi didn't relax her intense gaze. "I think the better question is: Do *you* like Ruth?"

Bo wouldn't answer that for the world. He couldn't answer. He'd never been so uncertain in his life.

Mammi finally broke eye contact to pour more syrup on her apple pancake. "You and Omi get along so well together. She's pretty and sensible and doesn't have a weakness for fast cars or out-of-towners. She wouldn't dream of hurting your feelings, and she makes *appeditlich* eggs. I think the two of you should be a couple."

Bo covered his mouth so he wouldn't spit apple pancake all over the table. He really had to quit eating at Mammi's house. There was always one food disaster or another waiting to happen. He took a gulp of milk to clear his throat. Did he want to date Omi? He was supposed to be dating Ruth, but lately all he could think about was Omi. All the time.

The color drained from Omi's face, but she tried to give Mammi a sweet smile. "I could never do that to Ruth."

Mammi frowned. "Do what to Ruth?"

"Ruth is my *schwester*. I could never steal her boyfriend."

Mammi seemed shocked at the very thought. "I'm not

suggesting you steal Bo from Ruth. Stealing is against the commandments. But we can both see that Ruth doesn't really appreciate Bo. In fact, she takes him for granite, and nobody likes to be taken for granite."

"For granted, Annie," Dawdi said.

Mammi nodded. "That too. She takes him for granite *and* for granted." Mammi's eyes got all mushy when she looked at Bo. "You're such a gute *bu*. You deserve a girl who adores you. I don't see Ruth being that girl. Don't you agree, Omi?"

Omi turned bright red again. "It's not my place to say."

Bo stared at Omi, trying to figure out what was going on in her head. Did she like him? Did she want to be his girlfriend? Was she as annoyed with Ruth as he was, or did she think he and Ruth made a *gute* couple? Did Omi want Bo to marry her *schwester*? Did she care one way or the other?

*Ach*, she cared. He saw the deep and undecipherable emotion in her eyes.

Mammi gave Omi a grandmotherly smile. "You're absolutely right. I'm sorry to put you in such an awkward position. I just get frustrated with Bo sometimes. I wish he had a little more self-respect than to follow after Ruth like a puppy dog. It has nothing to do with you." She dabbed her lips with her napkin. "Let's talk about something else."

The rest of dinner was less of a disaster than the beginning, but that was like saying mumps wasn't as bad as the measles. Mammi asked Bo what he liked about Ruth, and then she asked Omi what she liked about Ruth, and then she had everyone at the table say something nice about Bo. Even Bo had to say something nice about himself, and at that moment, he couldn't think of anything. He hadn't been honest with Ruth, he'd given Omi a scar, he'd kissed his girlfriend's *schwester*, and he'd been unfaithful to Ruth in his thoughts. He really had nothing *gute* to say about himself.

Bo finally resorted to asking Mammi about knitting and cooking, two of her favorite activities. Oysters and yarn were boring but safe, and he needed safe. They ate every last egg and both German apple pancakes while Mammi explained the difference between knitting and purling. Safe and boring.

Omi grew quieter and quieter until Bo worried she might not be feeling well. "Mammi, I need to get Omi home. It's been a long day."

Omi lifted her eyes briefly. "*Jah.* I can feel a headache coming."

Bo pulled his watch from his pocket. "Patricia should be here soon."

Omi took her plate to the sink. Mammi shook her head. "*Nae*, Omi. Felty and I will do the dishes. You and Bo go sit on the porch swing and wait for your driver."

"Are you sure?" Omi said. "I can help until she comes."

"I won't hear of it." Mammi smiled as if she had a *wunderbarr* secret. "It will give you and Bo some time alone together."

*Ach, du lieva.* Mammi didn't know when to say uncle. Bo jumped up like a shot, grabbed his hat from the hook, and helped Omi on with her jacket. They had to get out of there before Bo died of embarrassment.

They walked out on the porch, and Bo looked at his watch again. "She should be here in five minutes."

Bo wasn't especially keen to sit on the swing, mostly because Mammi had suggested it, and they both knew what she was scheming. But Omi wasn't feeling well, and Mammi was watching from the kitchen window. She tapped on the glass and waved as if they hadn't just walked out the front door. Bo waved back then motioned toward the swing. "We might as well sit. Mammi wants us to."

Omi's eyes flashed with unexpected amusement. It was the most enthusiasm she'd shown since they'd said silent grace. "We should always listen to your *mammi*. I don't know anyone quite as determined."

Bo sat, eager to make things less uncomfortable between them. "I'm sorry about my *mammi*. She says what she thinks, and sometimes it's embarrassing."

Omi smiled sadly. For sure and certain, Bo liked that smile, even if Omi didn't look particularly happy. "Never apologize for your *mammi*. She is the dearest, smartest woman I know, and she's lived long enough to earn the right to say whatever she wants. I think she's learned that life is too short to leave things unsaid."

Bo didn't know if he believed that. Some things should be left unsaid and undone, no matter how short life was. Would Ruth regret the time she wasted with Elam? Would Bo regret kissing Omi? Would Omi regret always stepping aside for her *schwester*? "Life is short, but it's also complicated."

She nodded. "I suppose you're right, but your *mammi* seems to have waded through the complexity and found the simplicity again. We could all learn something from her."

One corner of his mouth curled upward. "Like how to live through embarrassing situations?"

"Among other things."

"I've definitely learned that."

She giggled. "Don't be such a baby, Nebo Helmuth. I had a *dawdi* who took out his teeth and set them on the table before every meal. My *aendi* Becca burped on demand, and my *onkel* Paul stripped naked and ran outside to dance whenever it rained."

Bo's eyebrows traveled all the way up his forehead.

"Sounds like insanity runs in the family. You might want to go get checked."

She cuffed him on the shoulder. "It wasn't insanity. He said it cleansed his pores." She nudged her toe on the porch, and the swing moved back and forth. "Your *mammi* just wants to help you see things more clearly. No need to be embarrassed."

Mammi might have wanted him to see things more clearly, but Bo was more confused than ever, especially sitting so close to Omi. Omi wasn't just Ruth's *schwester*. She was interesting and attractive and exciting in her own way. She radiated goodness like a lantern radiated light, and she was so kind, as if she thought giving of herself was a blessing instead of a burden. She smelled like roses and springtime, and the way she unconsciously nibbled on her bottom lip drove Bo crazy. And who knew a scar could be so fascinating?

Did he love Ruth, or was that feeling an illusion? Did Omi like him, or was that wishful thinking?

He looked down the road and watched Omi out of the corner of his eye. He would have to gather his wits, take a step back, and think sensible thoughts. There was only one thing to do.

He was going to have to kiss Ruth.

# Chapter 9

Bo knocked on the Coblenzes' door, not sure if he hoped or dreaded Omi would answer. He wanted to see her something wonderful, but after all that had happened with the stitches and German apple pancakes and that whole embarrassing day, it would be kind of awkward if Omi came to the door first.

To his relief, Omi's younger *bruder* LaWayne answered the door and bloomed into a smile. "*Hallo*, Bo. Do you want to see my new scooter?"

Ruth suddenly appeared behind LaWayne and shooed him out of the way. "Not now, LaWayne. Bo didn't come to see you. He came to see me." She looked extra pretty in her pastel pink dress. It accented her smooth complexion and rose-petal lips. She was very good-looking, but his heart didn't trip all over itself like it usually did when he saw Ruth. He'd known it ever since German apple pancake day. Something was different between them, and it was all Omi's doing. Or maybe it was all his doing, because Omi hadn't changed. Bo had.

"Another time, LaWayne," Bo said, because no matter how badly he wanted to see LaWayne's new scooter, he wanted even worse to talk to Ruth and put this whole thing behind him one way or another.

LaWayne shrugged, gave Ruth the stink eye, and disappeared down the hall. Ruth beamed at Bo. She bounced on her toes like a horse eager to start a race. "Where are we going tonight? I've been a wreck all day. You said you had something special in mind, and I've been so excited I could hardly concentrate at Mrs. Womack's house. I missed three piles of dirt with the broom and almost forgot to clean both bathrooms."

Bo loved how excited Ruth got about things. His heart did a little hop. "I thought we could walk to the pond and watch the sunset. It's so beautiful this time of year."

Her face fell like one of Mammi's cheese-and-raisin soufflés. "The sunset? Why would we want to watch the sunset? They literally happen every day. You said it was going to be something special."

He forced a smile. "Just being with you is special."

She wasn't convinced, but she obviously didn't want to be rude. "I guess so. Let me get a sweater and some mosquito repellant." She came back a few minutes later with a black fleece sweater wrapped around her shoulders, smelling like mosquito spray. Maybe he wouldn't try to kiss her. Nothing put a damper on romance like the smell of DEET on a girl's neck.

He didn't realize she held a phone until it buzzed and the screen lit up. "You got a phone?"

She glanced at the screen and nodded. "A few weeks ago in case someone needs to call me. Mamm doesn't like me keeping it in the house, but I can't leave it outside or it will get stolen. Besides, I'm in *rumschpringe*, and she likes that I can call a driver and she doesn't have to borrow the phone at the neighbors down the road."

Bo wasn't sure why he was so irritated about a phone.

Lots of *die youngie* got cell phones during *rumschpringe*. It just wasn't something Bo would do, and he was pretty certain Omi wouldn't get one either.

They walked toward the pond, and Ruth told Bo about how LaWayne had bought a scooter even though their *dat* hadn't wanted him to. Then LaWayne had fallen on the scooter the very first day and scraped up his whole left side. "Dat said it was a *gute* lesson in humility and listening to your parents. Mamm said it was a *gute* lesson in wearing long sleeves." Ruth laughed. "LaWayne is a slow learner. I don't know that he learned anything."

Bo had always been drawn to Ruth's unbridled enthusiasm. She was fun to talk to, and she liked to laugh and tell funny stories. But tonight he couldn't enjoy being with her, not with everything that weighed on his mind, not with the conversation he was finally planning to have with her, not with his head full of Omi. And not with the guilt that his head was full of Omi instead of Ruth.

Ruth pulled out her phone and checked it for about the tenth time since they'd left her house.

"Expecting a call?" Bo asked.

She smiled sheepishly. "Um, no. Just checking. I get texts from people all the time."

No time like the present to have a hard conversation. "Like Elam?"

Her eyes widened, and she stopped walking. "What about Elam?"

He'd made up his mind before coming tonight that she wasn't going to put him on the defensive. Omi said if you didn't want to answer a question, you asked another question in return. "Why didn't you tell me about him?"

Ruth's expression hardened like cement. "Did Omi tell you?"

Bo had also made up his mind that he would leave

Omi out of the conversation as much as possible. "My *mammi* saw you driving around town with him. She bribed Raymond Fisher's *mamm* for information with some pot holders."

"Elam's just a *bu* from Cashton. He has a nice car, and he takes me riding in it sometimes."

Bo tried to keep his voice steady and sure. "Like the night of the gathering when you and Omi traded places?"

Ruth's eyes flashed with disbelief, but the disbelief soon gave way to irritation. "I knew I couldn't trust Omi to keep the secret. She's too honest."

"Omi didn't have to tell me. I knew the minute she walked out of the bathroom wearing your dress."

To his surprise, Ruth seemed relieved. "I've been mad at you all this time because I thought you couldn't tell us apart. A *bu* should know his girlfriend's face, even if she's a twin."

"I can tell the difference between you and Omi. It's not that hard."

"*Ach*, *vell*, that's *gute* to know. I'm *froh* you weren't fooled."

"It wasn't nice to try to fool me, Ruth."

She laughed, but she was clearly forcing it for his benefit. "It was just a joke. I wanted to go riding with Elam, and I didn't want to hurt your feelings."

"My feelings were hurt worse that you didn't tell the truth."

She was getting increasingly agitated but trying not to show it, as if nobody should care about her going on a ride with Elam. "Why are you so sensitive? It didn't mean anything."

"It meant something to me. I thought you were starting to like me. I liked you. A lot." It wasn't the whole truth.

He had been well on his way to love. "And what you did really hurt."

"You make me sound like a horrible person, Bo, but it was just a ride in a car . . ."

"That you didn't tell me about. Then you tried to deceive me by sending Omi in your place." He cleared his throat and softened his tone. "How do you think that made me feel?"

Ruth drew her brows together, as if she had to think very hard, as if the question confused her. The truth hit him like a ton of bricks. Ruth hadn't even considered how he would feel because Ruth rarely showed consideration for his feelings at all. "Why do you always think about yourself, Bo? How do you think I felt? I have a boyfriend who never wants to do anything fun. What was I supposed to do? Trading places with Omi was the easiest way."

"Easiest for whom?"

There was the slightest of pauses. "Everybody. I got to go driving with Elam, and I thought you wouldn't notice we'd switched. No hurt feelings, no missing out on the fun. See? Easier for everybody."

Bo's irritation was only heightened by the glaring evidence of Ruth's selfishness. Why had he ignored it? A fruit bat couldn't have been more blind. He took a deep breath and remembered to be kind. "It was only easier for you, Ruth. I got mad at Omi, and she didn't deserve it, then I wore a hole in my stomach wondering if you were going to break up with me. Omi felt terrible about deceiving me."

Ruth waved her hand in the air as if swatting away a cloud of mosquitoes. "Omi is fine. She feels guilty all the time. She feels guilty when her rolls don't rise properly. She feels guilty when she forgets to make her bed in the morning." Ruth checked her phone again. "If you don't like what I do with my free time, that's your problem, not mine. What is *rumschpringe* for if I can't even have a little fun?"

She made it sound so sensible, like he was the one in the wrong. Like he was the one ruining all her fun. He frowned. Maybe it didn't matter if he was right or wrong or if Ruth could argue circles around him. Maybe it only mattered that he was happy.

Right now, he wasn't happy.

He had always felt extra special that a girl like Ruth could be interested in a quiet, serious *bu* like him, but now he wasn't even sure that he wanted Ruth's love. Would he be relieved if she broke things off and chose Elam instead? Was it *deerich* to let a girl like Ruth slip through his fingers? Every *bu* in the *gmayna* wanted to marry her.

That's why he needed to kiss her.

The kiss was the most important thing.

After he'd kissed Omi, his thoughts, his desires, his orbit had unexpectedly shifted. Something had come to life inside him when he'd kissed Omi, and he hadn't been the same since. His heart had pounded like a drum, his insides had done somersaults, and his head had spun, leaving him dizzy and giddy and completely off balance. Ruth's appeal had somehow faded, and Bo had become a moth to Omi's flame.

He needed to know if kissing Ruth was as *wunderbarr* as kissing Omi.

Maybe his orbit would shift again.

He eyed Ruth. Why wait for a sunset to find out? "Ruth, can I . . . I want to kiss you. Can I kiss you?"

Ruth arched an eyebrow. "Right now?"

*Don't do it. You're not thinking clearly*, his conscience

screamed at him. He ignored it. Now was the best time in the world. Action was surely better than all this uncertainty. "*Jah*. Right now."

A playful smile grew slowly on her lips. "Okay, I guess."

His heart galloped wildly as he wrapped his arms around her waist and she placed her hands on his shoulders and closed her eyes. He bent his head and brought his lips down on hers. She smelled like mosquito repellant, but Bo tried to ignore it. Her mouth was soft and warm, and he could feel her smile as their lips touched. Bo closed his eyes and waited for the fireworks, but he felt nothing but Ruth's casual disinterest.

"That was nice," she said when they pulled apart. "I've been waiting for that kiss for weeks. I'm *froh* you finally got up the courage." She patted his arm. It was probably meant to be encouraging. "I was hoping it would have been somewhere more exciting like at the top of a Ferris wheel or at the lake during the fireworks. Next time, I get to pick the place." She studied his face and must not have liked what she saw. "It's okay, Bo. Don't worry about it. The kiss was *gute*. We just need to work on your romantic imagination."

Bo tried to smile even as a pit formed at the bottom of his stomach. He shouldn't have kissed Ruth. It hadn't changed anything, and deep down, he had known it wouldn't. The kiss hadn't been the most important thing. He'd just been fooling himself. He'd been so swept up in the *idea* of Ruth that he hadn't stopped to consider how he really felt about her. Ruth lit up every room she entered. She was like the sun, and every *bu* in the *gmayna* wanted to bask in her light.

But she wasn't Omi.

Bo's heart thumped an uneven rhythm. Ruth might have been as bright as the sun, but Bo had always preferred moonlight caressing the night with its soft, gentle glow. Omi was moonlight, subtle, persuasive, tender. It had always been Omi, even though Bo had been temporarily blinded by the sun.

Bo had been hasty and immature, but there was no use dwelling on his mistakes. All he could do was move forward, and he wasn't going to waste one more minute chasing after the wrong *schwester*. "We both know I'm not as exciting or interesting as you are. I'm getting in the way of your fun."

"You are, but I forgive you. We just have different ideas on *rumschpringe*."

"And different ideas on just about everything." He gazed at her, sad he was about to hurt her feelings and sad he'd wasted so much time already. "My *mammi* told me I should have more self-respect than to date someone who thinks I'm a nuisance or that I'm *in the way*." He tried to temper his words so they wouldn't hurt when they landed on her. "I don't think we should see each other anymore. You'd rather spend time with Elam, and I'd rather date a girl who likes me just the way I am."

He could tell she didn't believe him. She rolled her eyes. "Do you want me to apologize? Okay, I apologize. I apologize for wanting a little excitement in my life before I get baptized. I apologize that you were worried and almost got an ulcer. But, Bo, you know me better than this. I like to have a *gute* time, I like to make jokes, and I love cars, but I would never dream of breaking up with you. I've known since the day you drove me home from the gathering that you're the *bu* I want to be with. You're godly and steady and strong and the handsomest *bu* in the *gmayna* by far. You can always be sure of my love."

If she loved him, she sure had a strange way of showing it. Thank Derr Herr his eyes were open. He didn't love

Ruth Coblenz, and the truth set him free. "I forgive you, Ruth, and I hope you'll forgive me, but you and I can't date anymore. It's just not going to work out."

For the first time since he'd known her, Ruth was at a loss for words. She stared at him as if he had a bird nesting in his hat. Her look was so intense, he put his hand on top of his head just to make sure there wasn't something up there. He looked into the sky. The light was fading, but he'd rather get a cavity filled than watch the sunset with Ruth now. "*Cum*, Ruth. I'll walk you back." He turned and took a few steps the way they'd come.

Her feet were rooted to the ground. "Just . . . just . . . now wait a minute. Let's talk about this."

"We've done plenty of talking."

Still, she wouldn't budge. "I didn't realize how badly I'd hurt your feelings, and I understand that right now you feel like lashing out. I suppose if the shoe had been on the other foot and you had gone driving with another girl, I would have been a little jealous, but I certainly wouldn't have overreacted like you did. Even so, I shouldn't have disregarded your feelings."

"I forgive you, Ruth."

"I'm certainly not perfect and I am too lighthearted at times, but I can't imagine you really want to break up. Why did you kiss me if you want to break up?"

"I was curious."

"Curious? You don't kiss a girl because you're curious. You kiss her because you love her. When you kiss a girl, she thinks you love her. I'm sure you love me. We've had so many fun times together, and it would be a shame if you just threw away our special relationship."

He got a little testy that Ruth wanted to put the blame on him. "That was your decision, not mine."

"Breaking up is not my decision."

"You're the one who decided to go riding with Elam," Bo said. "You're the one who decided not to tell me that he comes up here every week to take you driving."

Ruth stomped her foot. "I told you I just wanted to have a little fun. If you were so mad about it, why didn't you say something sooner?"

He sighed. "You're right. I should have said something, but I was afraid you'd break up with me. I shouldn't have worried."

"Of course you shouldn't have worried. I would never break up with you."

"It would have been easier if you'd broken up with me. Mammi says I deserve better."

Ruth's eyebrows nearly flew off her face. "You deserve better than *me*?"

He raised his hands as if stopping traffic. "*Nae*. I deserve a girl who adores me."

"I adore you," she said weakly.

He shook his head. "If you adored me, you wouldn't be driving around town with Elam."

"That's not true."

Bo wasn't going to argue that point any longer. "You are a *wunderbarr* girl, and you know that any *bu* would be lucky to marry you, but it won't be me. I'm not sad or angry. Sometimes, things just don't work out between two people. It's nobody's fault. Lord willing, you'll find someone you truly love. Maybe it's Elam."

"It's not Elam," Ruth hissed. "He's handsome, but he only cares about having a *gute* time. He can't be serious about anything." Ruth obviously didn't grasp that she was also describing herself.

"*Ach*, *vell*, maybe it's not Elam." He started walking toward Ruth's house, hoping she'd follow him so he wouldn't feel bad about leaving her alone by the side of the road.

Thank Derr Herr, she quickly caught up with him. "I said I'm sorry, Bo. Isn't that enough?"

"It's enough, but I don't want to date you anymore."

She walked faster to keep up with him. "We don't need to rush into anything. If you're that mad, why don't we just agree to take a break and not see each other for . . . a month? For sure and certain, you'll miss me more than you think you will."

"*Denki*, but *nae*."

It didn't take them too long to get to Ruth's house because Bo was moving as fast as he could without actually running.

Bo fully expected Ruth to keep trying to convince him not to break up with her. Instead, she ran up her porch steps and opened her front door. "Remember, Bo, we're not breaking up, just taking a break." Before he could protest yet again, she ducked into the house and slammed the door behind her.

He should have known she'd pull a trick like that. She liked to pull tricks. But it didn't matter. He'd made himself very clear, and she had gotten the message, even if she didn't want to believe it. He looked up at the sky and smiled so hard his lips hurt. He was done with Ruth Coblenz. Now it was on to greener pastures and the girl who owned his heart.

It was time to give Omi those pot holders.

# Chapter 10

Omi got home from the bakery just in time to eat. She'd brought home day-old rolls, eight of them, just enough for everyone in the family to have a roll for dinner. Mamm had made fried chicken and buttered noodles, and the house smelled heavenly. "*Cum reu*, Omi," Mamm called. Omi hung her black bonnet on the hook by the door and went into the kitchen where the whole family was sitting at the table. Mammi smiled at her. "We just said prayers. We didn't know when you'd be home."

"I don't mind," Omi said, pulling a bowl from the cupboard and setting her rolls in it. LaWayne grabbed two rolls before she even put the bowl on the table. "Only one, LaWayne. There's enough for us to have one each."

"He can have mine," Ruth said, smiling as if she'd just offered to donate a kidney.

Mamm nodded at Ruth. "That's wonderful nice of you. These days, LaWayne eats more than the rest of us combined."

"It's because I got that scooter," LaWayne said, spreading about a fourth of a stick of butter on one of his rolls.

"I'm getting a lot of exercise, and exercise makes me hungry."

Omi didn't necessarily think it was the scooter. LaWayne was always hungry, just like every other sixteen-year-old *bu*.

"How was work today?" Dat asked. He was always curious how Raber's business was going and always concerned when the bakery had a slow day.

"So busy," Omi said. "We sold out of almost everything we made this morning, including those no-bake cookies that nobody likes."

"I like no-bake cookies," LaWayne said.

Omi shrugged. "Somebody likes them, because they were gone by four o'clock."

Mamm passed Omi the noodles. "Ruth had a *gute* day too. Bo Helmuth came over and they went for a walk." Omi concentrated very hard on getting those slimy noodles from the serving spoon to her plate. Why did news about Bo send her heart crashing to her toes? Bo and Ruth had been seeing each other for months. Omi should be used to it by now.

"That's nice," Dat said. "Did he get his soybeans in?"

"*Ach*, Perry." Mamm swatted away his question. "Ruth and Bo are in love. They didn't talk about soybeans."

"*Nae*, no soybeans." Ruth plastered a smile on her face as if she was trying a little too hard to be happy.

Omi studied Ruth out of the corner of her eye. It wasn't like Ruth to fake cheerfulness. Things always went her way, so she never had to pretend. Omi's heart did a double backflip. Anna Helmuth had told Bo that he deserved a girl who adored him. She'd also told him that he should drop Ruth like a hot potato. Had he taken her advice? Was that why he'd taken Ruth on a walk? A lump lodged in Omi's throat. She didn't dare hope.

"Have I told you how much I like Bo?" Mamm announced, gushing like a fountain. Mamm had been praising Bo up one side and down the other ever since she had found out that Ruth was secretly meeting Elam and riding around town in his car. Of course Ruth didn't know that Mamm knew what she'd been up to. Mamm and Dat were always reluctant to interfere with *rumschpringe*, but that didn't stop her from worrying about what Ruth was doing with her life. It was obvious that Mamm's best hope for Ruth was that she would settle down and marry Bo Helmuth. Bo was handsome and godly and obedient, and he didn't own a car. Bo would never jump the fence or lie to his parents or put a boom box in his buggy. He was every Amish *mamm*'s dream.

Mamm leaned toward Ruth and teasingly pumped her eyebrows up and down. "He'll make a fine husband someday."

Ruth's smile faltered but quickly regained strength. "He will. And there's a piece of property right next to Ben's house where Bo wants to build a house."

Omi pressed her lips together. Maybe she'd misinterpreted Ruth's fake smile. Bo and Ruth were obviously talking about where they were going to live after they got married. Maybe things were going Ruth's way after all. Omi lost her appetite. "You can have my roll too, LaWayne."

Elmer's jaw fell open. "No fair! I want another roll."

LaWayne made a face at Elmer. "You can have it. You don't need to act like a baby."

"I'm not a baby. I'm ten, and I'm a growing *bu* too."

"You certainly are, Elmer," Dat said.

Omi could barely eat, but she stayed at the table until the bitter end in case Ruth gave her any clues about what she and Bo had talked about on their walk. Mamm slid her chair from the table. "Omi, Ruth, you have dishes tonight."

Ruth didn't groan or try to talk Mamm out of making her do chores. She just sighed, picked up her plate, and set it in the sink. Dat and LaWayne cleared their plates and went to patch a leak in the barn roof. Elmer and Eva were assigned to sweep the sidewalks, and Mamm went off to her sewing room. Ruth filled the sink with soapy water and started washing dishes, slowly and unenthusiastically.

Omi pulled a dish towel out of the drawer. "You're not yourself tonight, Ruth," she said hesitantly. That was as close as she dared get to Bo.

Ruth huffed out a breath and glanced behind her, making sure no one else was listening. "Bo found out about Elam."

Omi was the one who'd told Bo about Elam, but she hadn't ever told Ruth that she'd told Bo. She suddenly felt ashamed of herself. She should have disclosed everything from the very start, even if Ruth had gotten angry. Even if Ruth was hurt that her *schwester* would betray her like that. Omi fingered the new scar on her forehead. "I know. I told him."

Ruth stopped swishing the rag around the plate. "You told him?"

"*Jah.*" Omi squared her shoulders and clung tightly to her righteous indignation. "I couldn't stand the way you were treating him, and I didn't want to make excuses for you."

Ruth's surprise turned into a red-hot glare. "How could you?"

"I just told you. I can't lie for you anymore, Ruth."

"Not telling Bo about Elam isn't the same as lying. And trading places was just a little trick."

Omi shook her head. "A little trick that hurt his feelings."

Ruth threw her dishrag into the water and foam splattered all over the clean plates drying on the rack. "That's another thing. Why didn't you tell me Bo figured out we'd traded places? I thought we'd gotten away with it, and now I feel foolish that the two of you were keeping it a secret from me."

Omi cocked an eyebrow. "He felt foolish too, Ruth. He thought we were making fun of him with that trick."

"*Oy,* anyhow," Ruth said, leaning against the counter and folding her arms. "All this time, and I didn't know. You should have told me, Omi. I could have fixed it before his thoughts ran away with him. He says he wants to break up."

Omi's heart tried to claw its way out of her chest. "He does?"

"He doesn't mean it."

"Bo isn't one to throw idle words around." Omi tried not to sound too hopeful.

"Maybe, but he also kissed me. I can't believe he would kiss me if he wanted to break up."

Omi felt sick to her stomach. "He kissed you?"

"He said he was curious. And then he said I take him for granted."

"You do," Omi said.

"That's not true. I adore Bo, and I told him so, but he doesn't believe me. He's got it in his head that if he breaks up with me, I'll appreciate him more."

Omi pursed her lips. There were so many things she wanted to say, but it wasn't in her nature to be vindictive.

"Maybe he's right. You don't seem to care about him as much as you care about Elam and his car."

Ruth's eyes flashed with irritation. "Of course I care. Bo is trying to manipulate my feelings, that's all."

Omi swallowed the rude thing she wanted to say and tried to help Ruth see what she could not see. "But, Ruth, *you* manipulated his feelings when you asked me to trade places with you."

"I did not. That's nothing like what he's doing to me. He wants to make me grovel, to make me beg him to take me back, but he forgets that I gave him a chance in the first place. If I hadn't decided to overlook his painful shyness, we wouldn't be dating."

Ruth thought she was doing Bo a favor by being his girlfriend, but Bo wasn't shy. He was quiet and thoughtful. If Ruth didn't know the difference, she didn't deserve Bo. Of course Omi didn't think Ruth deserved Bo anyway, but Ruth's ignorance only made it more true. Omi took a deep breath and tried to tamp down her temper. "I'm sorry he broke up with you. That must really hurt."

"He didn't really break up with me, and I'm not hurt. I'm irritated. I don't like being manipulated."

"I don't blame you, and Bo is very wrong to do that to you. You should break up with him. That would teach him a lesson."

Omi knew better than to think that trick would work on Ruth. "I wouldn't give him the satisfaction," she said.

Omi wanted to grab Ruth's arms and shake some sense into her. Instead, she pulled her *schwester* in for a hug. "I know you're angry, but I just don't think Bo would break up with you out of spite. He's not the type to intentionally hurt or manipulate anyone or to try to get you to panic so you'll beg him to take you back. Bo is better than that. He's kind and sensitive and trustworthy."

Ruth snorted. "Trustworthy? He didn't tell me he knew you and I had traded places. He's not trustworthy."

Omi hugged Ruth tighter. "So he has faults like the rest of us. He was hurt that we traded places. Very hurt. I know because I was there. I saw his uncertainty. He was afraid you didn't like him anymore. It tore him apart. It was even worse when he found out about Elam. He was terrified you'd break up with him."

Ruth's eyes pooled with moisture. "He really does love me."

Omi couldn't speak to that. She certainly hoped not. "I can't imagine he wants to see you grovel. He just doesn't want to be hurt over and over again every time you go riding with Elam."

Ruth sniffed back her tears. "Like a roller coaster. He doesn't like the roller-coaster feeling."

"I guess not."

Ruth pulled a tissue from the box by the sink and wiped her nose. "I guess I can understand that. I had no idea he'd be that upset, but I truly didn't think he'd find out." She scrunched her eyebrows together. "*Ach*, Omi, I didn't give him a very sincere apology." She laid her head on Omi's shoulder and whimpered. "I suppose I did take him for granted. I like Elam, but I'd trade Bo for Elam any day, with or without a car."

Omi clenched her teeth. She had been trying to make Ruth see how badly she'd hurt Bo, and all she'd managed to do was make Ruth more determined to get back together with him. Omi could only hope that Bo was even more determined than Ruth. Surely it was too late for Ruth to fix it.

Ruth dabbed at her eyes. "It's not too late. I just have to convince Bo that I've changed, that I don't care one bit for Elam."

"What will you tell Elam?"

Ruth frowned. "*Ach*, he was going to take me to the Fourth of July fireworks in Green Bay."

Omi turned her face from Ruth so Ruth wouldn't see the disgust in her eyes.

"I was hoping to keep it a secret until after the fireworks. They're so *gute* in Green Bay, and one of Elam's *Englisch* friends lets him park in his driveway so he doesn't have to fight the traffic." Ruth sighed. "I suppose Bo and I will have to settle for the Shawano fireworks. And I'll tell Elam I won't go driving with him anymore. There's plenty of other girls who want a ride in that car."

"But how do you know Bo will want to take you to the fireworks? He broke up with you."

Ruth didn't seem concerned. "He wanted to break up, but I told him we shouldn't rush into things. I told him we should take a break for one month. That should give him plenty of time to miss me. Wait and see. He'll beg me to take him back. I give two weeks. That will still give us almost two months before the fireworks."

Omi lost all hope. Ruth was pretty—way prettier than Omi because of her scar—exciting, and so much more fun. Bo would lose his resolve before he woke up tomorrow morning.

Once again the guilt and shame gnawed at Omi like an overly eager beaver. Ruth was her dearest, closest friend in the whole world. Omi should be happy that Ruth was going to get her happily ever after. But Ruth's happily ever after was the one Omi wanted, and she just couldn't muster any *gute* wishes.

She was a horrible *schwester*.

\* \* \*

"Here you go, Mrs. Clawson. All you have to do is thaw them on a cookie sheet for an hour and then bake as directed."

Mrs. Clawson's hands shook as she took the bag of frozen sweet rolls from Omi. Mrs. Clawson was in the early stages of Parkinson's disease, and her diagnosis had upset everyone at the bakery. But Mrs. Clawson didn't want anyone to feel sorry for her, and she refused to let the disease defeat her spirit. Despite hard things, she was the kind, cheerful person she'd always been. Omi was determined to follow her example, even if Ruth and Bo killed all her hopes and dreams. "Thank you, Omi. Are these the instructions taped to the bag?"

"Yes, and the frosting is in the bag." She grinned. "But don't bake the frosting with the rolls, or you'll have to scrape plastic off your cookie sheet."

Mrs. Clawson cocked an eyebrow. "You've obviously seen me bake before."

Omi giggled. "Do you want me to carry the bag to your car for you?"

"For heaven's sakes, no. I want to do it myself while I still can."

The bell over the door rang when Mrs. Clawson opened it. Omi's heart skipped a beat as Bo Helmuth held the door for Mrs. Clawson then came into the bakery. Bo didn't usually come to the bakery, but ever since he'd conked her in the head with that two-by-four, he'd come in almost every day to check on her.

The smile on his face almost knocked Omi over. "*Vie gehts?* It's a beautiful day, don't you think?"

Omi smiled back at him, even though she didn't feel much like smiling. "What brings you in today?"

If he kept looking at her like that, she would definitely fall over. "You want to know why I've come in? I thought you would have guessed by now."

She willed herself not to blush, but it wasn't easy, even if Bo was Ruth's boyfriend, sort of. "I'm guessing you came in for the jelly doughnuts. We make the best in Wisconsin."

He shook his head. "It's not the jelly doughnuts."

"A cinnamon roll."

"Nope."

A shiver of pleasure traveled up her spine. "Whatever you want, you should hurry and make your selection. We close in five minutes."

He clapped his hands together. "That's perfect, because I've come for you."

"Me?" She'd probably never been this close to fainting in her life.

He grinned like a three-year-old. "*Jah.* That's why I came at closing time."

"Um . . . okay," she said, unsure how to respond to such brazen attention.

He leaned against the front window and folded his arms. "I'll just wait right here."

She looked down at her hands, sure she was redder than the curtains in the window. "You should have something to eat while you wait."

"What have you got left?"

"Two chocolate cake doughnuts, an old-fashioned, one sweet roll, and a few dollar rolls."

He pulled a dollar bill out of his pocket. "How about a dollar roll?"

She put a roll in a white bag and handed it to him. "That will be fifty cents."

"Fifty cents? I thought they were dollar rolls?"

She couldn't help but grin. "I think they're named that because they're the size of silver dollars."

He chuckled. "Quite misleading, if you ask me."

"I thought I heard a familiar voice out here." Thomas Raber appeared from the back room with a small bag of powdered sugar in his arms. Thomas and his *fraa*, Gloria, owned the Sweet Stop Bakery, and each of their twelve children had worked here at one time or another. All their children were grown, but four of them still helped in their parents' business.

"*Hallo*, Thomas," Bo said. "Nice to see you."

"It looks like Omi's already set you up with a snack. What else can I do for you?"

"*Ach*." Was he blushing? "I've come for Omi, so I'm just standing around until you close."

Thomas's gaze flicked from Omi to Bo. "Since you've got nothing to do, I could use your muscle in the back."

Bo pushed himself away from the window. "For sure and certain. What can I do?"

"I need you to move a thousand pounds of flour."

Bo grinned. "I don't have that much muscle."

Omi averted her eyes. It would do no *gute* for Bo to catch her staring at his broad shoulders.

"*Nae*," Thomas said. "I need twenty fifty-pound bags moved from the wagon to the shelf. I can do it, but you're less likely to hurt your back."

Bo laughed. "I'd be happy to help. Lead the way."

Thomas winked at Omi. "Take your time closing up. I need him to finish all twenty bags."

Omi grinned. "I'll go wonderful slow."

Bo laughed again. "Glad to help."

An *Englisch* man rushed into the bakery one minute before closing and bought the rest of everything they had. It was a perfect day at the bakery when nothing was left over. It didn't happen very often. Omi wiped down all the counters and washed the trays then put everything where it belonged for opening tomorrow.

Just as she finished wiping the last tray, Bo and Thomas came from the back. Bo's face and shirt were dusted with flour. "That took longer than I thought," she said. "Are you sure you weren't stalling so you wouldn't have to help with the cleanup?"

Thomas leaned his hand on the counter. "*Nae*. After he loaded the flour, I had him dump the sugar into the bin and break down a dozen boxes. Strike while the iron is hot, I always say."

Bo brushed some flour off his shoulder. "Remind me to wait outside next time."

Thomas tapped his finger to his temple. "I'm smarter than most people think. I know an opportunity when I see one."

Bo grinned at Omi. "Shall we go? I brought my buggy."

"You want to drive me home? I only live three blocks that way."

Bo glanced at Thomas. "I do."

Thomas waved them out the door. "Go, go. I'm too old to care what you're up to."

Both Bo and Omi laughed at that, and Omi's heart galloped even faster. Even though they could never be a couple, she couldn't keep herself from smiling. She and Bo had been through a lot together, and she'd enjoy the moments he wanted to spend with her.

She already lived with the heartbreak every day.

Bo seemed to bounce down the street to his buggy. He slid open the door and motioned for Omi to get in on his side. Then he jumped in next to her.

"This is a lot of trouble for three blocks."

He picked up the reins. "You're injured. Why should you walk when I'm willing to drive?"

"But why?"

He ignored the question and guided the horse down the road. "How's your head feeling?"

Omi's hand automatically went to her forehead. "*Ach*, the scar is a little tender but only when I touch it. It fades a little more every day. Dr. Patel did a *gute* job."

"She did," he said, his eyes shining. "I think it looks really cute."

Omi eyed him skeptically. "It does not."

"It does. I'm sorry it happened, and I'm sorry it's my fault, but I think it looks really attractive on your face, with the added advantage that no one will confuse you for Ruth ever again."

Omi nodded. "Ruth is almost irritated about that."

"I bet she is." He said it with a tinge of amusement in his voice. He seemed to have gotten over his bitterness.

"It really wasn't your fault. I was mad at you and sort of charged you like a bull."

He fell silent for a few minutes. "I know why you were mad at me."

"I'm not proud of it. You wanted to be honest with Ruth, and I was trying to talk you out of it."

"That's not why you were mad at me. You were mad because I made excuses for Ruth that I wouldn't have made for anyone else. You were mad that I didn't have enough self-respect to break up with her right then and there."

Omi smiled weakly, and she cleared her throat. "I guess that's about right."

"That is exactly right. You were right."

"I was right about being exactly right?"

"Exactly," he said.

Omi grinned in spite of herself. "What exactly are you trying to say here?"

"Just that I'm a little bit smarter than I was that day at the barn raising."

She nodded. "You should be. I hope you've learned that when you have long boards propped on your shoulder, never turn without looking."

He chuckled. "I've definitely learned that. But there's more."

"Go on."

He turned in the opposite direction of Omi's house. "Do you mind if I show you something before I take you home?"

Omi's heart did a flip. "I suppose. Where are we going?"

"It's a surprise."

She rolled her eyes. "You're just full of surprises." Speaking of surprises . . . "Ruth says you broke up with her."

He burst into a smile. "No explanations yet. We're almost there."

Omi blew air from between her lips. Bo was kind and handsome and thoughtful, but he could be very aggravating without even trying. They pulled onto a little turnoff and headed into a thick grove of trees. The grove gave way to a meadow of late spring wildflowers and tall grass. Smack-dab in the middle of the meadow sat a stone bench that looked like it had been there for hundreds of years.

Bo glanced at her, his face full of light. "I found this place years ago when I was out exploring with my *bruderen.* It's the perfect spot for a wrestling match. Or a nap. We mostly used it for Hide and Seek and spying on rabbits and bears. We never saw a bear, but we saw plenty of rabbits."

"It's beautiful," Omi said. "And exactly why did you bring me here?"

"Not yet."

She was tempted to stomp her foot as she got out of the buggy. "Not yet what?"

She nearly jumped out of her skin when he took her hand and tugged her to the bench. He motioned for her to sit, then ambled a few feet away and broke a Purple Prairie Clover from its stem. He came back to the bench, sat down next to her, and handed her the flower. She instinctively put it up to her nose, though wildflowers didn't usually smell especially sweet. The gesture was more to cover her face from his view because if her face got any hotter, steam was going to start rising from her cheeks.

What was he up to? She didn't dare hope that it was exactly what it looked like. Maybe Bo brought all his friends and relatives here and picked wildflowers for each of them.

He pulled something red and fluffy from his pocket. "First of all, I want to give you these pot holders."

She took them and smoothed her hand along the extra soft yarn. "These are so pretty. *Denki.* I can use them when I bake."

He suddenly seemed too serious. "*Gute.* I hope you really enjoy them."

"I will," she said, because he seemed to care very much about a pair of pot holders.

A long pause. Should she say something to break the awkward silence? "Omi, I've been an idiot."

She stretched her lips over her teeth. "You brought me all the way out here to tell me this?"

He laughed nervously. "I brought you all the way out here because I wanted to be alone." He took her hand, and she flinched. He grimaced. "I'm sorry. Am I making you uncomfortable?"

Wildly uncomfortable. "I don't mind."

He grew even more serious. "Omi, I was completely fascinated with Ruth. She's fun and exciting and . . . I guess I've already told you. But something happened to me that night we kissed. It was like I got hit by lightning." Doubt saturated his expression. "Please tell me I'm not the only one who felt that way."

Omi was suddenly light-headed. "I . . . *jah*, it was . . . that kiss . . . I've never felt anything like it."

He threw back his head and laughed. "*Ach*, Omi, you don't know how badly I've wanted to hear you say that." He squeezed her hand. "It's all clear now, and I was so blind. I fooled myself into thinking I was in love with Ruth. I made excuses for her behavior, even though I knew it was wrong. Do you remember how surprised I was that you had helped her deceive me, but I wasn't at all surprised that the whole thing had been her idea. I began to see that you have more kindness, consideration, and integrity than Ruth ever will. Ruth is fun and exciting, but in the ways that are important, you are ten times the girl Ruth is."

Omi hadn't known what to expect when she sat down on the bench, but Bo's little speech was beyond her wildest dreams. For ten glorious seconds, she felt as if she could fly, but the feeling was brief, and she pulled her hopes back to Earth before they got too high. "Ruth says you kissed her."

Bo eyed her hesitantly. "I did. I wanted to see if kissing you was the reason for my wild happiness or just kissing in general." He smiled. "It was definitely kissing you. I felt nothing special when I kissed Ruth except the sting of DEET in my nose. She didn't feel anything either, though she wouldn't admit it. She said it was because we weren't in a romantic place, but it was because neither of us was with the right person." He smoothed his thumb across the back of her hand. "Omi, I know this seems sudden, but it's been coming on for weeks. Can I date you? Can I drive you home from the next gathering? I want to date you, and I'll be devastated if you don't feel the same way."

Omi had never been so completely happy or so completely miserable in her whole life. Bo Helmuth wanted to date her! It was *wunderbarr* and glorious, a dream come true.

But the person Omi loved most in the world wanted to marry Bo. Ruth would be heartbroken if Omi stole Bo right out from under her nose. It was horrible and heartbreaking.

What could she do?

Omi wasn't prone to fits of anger or elation, but she couldn't stop herself from cuffing Bo on the shoulder and growling her displeasure. "You're an idiot, Bo Helmuth."

The amorous look on his face disappeared, and his eyes got as round and as big as dinner plates. "I already know that. I just told you so."

"You don't know the half of it. I have loved you ever since fifth grade, and you completely ignored me. You were so enamored with my *schwester* that you barely knew I existed."

"That's not true. We were always friends."

Omi snorted in derision. "Friends? Ruth was the center of your world. I was a dirt clod. Ruth is brighter and more exciting, and you were like a cat, always chasing the shiny object and ignoring the cat food."

He drew his brows together. "You're not cat food."

She groaned and waved her hand in the air. "*Ach*. You know what I mean."

"*Nae*, I don't."

"You ignored and overlooked me. Can you imagine how that made me feel?"

Omi took perverse satisfaction in Bo's complete shock and growing remorse. He *should* feel regret for being an idiot. His shortsightedness had ruined any chance of happiness that Omi might have had.

He spread his hands in front of him. "There are no words to tell you how sorry I am for the pain I put you through, but I see you now, Omi. Aren't you *froh* I came to my senses?"

The anxiety and confusion on his face melted her righteous indignation. She exhaled slowly and laid her hand over his. His eyes flashed with surprise. "I am *froh*, Bo. I have been wanting to hear you say those very words for a long time. But it doesn't matter anymore. It's no use crying over spilled milk."

"Of course it matters. I've broken up with Ruth. Now you and I can be together."

With her anger spent, she made a valiant effort to hold back threatening tears. "If only you had dated me first, instead of being so infatuated with Ruth! Ruth still wants to marry you. She still thinks you're dating."

"I broke up with her," Bo said through gritted teeth. "Besides, I don't care what Ruth thinks."

"I do. She is insistent that the two of you are just taking a break. If you start to date me, she'll say I stole her boyfriend. She will see it as the worst kind of betrayal. For all her faults, I love her dearly. She's not only my twin *schwester*, but my closest friend. You and I can never be together because I would never intentionally break Ruth's heart." She managed to keep the tears at bay, but her chest ached so badly, it hurt to take a breath.

Bo fell silent, frowning as if there would never be any happiness in the world ever again. The chirping birds and buzzing bees filled the silence between them. "I see why you're so mad at me."

"I shouldn't have lashed out like that. Anger solves nothing, and I'm sorry for losing my temper."

"Don't apologize." His lips twitched upward. "At least I know you have strong feelings for me."

"Very strong." She couldn't help but grin. He always tried to find the good in every situation, even if there wasn't one.

He squinted and fingered the stubble on his chin. "I don't want to argue with you, but you're wrong when you say we can never be together."

"I'm not wrong, and hoping otherwise will just lead to more heartache."

"What if Ruth decides that I'm too boring and wants to break up with me?"

Omi shook her head. "She would never do that. You're too irresistible."

He gave her a brilliant smile. "You think I'm irresistible?"

"It's not a reason to rejoice, Bo. Ruth thinks you're irresistible too. It's why she can't accept that you've broken up with her."

"Okay, then," he said. "Let's assume I'm irresistible." He pumped his eyebrows up and down and made Omi laugh in spite of herself. "What if Ruth finds someone she likes better than me? What about Elam? She must like him, or she wouldn't have missed the chance to be with 'irresistible' me."

Omi rolled her eyes. "Okay. I shouldn't have said anything about your being irresistible. Your head is going to swell to twice its size."

"But what about Elam? If Ruth married Elam, she wouldn't care if you and I dated, would she?"

A glimmer of hope pricked Omi's heart. "That might work. But it won't be Elam. He's very *gute*-looking, but Ruth likes his car better than she likes him. He'd have to sell the car before he can get baptized and marry Ruth. She'll lose interest wonderful fast."

Bo snatched up her hand again. "Omi, I think I love you."

She caught her breath. "I think I love you too, but . . ."

"*Nae, nae,* don't say 'but.' We love each other. I know we can make this work so everyone, including Ruth, is happy."

"Okay," she said, trying not to let her hope run away with her common sense. "What should we do?"

"First of all, can you and I still be friends? I mean, I don't want Ruth to suspect anything, but I'll go crazy if I can't be with you."

She nodded. "I suppose we can, but I won't lie to Ruth, and I won't sneak around like a thief. We have to be honest and careful."

"Careful as a mouse stealing the cheese from a mouse-trap."

She smirked. "That sounds about right."

"Second of all, it's time to call on the best matchmaker in Wisconsin. If she can't help us, no one can."

# Chapter 11

Bo jogged up Mammi's porch steps, tapped on the door, and opened it before anyone could answer it. *"Hallo!"* he said, announcing himself as he walked into the house. He was determined, excited, hopeful, terrified, and eager to get started. Or eager to get Mammi started.

Mammi and Dawdi sat at the table across from each other, each staring at the gallon-size glass bottles sitting in front of them. Dawdi glanced at Bo, smiled, and quickly returned to staring at his bottle. Mammi set down a stick she'd been holding, stood, and gave Bo a warm hug. "I'm *froh* you're here," she whispered into his ear. "Your *dawdi* is trying a new hobby, and you're going to have to put me in an asylum before the day is done."

A book and several sheets of paper sat on the table next to the bottles, along with four different types of glue, a pair of scissors, two spools of thread, and a pile of dowels and blocks of wood. Bo smiled and sat at the head of the table. "This looks fun. What are you working on?"

Dawdi picked up his bottle and peered into it from the opening in the neck. "We've decided to tackle something really challenging."

Mammi's smile was all affection and irritation. "I haven't

mastered painting or chair yoga, but Felty thinks I need something else to keep me busy so I won't interfere in other people's lives."

"I never said that, Annie-banannie. I just think trying new things keeps you young."

Mammi picked up her bottle and looked into it just as Dawdi was doing. "*Ach*, Felty, you are so thoughtful about my health, but I don't need any new hobbies. Matchmaking keeps me plenty young, and it has the added benefit of helping our poor, lonely grandchildren. Putting a model ship in a bottle doesn't help anyone."

"But it's fun," Dawdi said, as if he didn't even believe it himself.

Mammi shrugged in resignation. "I'm usually very *gute* with my hands, but this is even beyond my skill. You have to make a model ship with masts and sails and ropes and somehow stuff it into this bottle without breaking it. Reasonable people don't even dare try."

Bo tapped on Mammi's bottle. "It sounds hard. But half the fun of a project like this is figuring it out."

Mammi stared at Bo for a few seconds. "That's not fun at all. It's just frustrating."

"Let's try it, Annie. I think we might find out we enjoy it."

Mammi didn't look convinced. "I'll do anything for you, Felty. I'm just complaining a little first. People who don't complain don't get any pity."

Bo chuckled. "You have my pity, Mammi."

Mammi patted Bo on the cheek. "I can always count on you. You're such a fine young man."

Mammi picked up a pencil and opened the notebook sitting on the table. "What if I made a buggy in a bottle instead of a ship?" She chewed on the eraser, drew a square in her notebook, and chewed on her eraser some more. "It wonders me if I could get a horse in the bottle."

Much as Bo would love to sit and watch Mammi attempt to draw a buggy, he was a man in love, and his desperation made him impatient. "Mammi, I hate to interrupt your work, but I'm in trouble."

Mammi furrowed her brow in deep concern. "No need to apologize. You know I'm happy to drop everything to help one of my grandchildren. What is the problem?"

"I've made a mess of things with Omi and Ruth, and I need your help."

Mammi nodded as if she already knew his whole story. "*Ach*, I was afraid this would happen, but there was no way to avoid it. You have to go to school, or you won't learn the lessons."

"I like Omi a lot."

Mammi smiled serenely at Dawdi. Dawdi smiled back. "Omi is such a sweet girl. Always cheerful and willing to help. She's easy to like."

Mammi and Dawdi had known all along. Bo was the one who had been blind. "I like Omi, so I broke up with Ruth."

"That was smart."

"I broke up with Ruth, but Ruth still likes me, and Omi won't date me because she doesn't want to hurt Ruth. But I like Omi, and if I lose her, I'll never be happy again."

"I'm so *froh* your love life is going badly," Mammi said. "It means we get to see you more often." She propped her elbows on the table and laced her fingers together. "So you need me to find a match for Ruth."

Bo let out a slow breath. He and Mammi understood each other perfectly. "*Jah*."

"And the sooner the better, I expect."

"If it wouldn't be too much trouble."

Mammi peered at Dawdi. "I'm afraid I'm going to have to put the ship project on hold, Felty. Bo's future happiness needs my full attention."

"So you want to abandon ship?" Dawdi laughed. Neither Mammi nor Bo were quite sure what was so funny. Dawdi's smile faded. "It's a military joke."

"*Denki* for sharing it with us, dear." Mammi tore the page with the square she'd just drawn out of her notebook and picked up her pencil. "Okay, then, Bo. We've got to make a list." She looked up at the ceiling. "Two lists." She looked heavenward again. "Three lists. We've got to make three lists."

"Okay?" Bo said. He wasn't sure how many lists they needed, but Mammi was the expert so he'd go along with whatever she said.

"First we need to make a list of Ruth's *gute* qualities. Then we need a list of her bad qualities. Finally, we need a list of all *die buwe* in the *gmayna* and all *die buwe* who live within twenty-five miles."

"I don't know all *die buwe* within twenty-five miles," Bo said.

"We just have to go with what we know and pray that Gotte will guide us in our search. Does Omi have any ideas?"

"Of *buwe*?"

"*Jah*. She knows Ruth better than anyone."

Bo frowned. "We didn't really talk about it."

Mammi shrugged. "*Ach, vell,* let's make our list as best we can, and you can talk to Omi later. If we all put our heads together, I'm sure we can come up with a *wunderbarr* list." She drew three lines at the top of the paper. Above the first line, she wrote: "Good Things About Ruth." Above the second line was: "Opportunities for Growth." She smiled at Bo. "This is where we will list Ruth's bad qualities, but 'opportunities' sounds nicer, don't you think?" On the third line she put: "Possible Husbands, Ages 17-35."

"That seems a little old, Mammi."

Mammi didn't hesitate. "It's going to be hard enough finding Ruth a husband without counting out the widowers and desperate bachelors. She's not sweet or kind like Omi, and I doubt she knows how to make German apple pancakes."

Mammi was right, and Bo suddenly got very discouraged. Who in the world would they convince to marry Ruth? At one time, he had thought Ruth was the most *wunderbarr*, most desirable girl in the whole world. Now that he knew her better, he couldn't imagine anyone falling in love with her. "She cleans four houses every week," he mumbled.

Mammi perked up. "I'm putting that on my list. Tidiness is a *gute* quality." She scrunched her lips together. "I'm writing 'hard worker' even though I don't know if she's really a hard worker. I think we should give her the benefit of the doubt."

Mammi wrote "tidy," "fun," "adventurous," and "pretty" on her list. Dawdi suggested "clever" and "doesn't smell bad." Bo added "*gute* laugh," "full of life," and "nice teeth."

The "Opportunities for Growth" list was easier, but Bo didn't want to pile on the bad qualities, so he only made three suggestions: "selfish," "tricky," and "only looks out for herself," which was kind of like selfish, but Mammi wasn't picky about what went on her list.

They patched together a list of Ruth's *gute* qualities and her "opportunities for growth" then started in on a list of *buwe*. Mammi wrote "Vernon Schmucker" at the top of the list.

Vernon was almost forty years old, a hundred pounds overweight, and completely unaware of his "opportunities for growth." "*Ach, nae*, Mammi," Bo said. "Vernon is too old, and Ruth won't even look twice at him."

Dawdi shook his head so hard, he fanned up a breeze. "Absolutely not, Annie. Vernon is not setting foot in our home again unless it's for church."

Mammi stuck out her bottom lip. "But I feel so bad for him. I've tried to match him with four of my grand-daughters, and it's never worked out. I feel I owe him something."

"*Cum*, Annie. Bo is a *bu* in love. He needs to find Ruth a husband as soon as possible. Vernon will just waste precious time."

Mammi sighed and crossed Vernon off her list. "You're right, Felty, as always, but now there are no names on our list." Mammi tapped the pencil on the notebook. "What about Elam? He's the one who started this whole mess."

Bo propped his elbow on the table. "I should probably thank him. In a roundabout way, he brought Omi and me together . . . even though we aren't really together yet."

Mammi considered it for a minute. "He's been very useful so far."

"Omi says Ruth likes Elam's car better than she likes Elam."

Mammi wrote his name on the list. "I don't think we can count him out. And look, Elam spelled backward is 'male.' For sure and certain Gotte is trying to tell us something."

Bo didn't know what Gotte was trying to tell them, but Mammi was the expert. He wouldn't question her methods. "Menno Glick has nice hair."

"Does Ruth like hair?"

"It can't hurt."

Mammi wrote Menno on the list and put "hair" next to his name. Then she went back and put "car" and "handsome" next to Elam. "Lists are better with more information." She narrowed her eyes. "What about Raymond Fisher? He's Elam's cousin, and he introduced Elam and Ruth. I just gave his *mamm* some very nice pot holders. I think that could help us." She wrote "Raymond," "pot holders," and "brave" on her list.

"Why brave, Mammi?"

"*Ach*, he killed a snake in his barn last summer, then on a dare, he cooked it and ate it. That's bravery if I ever saw it." She tilted her head as if thinking deep thoughts then wrote "willing to do disgusting things" next to "brave." "You never know what information will be useful later on."

Next to Dade Nelson Mammi wrote "missing two teeth." Next to Jesse Riehl she wrote "can't whistle" and "eats raw eggs for fun." Mammi knew a lot of random information, even though Bo didn't see how it could be useful. Then again, who knew what Ruth might find interesting?

Once they had a list of ten *buwe*, Mammi smiled and closed her notebook. "This is a very *gute* start. While Felty works on getting a ship into his bottle, I'm going to rank these *buwe* in order from most promising to least promising and start passing out pot holders."

Bo leaned back in his chair. His head hurt from concentrating so hard. "What do you want me to do?"

"Make sure all *die buwe* know you've broken up with Ruth. Plant the idea in their heads that Ruth is available. But you have to be careful, because if they wonder why you broke up with Ruth, they might ask uncomfortable questions. Don't lie, but you want them to believe that Ruth would make a *gute fraa*."

"I don't know if I can do that—trick someone into marrying Ruth just so I can date Omi."

"It's not a trick. Someone out there is more than willing to marry Ruth, but you can't start a fire without a spark." Mammi opened the notebook and pointed to list number one. "Ruth has gute qualities. Someone who isn't too picky is bound to fall in love with her." She frowned. "It wonders me if I should put Vernon Schmucker back on the list."

"Don't do it, Annie."

# Chapter 12

"Do you think Bo will be there today?" Ruth said, smoothing her hand down her dress.

"I don't know," Omi said.

Ruth got that glint in her eye like she knew a secret Omi didn't. "For sure and certain he'll be there. His *mammi* likes to match her grandchildren, and it's natural that she would be trying to get me and Bo married. That has to be why she invited us to her house. Bo probably even asked her to invite me because he wants to get back together but is too proud to ask."

Omi usually couldn't get enough of Bo Helmuth. She loved thinking about him, talking about him, watching him from across the room at *gmay*, even dreaming about him. But today, the last thing Omi wanted to hear about was Bo, mostly because Ruth wouldn't stop talking about him. *I just love Bo Helmuth. He's surely regretting all those horrible things he said to me. When we get married, I'll have the most handsome husband in the* gmayna. *Won't all the other girls be jealous?*

Omi had tried to discourage Ruth, talk her out of liking Bo so much. It wasn't just because Omi liked Bo and Bo liked Omi. Omi truly didn't want to see her *schwester* get hurt, and Bo didn't love Ruth. When Ruth finally realized it, her hopes for Bo were going to be dashed to pieces. Not only would she be heartbroken, but she'd feel like a fool.

Omi couldn't worry about Ruth's heartbreak when she had her own sorrow to deal with. Ruth talked about how much she missed Bo, but Omi felt the ache of longing clear to her bones. Even surrounded by family, the loneliness closed around her. She loved Bo so much, but had no one to confide in, no one who could feel sorry for her or even tell her everything was going to be okay. Marilyn had left for Pennsylvania last week to be with her boyfriend, and the mail was too slow when someone needed to talk about love.

What if Bo couldn't make things right? What if Ruth never found a husband? What if bitter memories were the only thing Omi had to look forward to? What if she died an old *maedel*?

She took a shuddering breath and tried to think happy thoughts. Bo loved her. Bo loved her! He said he would fix things. His *mammi* was working on a plan. What could possibly go wrong?

They strolled up Huckleberry Hill toward Anna and Felty's house. It was a beautiful afternoon, clear, sunny skies and mild temperatures. Anna had invited them to a Popsicle party, which sounded strange and maybe fun. What was a Popsicle party, and why did Anna want Omi and Ruth to be there?

Lord willing, it had something to do with Bo's plan to find Ruth a husband. What did Anna have up her sleeve? Would it work? Would Ruth suspect they were plotting against her?

They reached the top of the hill where four buggies were already parked. Ruth caught her breath. "For sure and certain Bo is here." She grabbed Omi's hand. "Will you help me?"

"Help you what?"

"Divert Anna's attention so Bo and I can sneak away. We need to have a serious talk."

Omi sighed clear down to her toes. "Ruth, you know I love you, but Bo hasn't so much as looked at you for three weeks. He's stopped coming over, and he doesn't even say hello at *gmay*. How many times do I need to tell you? He doesn't want to be your boyfriend."

Ruth didn't like hearing such talk, ever. "Omi, I know Bo a lot better than you do, and I know how his mind works. I hurt his feelings, and he's giving me some time to think about it, to regret it. He wants me to get frustrated and beg him to take me back." She stopped short and looked at the house. "I guess it's working. I am frustrated, mostly frustrated that he's letting this go on much longer than it has to. I'm ready to take him back, and I know he wants to date again. He kissed me, you know."

"*Jah*. I know."

"You don't kiss a girl and break up with her if you're not planning to get back together." She pressed her lips together. "I've been patient, but he'll always miss me more than I miss him. It won't be much longer now." She smiled as if she had a lovely secret. "Lord willing, today is the day."

"You said you don't want to get back together with Bo until after the Fourth of July. Aren't you still planning to go with Elam to Green Bay?"

Ruth swatted away that concern. "That's only if Bo and I haven't gotten back together before then. He's still got almost two months. It will drive Bo crazy with jealousy if I go to Green Bay with Elam. Lord willing, Bo will come to his senses before then. I'd much rather watch fireworks in Shawano than go to Green Bay with Elam anyway."

That wasn't exactly what Ruth had told Omi the last time they'd talked about fireworks, but Ruth had every right to change her mind. And Omi had every right to be irritated. She was loyal to her *schwester*, but that didn't mean she had to like her very much right now.

Ruth grabbed Omi's arm. "Come on, Omi, just help me find a way to be alone with Bo."

Omi pulled her arm from Ruth's grasp. "I'm sorry, but I'm done interfering. The last time you talked me into helping you, I ended up being completely mortified. I won't do it again."

Ruth glared in Omi's direction. "Do you love me or not, Omi, because that's what it all comes down to."

Omi felt the familiar twinge of guilt, resentment, and frustration she always felt when Ruth accused her of not caring enough. She huffed out a breath and swallowed her guilt. "I'm not helping. Bo isn't even your boyfriend anymore."

Ruth came to a swift halt and frowned. "What is he doing here?"

"Who?"

She pointed to a faded red car parked behind one of the buggies. It had been hidden from view until they'd gotten to the top of the hill. "Elam is here."

Anna had invited Elam? Elam had actually come? Things were getting more and more interesting by the minute. "Do you want me to help you two sneak away? Maybe you can make plans for the Fourth of July."

Ruth looked at Omi as if she'd said something very offensive. "You'll help me sneak off with Elam but not Bo?"

Omi felt her face get warm. "That's about right."

Ruth stuck her nose in the air. "Some *schwester* you are. Despite what you think, I'm smarter than that. If Bo is here, he'll be hurt if I leave with Elam. I wish he weren't so touchy, but it can't be helped, especially if I want him to come back to me."

"Does Elam know about Bo?"

"Of course. You always think the worst of me, Omi. I told you, Elam cares more about his car than he does about me, and I care more about his car than I do about him. Raymond told Elam all about me and Bo and that we're planning on getting married. You've got to help me get rid of him."

"Bo or Elam?"

Ruth scowled. "Elam, of course."

"Anna invited him. We can't just uninvite him."

"Come on, Omi. Just help me. If only you didn't have that scar, you could trick Elam into taking you out for a drive and leave me here with Bo."

"It's really too bad," Omi said, pressing her fingers to her new scar. The Bible said to give thanks in all things. She said a little prayer of thanks for her scar.

Ruth squared her shoulders. "I'll think of a way. Just stay close if I need to act fast."

Omi gave Ruth a little curtsy. "Yes, Your Majesty."

Ruth nudged Omi with her hand and giggled. "Okay, I'm sorry. I didn't mean to get bossy. I just love Bo so much, and I've already messed it up once."

Omi cocked an eyebrow in surprise. Ruth rarely owned up to a mistake. "Stop trying to make everything go according to your plan. Just try to have fun."

"I know how to have fun," Ruth insisted. "But I also need to impress Bo and get rid of Elam. It's a lot of pressure, and

I need to be able to count on your help, Omi. Is that too much to ask of a *schwester*?"

"You're not the boss of me," Omi said in her best six-year-old voice, just like she used to do when they were little girls.

Ruth smirked. "But we stick together, no matter what."

"Like that time you went riding with Elam and left me to fend for myself with Bo?"

"Okay, okay, that wasn't very nice, and you did warn me it wouldn't go well. I should have listened." Ruth sighed. "But I sure did have fun in Elam's car."

"I can smell the remorse from here."

Ruth laughed and draped her arm around Omi's shoulder. "You know I love you, right?"

Omi knew it, but that didn't make Ruth's behavior more acceptable. "Let's get in there before all the Popsicles melt."

"I want banana flavor."

"Save at least one banana for me. They're my favorite too."

Anna opened the door as Omi and Ruth walked up the porch steps. "It's the Coblenz *schwesteren*! I'm *froh* you could come. We are already having too much fun for our britches."

"Who's here?" Ruth said, untying her black bonnet and slipping it off her head.

Anna clapped her hands. "*Ach*, just about every *bu* in the district." She ushered Omi and Ruth into the house. "Welcome to our Popsicle party."

Five *buwe* and Felty sat around Anna's kitchen table each with a pile of Popsicle sticks in front of them. Another huge stack of sticks sat in the center of the table. Ruth leaned close to Omi and whispered, "I think we got the wrong idea about the Popsicle party."

Raymond Fisher, at the far end of the table, jumped to his feet when Omi and Ruth walked in the door. "*Hallo*, Ruth. *Hallo*, Omi. *Gute* to see you." Raymond, Elam's cousin, was a quiet boy with straight brown hair and blue eyes. He constantly wore a mischievous smile, as if he were planning a new way to get into trouble.

Elam sat next to Raymond, with Jesse Riehl next to him and Dade Nelson next to Jesse. Vernon Schmucker sat by Dade. Omi recoiled slightly at the sight of Vernon. He was an overeager bachelor who couldn't take a hint that a girl wasn't interested in him. Omi would have to steer clear. Vernon didn't need one iota of encouragement.

Were these *die buwe* Anna had chosen for Ruth? Except for Elam, they had all been in the district their whole lives. Omi couldn't see any of them catching Ruth's interest. And Vernon Schmucker was unacceptable. What had Anna been thinking?

Felty waved at them with a stick then lowered his head over the project he was working on.

Ruth sort of cranked a smile across her face. "That's a lot of Popsicle sticks."

Anna beamed like a flashlight. "Felty and I are trying a new hobby. It's called Popsicle sticking. I made it up, and that's what we're calling it now. It's making crafts with Popsicle sticks. I invited a few people over to share the fun with us."

Jesse, Dade, and Raymond attempted encouraging smiles in Anna's direction. For sure and certain they were all completely confused as to why Anna had invited them to her house to play with sticks. Elam just stared out the window at his car, and Vernon was completely engrossed in his pile of Popsicle sticks. No doubt he was planning something grand.

"What are you making?" Omi asked.

Anna pulled a Popsicle stick from her apron pocket. "There are dozens of things you can make with a few Popsicle sticks and a little glue. And paint if you want some color."

Elam gave Ruth a pained expression. He obviously hadn't come for the crafts.

Vernon had the largest pile of sticks sitting in front of him. "I'm making a tackle box for my fishing flies."

"*Ach*, *vell*," Anna said. "You'd better get started on that right quick."

Felty nodded. "We don't want you here all day."

"Where's Bo?" Ruth asked, not one to beat around the bush.

Anna's smile faltered. "*Ach*, he had to plant or plow or something to do with the farm. I'm wonderful disappointed he couldn't come. But don't worry. He said if he finishes early, he'll race right up here. He's wonderful excited about Popsicle sticking. He wants to try making a cell phone stand. I'm not sure why he wants to make a cell phone stand since he doesn't have a cell phone, but that's what he said."

Ruth smiled as if she was the keeper of some *wunderbarr* secret. She leaned over again and whispered in Omi's ear. "He wants to make one for me."

Omi hissed and slapped at Ruth's shoulder. "Stop that."

Raymond came around the table. "What do you want to make, Ruth?"

"I don't know," Ruth said. It was immediately obvious that she didn't have any desire to learn Popsicle sticking. "What is there to make?"

Anna picked up a book that had been sitting on the counter. "*Ach*, Ruth, you are going to be astonished. You can make a napkin holder or a bird feeder or a cute pot for a small plant. There's also a bookmark, a fan, or a little box with a lid."

"I'm making a ship in a bottle," Felty said.

Anna smiled sadly at Omi. "He hasn't given up on that dream."

Raymond handed Ruth a stick. "I'm making a catapult so I can shoot spit wads at Elam."

Elam gave Raymond the stink eye.

Ruth grinned playfully at Elam. "That sounds kind of fun."

"Do you want to help me make it?" Raymond said.

Ruth shrugged. "Okay."

Raymond and his *dat* fixed RVs, motorboats, and cars as a business, even though the Amish didn't believe in owning vehicles. Raymond was wonderful *gute* with his hands, and if anybody could figure out how to make a catapult out of Popsicle sticks, it was him. Raymond went to the hall closet and pulled out two folding chairs. He set one up next to him and another next to Elam. Since Ruth and Raymond were working together, Omi got stuck next to Elam.

He sat there twirling two Popsicle sticks in his fingers. Omi didn't know what he planned to make, but he seemed completely disinterested. "I'm Omi," she said, because even though she'd heard a lot about him, they'd never officially met.

He leaned back lazily in his chair. "Raymond wasn't kidding. You and Ruth look exactly alike."

Omi could see why Ruth was so fascinated with Elam. He wasn't as handsome as Bo, but there was a certain symmetry to his face that was very pleasing. His nose was on the large side, but it fit well on his face. He had a deep dimple on his right cheek, and beautiful white teeth. He also had flawless, smooth skin, as if he'd never had a pimple in his life. Then, of course, there was his car, which Ruth adored most of all.

"What are you going to make?" Omi asked, grabbing a handful of Popsicle sticks from the center of the table.

Jesse Riehl pointed across the table. "Omi, would you pass the glue?"

Omi handed Jesse the glue and eyed Elam, waiting for a response to her question. He glanced out the window. "Popsicle sticks aren't really my thing."

*Popsicle sticks aren't really my thing*? Elam had a car, and he talked like an *Englischer*. So far, Omi wasn't impressed, even if Ruth liked him.

Ruth was very interested in Elam's project or lack thereof. Bo wasn't here, so it made sense she'd try to flirt with the next best thing. "You should make something for your car, something to hang on the mirror."

Elam nodded, as if he was thinking about it. "I guess."

Dade Nelson hadn't taken his eyes from Ruth since she'd walked in the house. "I want to make a little box for my *dat* to put his fishing flies in. Do you like fishing, Ruth?"

Vernon looked up. "I already told you, that's what I'm making. You can't copy me."

Dade frowned, pursed his lips, and spread a dab of glue onto one of his Popsicle sticks. Apparently, he had no intention of changing his project.

Raymond painted four sticks red while Ruth watched. "Anna, do you have a plastic lid, like one off a gallon of milk?"

"I have the metal lid from Felty's ship-in-a-bottle bottle."

"That will work."

Felty's brows crashed together. "I'm going to need that lid, Annie."

Anna didn't seem concerned. "I'll buy you a new one as soon as you get your ship into the bottle."

Ruth gazed at Elam. "You could make a fan."

Raymond and Ruth discussed how to make a catapult while Jesse asked Felty's opinion on what color to paint his napkin holder. Anna held a stick steady while Vernon glued it to another one.

Elam smoothed his stick between his fingers. "I think I'll make a bookmark." He smiled curtly at Omi and set the stick on the table. "And now I'm done." He folded his arms and leaned back in his chair. "Ruth, do you wanna go driving around the lake with me?"

Anna didn't seem insulted that Elam didn't like Popsicle sticking. "The lake is so beautiful this time of year. Stay for the sunset. It's very romantic."

Ruth looked as if she would spring from her chair at any moment, but she hesitated, torn between going with Elam and waiting for Bo, who might not even come. Ruth was smart enough to know that if Bo came and she was off with Elam, it would be the end of everything between them. It was already the end of everything, but Ruth refused to believe it.

Omi didn't know if she'd rather Ruth stayed or went, but she felt a little sorry for Raymond. Ruth shouldn't just abandon him. "What about your catapult?" Omi said.

"I don't mind finishing it myself," Raymond said, putting his head down and fiddling with the rubber bands Anna had given him. He didn't look up. Not once.

"It's wonderful romantic by the lake," Anna said.

Ruth pressed her lips together. "I guess I'd better stay here just in case . . . Raymond needs my help."

Elam shrugged. "How about you, Omi? You wanna come? There's a spot where the police don't patrol, and I got going ninety miles an hour once."

Ruth gave Omi one of her "Your Majesty" looks. Ruth didn't want Elam to be here if Bo came. But if Bo didn't come, Ruth would have no one else to flirt with. It was a problem for sure, but it wasn't Omi's problem, and she had no desire to ride in Elam's car. She gave Elam a half smile. "Going that fast makes me nervous."

"We don't have to go fast." Elam leaned closer to Omi. "I've got to get out of here," he whispered.

Omi leaned away from him as if he'd pinched her. *Ach*, first Ruth and now Elam. The whispering was driving her batty. What was wrong with those two?

"I'll go with you," Vernon said, his gaze flicking from Anna to Elam and back again.

A look of horror overtook Elam's handsome features, that charming dimple digging into his cheek. Vernon had struck him completely mute.

Felty glanced up from his ship. "That is the best idea I've heard all day."

Anna got excited about just about everything. "*Wunderbarr*. Vernon loves the lake. He's spent many happy hours there fishing. It wonders me if he wouldn't want to go around it twice."

Omi stared at Anna. Just what was her plan here? Neither Elam nor Vernon would have a chance to fall in love with Ruth if they weren't in the same room with her. Omi covered her mouth to smother a burst of laughter. Vernon and Elam riding around the lake together would surely be a sight to see.

Odd, awkward, and wonderful strange.

Omi couldn't speak without laughing, so she stayed quiet. Besides, there were no words.

Elam stood up so fast, he cracked his knee on the table. "I've got to get back to Cashton."

Vernon frowned. "I thought you wanted to drive me around the lake."

"Not today," Elam said, stuffing his "bookmark" in his pocket.

"Could you at least give Vernon a ride home?" Felty said.

Vernon made a face. "I brought my buggy."

Felty huffed out a breath. "I guess that's the end of that."

Ruth seemed to both regret and rejoice that Elam was leaving. "Maybe I'll see you some other time?" Some other time when Bo wasn't around.

Elam nodded. "Okay. Soon."

He raced out the front door as if he was running from a pack of wild dogs. At least he remembered to take his craft project.

Anna smiled and sat down next to Omi. "*Vell.* That just leaves more Popsicle sticks for the rest of us. And more cheesy jalapeño raisin bread. That's right, everybody, I made two loaves of cheesy jalapeño raisin bread for our Popsicle sticking party."

Raymond and Dade both expressed utter delight at the thought of cheesy jalapeño raisin bread, and Omi smiled at their valiant attempts to seem sincere.

While Anna sliced bread for everyone, Ruth and Raymond finished their catapult. Raymond grinned. He seemed to have cheered up considerably since Elam left. "Anna, do you have any M&M's? We need something to launch."

"I have raisins."

Raymond eyed Ruth. "Are raisins okay?"

"Sure," Ruth said. "I don't even know what we're doing with them."

Anna gave Raymond a handful of raisins. Raymond put one raisin in the bottle lid, braced the horizontal sticks in the front with his free hand, pushed down on the top Popsicle stick, and let it go. The stick sprang forward and launched the raisin all the way across the table, hitting Vernon in the forehead. Vernon snapped his head up in surprise.

Ruth squealed in delight. "Raymond, you're so clever. Can I try?"

Looking very pleased with himself, Raymond handed Ruth a raisin, and she set it in the lid. She pulled back the stick and released it. The raisin flew into the air and conked Vernon in the chin.

Indignation popped all over Vernon's face. "You could have put out my eye."

Everybody at the table but Vernon laughed. Ruth laughed the loudest. "Raymond, go sit where Vernon is sitting. I want to see if I can get one in your mouth."

Raymond laughed. "*Gute* idea." He went to Vernon's end of the table and tapped Vernon's shoulder. "Could you move over please?"

Vernon straightened his spine. "This is my spot."

Raymond had the perfect demeanor for someone as stubborn as Vernon. "Okay, friend, but Ruth is going to keep launching raisins. If you don't want to lose your eye, you should move over."

Vernon gathered up his half-made box and scooted to Elam's chair, where there was the least danger of his being hit by a flying raisin.

Raymond sat down and opened his mouth. Ruth catapulted another raisin in his direction. He leaned forward but the raisin bounced off his nose. Ruth howled with laughter. "Try again," he said.

She shot another raisin, and this time Raymond caught it in his mouth. Everyone but Vernon threw up their hands and cheered. Raymond had just invented a new game, and

Ruth was ecstatic. They all took turns launching raisins and catching them, except for Vernon of course. Raymond was the best at catching, Jesse and Ruth were both *gute* launchers. Omi hadn't seen Ruth so genuinely happy in quite a long time.

After about fifty raisins, Ruth came to rest in a chair, and Raymond stuffed a piece of Anna's cheesy jalapeño raisin bread into his mouth. "That was fun, but I know something even better."

Ruth's eyes lit up. "What? Whatever it is, I want to do it."

"I help an *Englisch* friend with his boat sometimes, and he said I could use it whenever I want it. Do you want to come out for a ride with me?"

Vernon actually raised his hand. "I do. I do." He really was oblivious sometimes.

"I wouldn't hear of it, Vernon," Anna said. "You need to stay here and finish your Popsicle box. You don't want a closet full of unfinished projects."

Vernon frowned. "But what about the boat?"

Anna placed a firm hand on Vernon's shoulder. "There will be other boats."

Dade set a single raisin on the table. "I've got to go milk the cows, but *denki* for inviting me to Popsicle day. It was funner than I thought it would be."

"It usually is," Anna said. "Unless you're trying to build a ship in a bottle. Then don't even bother."

Jesse and Raymond exchanged a look. Jesse cleared his throat. "I'd love to go on the boat, but I want to rush right home and show my *schwester* this napkin holder. She'll be so excited."

Omi was pretty sure Lily Riehl wouldn't get too worked up about a napkin holder, but it was a *gute* enough excuse to get Jesse off the boat. Omi studied Raymond Fisher out of the corner of her eye. There was nothing flashy about Raymond, but he could fix cars and catch raisins with his teeth. And he knew someone who had a boat. If that wasn't exciting enough for Ruth, Omi didn't know what was.

Ruth hurriedly handed Omi her catapult and asked her to take it home. Omi watched from the window as Ruth jumped into Raymond's buggy and they drove off down the hill.

Omi couldn't help but smile.

For the first time in a long while, Ruth seemed to have forgotten all about Bo.

# Chapter 13

Bo led the horses to the barn while Ben rested in the wagon. They'd been spreading mulch on the soybeans all day, and Ben was completely spent. He always tried to hide when his legs got shaky or his head started hurting, but Bo knew his *bruder* well enough to recognize when Ben had overdone it or even when he was having a bad day.

Bo pulled the wagon into the shade and unhitched the team. "You okay back there?" he asked in a loud voice.

Ben's head appeared above the top box board. He'd been lying down in the wagon. Bo frowned. Ben must have been feeling pretty bad, because even though he sometimes hitched a ride in from the fields, he seldom lay down because he didn't want to appear weak, not even in front of his family. "I'm okay."

Bo pulled a bottle of water from the shelf just inside the barn and handed it to his *bruder*. "It wonders me if you didn't overdo it today."

Ben took a swig of water and waved away Bo's concern. "Don't worry about me. Worry about finding a girl willing to live with that face of yours for the rest of her life."

Bo chuckled. "I worry about that all the time, but

there's enough room in my head to worry about two things at once."

Ben finished the bottle and handed it to Bo. "Do you know how much I hate being a burden on my family?"

"You've never been a burden, and everything happens according to Gotte's will. Your sickness is teaching all of us."

"Teaching you all how to do more than your fair share of the work."

Bo grinned. "Hard work never killed anybody, and Gotte told Adam he'd do a lot of sweating."

Ben slid out of the wagon and wobbled toward the barn. "I'd like to help you with the horses, but I'm afraid I'll end up on the ground in a heap. I'm sorry."

Bo patted Royal, their Percheron, on the nose. "It takes a humble man to let people help. I admire you for that."

"I'd rather help than be helped," Ben said.

Bo started unhitching the team. "I know you would. So would I. That's why I'm more than happy to be on this end instead of yours."

Ben wiped his face with his red bandanna. "Omi's coming over tonight. Are you going to be there?"

Bo's heart raced at the sound of her name. He hid his face behind Royal's head. "Who wants to know?"

"A concerned *bruder*."

Bo led Royal and then Rowdy to their stalls and came back for the hose. "If you keep talking about it, Ruth is going to find out."

Ben leaned against the barn wall. "Find out that you love Omi? That shouldn't be anything you have to hide."

"You know why we have to keep it a secret. Omi doesn't want Ruth to get hurt."

Ben scrubbed his hand down the side of his face. "If

only Ruth had as much consideration for Omi's feelings as Omi has for hers."

"It's my fault. I was *dumm* and started dating Ruth first. She got her hopes up."

Ben's mouth twitched in amusement. "You're such a catch."

Bo rolled his eyes. "For some reason, Ruth has her sights set on me. I'm nothing special."

"I agree."

Bo laughed and grabbed the hose. "Nothing like a big *bruder* to keep me humble."

"Somebody has to do it." Ben folded his arms, and Bo could see them trembling slightly. "It just doesn't seem fair. Omi is a sweet girl, but she shouldn't give up her own happiness just to spare Ruth's feelings."

"You and I know all about strong family bonds. Ruth thinks she and I are going to get married. If Omi and I started dating, it would feel like a betrayal."

Ben made a face. "*Ach, bruder*, you and Omi are already dating. Ruth is the only one who doesn't know."

Bo frowned. "I hope nobody knows but you and Emma. *Denki* for giving us a place to meet." Omi still insisted that she only wanted to be friends, so Bo just happened to show up at Ben and Emma's house on the nights Omi was there. Ruth didn't suspect because Omi had gone to Emma's house two nights a week ever since Lindy was born.

Ben chuckled. "Emma likes you. I would have kicked you out weeks ago."

"*Denki* for being such a *gute bruder*," Bo said wryly. "We just need to find somebody for Ruth to fall in love with. Mammi's working on it."

"That may be the only thing that will help," Ben said. "Some of the relatives don't like Mammi's meddling, but she got me and Emma back together. And Martha Sue and Yost. And Jethro and Mary Ann and about a dozen others."

"She's my only hope." Bo turned on the hose. "I need to water the horses, and you need to go lie down before you fall over."

"That could definitely happen." Ben hobbled toward the house. "I'll see you later."

Bo drew his brows together. "You need help?"

"Maybe watch after me until I make it home. If I fall over, come scoop me up."

"Will do."

Bo watered and fed the horses and brushed them down. Just as he was leaving the barn, Omi walked in like a vision with a plate of cookies. His heart galloped like a colt. "*Hallo*." That was all he could say. She'd stolen his ability to think.

"*Hallo*," she said. "I brought you some cookies because you're so handsome."

"That's a *gute* reason to bake cookies."

She giggled. "As *gute* a reason as any."

"What kind?"

She handed him the plate. "Pumpkin chocolate chip. I know you like them."

He peeled back the plastic wrap over the top. "I can't think of one thing you make that I don't like." He grabbed a cookie and took a bite. "*Appeditlich*, Omi. *Denki*."

Her lips curled upward. "Are you coming to Emma and Ben's tonight?"

"I wouldn't miss it."

The gate to the fence that surrounded Ben's yard made a loud clap as it swung shut. Bo and Omi peeked around the corner of the barn. Ruth was heading right toward them with a plate in her hand. They stepped back and out of sight, and Omi's face drained of color. "She can't find us together."

"She knows we're friends. It will be okay." But Bo couldn't feel completely confident that Ruth wouldn't get suspicious.

Apparently, Omi couldn't either. Her eyes flashed in panic, and she darted for an empty stall, leaving Bo holding a plate of cookies he wouldn't be able to explain.

Ruth came around the corner of the barn and bloomed into a smile when she saw Bo. "I hoped I'd find you here." She tilted her head and studied his face. "It looks like it's been a hard day's work."

Bo surreptitiously slid Omi's cookies onto the shelf with the water bottles. If Ruth asked about them, he didn't know what he would say. "What are you doing here?"

"Omi made some pumpkin chocolate chip cookies this morning. I know they're your favorite." She handed him the plate, and he was *froh* he wasn't still holding Omi's gift.

"*Denki*. That's very nice of you to think of me." He took a bite of one of Ruth's cookies. At least if she smelled pumpkin chocolate chips on his breath, she wouldn't get suspicious.

"I have missed you something wonderful, Bo."

"You see me at *gmay* every other week." He simply wasn't in the mood for Ruth. He wasn't in the mood to be polite or kind or tactful, but it didn't matter if he was in the mood or not. The test of true character was how you behaved when you didn't feel like it.

She sidled closer than she should have. "Have you missed me?"

He took a step back. "I'm sorry, Ruth. You know I don't want to be anything more than friends."

She winced. "You don't mean that."

Bo resisted the urge to glance at the stall where Omi was hiding. "I don't know what to say, Ruth, and I really need to be going."

Ruth ambled into the barn, passed the stall where Omi hid, and sat down on a milking stool. "I'm not leaving until you talk to me, and I mean really talk."

"We've already talked."

She propped her elbows on her knees and leaned forward. "Look, I understand how angry you are. I was wrong to deceive you, and I was wrong to go driving with Elam all those times. But, Bo, the break has already been two months long, and it was only supposed to last for a month."

"It wasn't a break, Ruth."

"I've done a lot of thinking and praying and repenting, and Omi and Mamm have preached and preached until I thought my ears were going to fall off. I've changed, Bo. I'm still the girl you fell in love with, but I'm wiser and more mature now, and I think you should forgive me. It's not Christian to hold a grudge."

It was a splendid apology, especially for Ruth. But it didn't matter. "I forgive you, Ruth. I already told you that."

She narrowed her eyes. "Then why won't you take me back? When are you going to stop punishing me for my mistakes? How much longer do I have to wait? How miserable do you want me to get?" She wrapped her arms around her knees. "You've proved your point. It's time for us to put this trouble behind us and get back together."

"I'm not punishing you, Ruth. I just don't want to date you anymore."

"Why not? I'm fun and nice and pretty, and you always seemed to have the best time when we were together."

Bo wasn't about to list out all of Ruth's faults. It would be rude, and it would take way too long. He pressed his lips together and immediately chastised himself for that unworthy thought. Bo had just as many faults as Ruth or anyone else—except for maybe Omi. She was as near perfect as a girl could get. "Look, Omi, sometimes things don't work out between a *bu* and a girl. They both need to find other people to date."

Ruth eyed him as if she was trying to bore a hole through his skull. "You called me Omi."

His heart tripped over itself. "Did I?"

She stood up and squared her shoulders. "I didn't want to have to do this, but if you don't swallow your pride and quit punishing me, I'm going to let Elam take me to Green Bay for the fireworks in two weeks." She folded her arms and eyed him as if she'd just beat him at a board game. "Won't that just put your knickers in a knot."

He probably smiled a little too eagerly. "You're going to fireworks with Elam? That sounds nice. Are you a couple?"

"Of course we're not a couple. How can Elam and I be a couple when you and I are a couple?"

"Ruth, we're not a couple. Please go to Green Bay with Elam and have fun. This is the time of your life when you should be having fun."

"You should be having fun too," she said.

"I have plenty of fun, just not with you anymore."

To his surprise, moisture pooled in her eyes and a single tear crept down her cheek. "I can't understand you, Bo. For months you were devoted to me, and then all of a sudden, you don't want anything to do with me." She took a tissue from her apron pocket and dabbed at her nose. "I was just joking. I would never go to Green Bay with Elam. I love you. I'm completely faithful to you, and I'll never be happy again if you don't come back to me."

Bo sighed. "You are one of the happiest, most energetic people I know. You should always be smiling."

Her eyes lit up with hope. "You wouldn't say that if you didn't still like me."

"I like you fine, but I just want to be friends. I wish you no ill will. I want you to find happiness."

She batted her eyelashes. "Whether I'm happy or not is up to you."

"Actually, it's up to you. I hope you'll choose to be happy even though you and I aren't together anymore."

The tears grew plumper and heavier, carving two paths down her cheeks. "I don't understand. We belong together. Why can't you see that? Someday you're going to look back and regret everything you said, regret not forgiving me. By the time you realize you love me, it will be too late. I'll be married to someone else, and you'll be sad and lonely the rest of your life."

Bo wasn't made out of stone, and the sight of a girl crying always softened him up. "Don't cry, Ruth. I'm truly sorry you're upset."

"Not sorry enough," she snapped.

He hardened like a block of cement. "If our relationship was that important to you, you wouldn't have gone riding with Elam."

"I told you I was sorry."

"You can make your own choices, Ruth. You can even repent and ask forgiveness. But you can't control the consequences of your actions. Because of what you did, I started to doubt you. For sure and certain I was hurt, and the longer I let it fester, the bigger it got, especially since you kept seeing Elam. I had to let you go to protect my own heart. Don't you see, Ruth? I can't be sure of you, and I have more respect for myself than to wait around for you."

Ruth stood and jabbed her forefinger to her chest. "I'm right here, right now. I'm not asking you to wait."

*Ach*, Ruth was energetic, enthusiastic, *and* persistent. Bo wasn't going to waste more breath. But how could he convince Ruth to go away? Omi was surely tired of crouching in that stall waiting for them to finish their conversation.

He eyed Ruth. Her arms were folded tightly, and she looked about as immovable as a telephone pole. For sure and certain, she wouldn't leave until he did. "I need to get home. Mamm always serves dinner at five sharp."

She acted irritated that he hadn't acknowledged what she'd just said. "So. Will you take me to the Shawano fireworks or not?"

"*Nae*, Ruth. I'm not taking you to anything ever again." It sounded more impolite than he meant, but he was frustrated and fed up.

Her eyes flashed with anger. Did she really think he would say yes? "Fine. Then I'm going to Green Bay with Elam. I hope you're happy. Don't come crawling back to me when you're drowning in regret."

He wouldn't go back to Ruth, and he wouldn't ever regret breaking up with her, but he'd said enough, and whether Ruth knew it or not, the more she said, the more she hurt herself. She would be the one to regret this conversation, and he wouldn't pile any more shame on her head.

Ruth balled her hands into fists at her side, turned on her heels, and marched out of the barn. Bo watched until all he could see was the dust kicked up by her shoes as she stomped down the dirt road.

Omi came up behind him. "*Ach*, Bo, I hate to see her so sad."

Bo wanted to urge Omi not to be upset on Ruth's

account. Ruth had made her own choices. But Omi loved her *schwester* as much as Bo loved his *bruder*, and he couldn't just tell her to turn off her feelings. "*Cum*," he said, pulling the second plate of cookies from the shelf. "Let's take our cookies to Ben's house. We can eat until we're sick and do some Popsicle sticking."

That teased a smile from her lips. "Popsicle sticking? What do you know about Popsicle sticking?"

"Nothing. Mammi gave me a hundred Popsicle sticks and told me to make you something nice. I want to be obedient, but I don't know how to make anything out of Popsicle sticks but a bookmark."

"You're in *gute* company. That's what Elam made."

Bo grimaced. "Let's not talk about Elam."

Omi nodded. "We won't have time to do much talking. Popsicle sticking takes a lot of concentration, and I want you to make me a bird feeder. It's the last project in your *mammi*'s book and the hardest. You'll need all your brainpower just to make the roof."

"Okay," Bo said. "But if I'm making a bird feeder, I get at least half the cookies."

# Chapter 14

Omi's family always went to the lake to watch the Shawano fireworks, where a whole group of Amish congregated. Omi pulled a blanket out of the van as well as a picnic basket loaded with snacks and treats for the family. LaWayne carried another picnic basket filled with more treats and snacks. Mamm was determined that everyone would eat well at the fireworks display, even though they'd just finished dinner. They had come to the lake in a van with another family from Bonduel because there wasn't room to park a buggy, and the horses didn't like the fireworks all that much.

The Fourth of July was maybe the only night of the year when droves of Amish people stayed up later than ten o'clock. Everyone loved the fireworks, and *Englisch* and Amish alike came from all the surrounding areas to watch the show over the lake. The family found a spot where Omi's *schwester* Eva helped her spread out the blanket, and Mamm set up two camping chairs for her and Dat. Donald Prince, the *Englischer* who had driven them to the lake, pulled out his own camping chair and set it up next to Dat.

Discontent and irritated, Omi set the picnic basket on

the blanket and opened it. She handed a can of pop to each of her siblings, though she didn't take one for herself. She didn't like pop, and she wasn't in a festive mood anyway. Ruth had made good on her threat and gone to Green Bay with Elam. At four o'clock, Elam and Raymond Fisher had pulled up in Elam's junky car, and Ruth had jumped in as if she hadn't a care in the world, as if she hadn't told Bo just two weeks ago that she wouldn't go riding with Elam ever again.

Omi wasn't especially mad about that, even though Ruth's dishonesty and impulsive nature were aggravating. She should probably be happy that Ruth had gone to Green Bay. Omi and Bo might find some time to be alone together tonight, and Ruth might decide that she wasn't in love with Bo after all. Lord willing, Elam would capture Ruth's heart under the stars.

*Nae*, Omi wasn't irritated that Ruth had gone to Green Bay. Omi was troubled about something she'd heard Bo say to Ruth. She'd been thinking about it for two weeks, and she'd stewed about it for so long that the stew was bubbling over the pot and onto the stove. Did Bo really like Omi as he claimed, or was she just the next best thing to Ruth? Wringing her hands, she scanned the growing crowd in the gathering darkness looking for Bo. They'd made a plan to spread their families' blankets next to each other so they could sit together and watch fireworks without arousing any suspicion. But she couldn't see the Helmuth family anywhere.

LaWayne and Elmer settled down on the blanket even though the sun had barely set and fireworks were at least half an hour away. LaWayne stretched out on his back and propped his arms under his head. Elmer did the same, because LaWayne was Elmer's favorite person. He wanted to be just like him.

Omi's heart skipped when Anna and Felty Helmuth marched toward her, followed by Emma carrying Lindy, Ben holding Mary's hand, Bo, and finally Bo's parents. Bo had about five camping chairs slung over his shoulders plus a denim blanket tucked under one arm. Emma carried a diaper bag, and Anna and Felty each toted a long black tube attached to a metal stand.

Felty unfolded his metal stand, which consisted of three legs, and set it on the ground. He then attached his tube to the stand. He took Anna's stand and set it up next to his.

Anna waved at Omi. "I'm *froh* we found you," she said breathlessly. "We've been following Bo round and round in circles, and I was afraid my arms would give out before we got here. But Bo was carrying most of the heavy stuff, so I couldn't complain."

Omi glanced at Bo, and her heart jumped and leaped and danced. She tried not to look as overjoyed and uneasy as she felt. "What did you bring, Anna?"

Anna patted her black tube as if it was an old friend. "Felty and I are trying a new hobby. It's called astrology. Supposedly you need these telescopes to look at the stars, though I don't see why we can't just stand here and look at the stars with our naked eyes." She clamped her mouth shut, and her eyes got wide. "I didn't really mean 'naked.' I meant that I don't know why we can't look at the stars with our plain eyes. I hope you're not offended."

Omi laughed. "Not at all, Anna. I've heard that a telescope can help you see all sorts of things you wouldn't see otherwise."

Anna sighed. "I guess, but it sure seems a trial to haul all this equipment to look at stars when we're here for the fireworks."

"I think it's called astronomy, Mammi," Ben said.

Anna tilted her telescope and looked into the eyepiece.

"*Nae*, Ben, astronomy is when people try to tell your future in the stars. There's a whole bunch of strange creatures that gallop across the sky and tell people if they should get a new job or date someone else. I don't want to know my future. I'm pretty sure I'm going to die, and I don't need anyone confirming it for me."

"You're not going to die for a long time, Annie," Felty said.

"I know, dear, but it's going to happen to all of us. I don't need astronomy to tell me that."

"Or astrology," Ben said.

Anna nodded enthusiastically. "Exactly, Benjamin. If we'd all just live our lives and try to stay out of each other's business, we wouldn't need to look at the stars at all."

Omi stifled a smile. Anna was neck-deep in everybody's business, including Omi's. She obviously didn't live by her own advice.

Bo set down his armful of chairs, and Omi helped him spread the blanket right next to hers. Their eyes met, and Bo gave her a quick smile. She smiled back, but the smile didn't quite reach her heart. Did Bo really like her, or was she just a temporary girlfriend until Ruth came to her senses? He gave her a puzzled look, as if he wasn't sure what to make of her expression. She shook her head slightly. They could talk about it later when everyone was engrossed in the fireworks. Ben and LaWayne helped Bo set up all the camping chairs, and Anna and Felty immediately sat down and gazed into their telescopes.

"What am I looking for, Felty?" Anna said.

"You'll know it when you see it, Banannie," Felty mumbled.

Anna frowned. "That doesn't sound very productive."

"We're not trying to be productive, Annie. We're having fun."

Anna glanced in Felty's direction. "You can call it whatever you want, Felty dear."

Omi sat on the far right side of her blanket, and Bo sat on the far left side of his, which meant they were sitting right next to each other as close as they dared. She handed Bo a can of soda. "We brought a dozen," she said.

He flipped the tab on his can and leaned closer. "You seem a little out of sorts tonight. Is everything okay?"

"*Ach*, I guess I'm just put out with Ruth. She went to Green Bay after all."

Bo took a sip of soda. "I was pretty sure she would. I hear the fireworks are really *gute* in Green Bay."

"But she told you she wouldn't."

"I didn't believe her, so I'm not really counting it as a lie."

Omi smiled weakly. "I'm *froh* you don't hold it against her."

Bo studied her face. "I think we should go for a walk."

"But you just got here."

He cocked an eyebrow. "It's a nice night for a walk."

She felt her face get warm. "Okay."

Bo stood and brushed off his trousers. "Mamm, Omi and I are going to walk around and see if we can find any friends."

Bo's *mamm* nodded, too busy with her grandchildren to care.

"I want to come," Elmer said, jumping to his feet.

Anna lifted her head from her telescope. "Elmer, would you like to see the moon up close."

Elmer's attention was immediately diverted. Bo motioned to Omi, and they slipped away without anyone else noticing, or at least they didn't seem to notice. Bo led her down toward the lake for a few hundred feet, then he glanced in the direction of their families and walked toward the parking lot.

"Where are we going?" Omi said.

"The parking lot is full of cars and empty of people. Let's go stand behind that van where no one can see us."

Omi followed him up the slope to the parking lot. When they got closer to the cars and farther from the crowds, Bo reached out and took her hand. She almost jumped out of her skin. "You know, somebody is going to see you."

He grinned. "It's too dark, and they're all facing the other way."

Omi laughed quietly, willed her heart to stop racing, and laced her fingers with his. Her hand felt so *gute* in his. *Ach*, how she wished this feeling could go on forever. "You're wonderful bold, Bo Helmuth."

He stopped behind a van, and they were as protected from prying eyes as if they'd been invisible. "So Ruth has gone to Green Bay."

"She was wonderful mad this morning. She said she was going to go to Green Bay with Elam and Raymond to make you jealous."

"I guess she can try that if she thinks it will work."

Omi suddenly felt very small. "Will it work?"

He looked at her as if she was crazy. "Are you kidding?"

Omi swallowed past the lump in her throat. "Bo, I want you to tell me the truth. The whole truth."

"I always try to tell the truth."

"You told Ruth that you broke up with her because you had to protect your own heart, and that you were done waiting for her."

"*Jah*," he said tentatively.

"But Ruth wants you back. She cried and everything. She's very sincere."

Bo scrubbed his hand down the side of his face. "She

has a strange way of showing it. She went to Green Bay with Elam."

"She went to Green Bay to make you jealous."

"I know. But, Omi, I'm not jealous. Her behavior only makes me more certain that I was right to break up with her."

Omi winced and wrapped her arms around her waist. "She's determined to be the best-behaved girl in the *gmayna* from now on. She thinks you're trying to teach her a lesson. She still thinks she has a chance. She told me so herself this morning." Omi couldn't look him in the eye. "Does she?"

"Does she what?"

"Have a chance with you?"

The horrified look on his face gave her some comfort. "Omi, how could you ask that? Ruth and I are finished."

"I can't help but wonder, what would have happened if Ruth hadn't traded places with me."

"But she did."

"If she hadn't treated you the way she did, would you two be engaged by now?"

Bo fell silent and his frown etched itself into his face. "I can't say for sure, Omi. I like to think I'm smarter than that. I like to think I would have eventually realized the truth about Ruth without being forced to see it."

Omi kicked at the gravel at her feet. "Did you break up with Ruth because of Ruth or because of me?"

"I don't understand."

She exhaled all the air from her lungs. Did she really want to know the answer? "Ruth and I had another fight this morning. She says it's just a matter of time before you get back together, and I can't help but think that I will never be your first choice, that maybe if you found a way to forgive Ruth, you would realize that she is the girl you love and the one you want to marry."

"That's not . . ."

She held up her hand. If she didn't say everything now, she wouldn't be able to say it later. "Maybe you're not telling me what is really in your heart because you're trying to spare my feelings, but I don't want you to spare my feelings."

Bo growled like a mountain lion. "Omi, we both know I'm not that nice. I don't do things just to spare people's feelings. If that were the case, I'd already be back together with Ruth."

That made Omi feel a little better. Bo would always tell her the truth. "What if Ruth is true to her word, if she quits going off with other boys, if she stops playing childish tricks on you? She is still as fun and energetic and beguiling as ever. In a few months when she's proved she's a better girl, will you regret losing her? Will you be sad you got together with me?"

Before she could say another word, he swept her into his arms and kissed her forcefully, as if his lips could prove a point he couldn't make with his words. She forgot her own name. Thank Derr Herr she remembered it when he pulled away. "Omi, Ruth hurt me. She hurt me very badly, but I liked her so much I was willing to forgive all of it. *Mammi* said that Ruth took me for granted, but I took you for granted, and it almost cost me a lifetime of happiness. Ruth was never the one. I broke up with her because I fell in love with you."

Omi certainly didn't want to argue with that. She nibbled on her bottom lip. "Okay."

He nudged her away from him, cupped his hands around her upper arms, and grew serious. "Here is the most important question. Are you saying this because you secretly want to get rid of me? Because it doesn't matter what you say, I will never get back together with Ruth. I don't love her. She doesn't love me. That's why I hope she falls in love with Elam. Maybe it will happen tonight. Fireworks are romantic."

Omi shook her head. "Your *mammi* had quite a group of *buwe* at her house the other day Popsicle sticking. Ruth and Elam both adore Elam's car, but they're not especially fond of each other."

Bo smoothed his finger down Omi's cheek. "Mammi is working on it. I know she'll find someone for Ruth."

"Lord willing, because I feel guilty enough already."

Suddenly, Ruth appeared from between two cars in the parking lot. "What is this?" she hissed.

Omi was so startled, she might have left the ground when she jumped backward and away from Bo. Bo dropped his hand to his side and sort of leaned against the car behind him. *Ach!* They'd been caught.

Ruth's eyes flashed with fire. She pointed an accusing finger in Omi's direction. "I should have known you were trying to steal my boyfriend. You practically begged me to go to Green Bay with Elam, and now I know why."

"That's not true, Ruth. Mamm and I both encouraged you not to go."

"You did not," Ruth insisted. Omi shut her mouth. It was useless to try to talk Ruth out of something she didn't want to be talked out of. Bo had tried to break up with her two times already, and she wouldn't let him do it.

Bo tried to smooth things over. "How were the fireworks in Green Bay?" he asked, even though it was obvious the fireworks hadn't started in Green Bay.

Ruth glared at him. "I went to make you jealous, Bo. All I can think about day and night is you and how much I love you and want to be with you. Halfway to Green Bay I realized that the reason you broke up with me was because of Elam and his car. You think I love Elam. You can't trust me. I wanted to prove to you that I had really changed, so I told Elam to turn the car around and bring me back to you." Her anger evaporated faster than dew in the sunshine, and she burst into tears. "And now I find my devious *schwester* trying to steal you."

Bo held up his hands. "She's not trying to steal me, Ruth. I love Omi, and we've been keeping it a secret from you because we didn't want you to be upset."

Omi winced at the word *love*. Ruth wouldn't like it, but it was true all the same. She loved Bo too. She also loved Ruth, and she and Ruth were not only *schwesters*, they were twins. Their bond felt stronger than life itself.

Ruth slapped a tear from her cheek. "I can't think of anything more cruel than keeping a secret from your twin *schwester*."

Omi felt sick to her stomach. All her worst nightmares were coming true. "I'm sorry, Ruth. I never meant to hurt you. Bo and I really like each other, and you didn't want to let him go. We wanted you to find another *bu* so you wouldn't care if I dated Bo."

"He's my boyfriend. How could you do this to your own *schwester*? What have I ever done to you?"

Omi tried to explain herself, though it was clear Ruth wasn't in any shape to hear a reasonable explanation. "It's not like that. The night we traded places, Bo was ready to forgive you. But then he got mad, and we kissed, and we kept running into each other. We had a lot of opportunity to talk. Then he conked me on the head and had to take me to the doctor. We just . . . we just started liking each other."

Ruth's mouth twisted with anger. "You kissed?"

Oh, dear. The horrible secret Omi had successfully kept from Ruth was now out. Her mouth went dry. "That first night. Bo was pretty mad."

Ruth turned on Bo. "You told me you knew it was Omi from the beginning."

He cleared his throat. "I did."

Ruth's voice rose in pitch. "And you kissed her anyway?"

"*Jah*. I was mad."

Omi couldn't let Bo take the blame. "He asked if he could kiss me. I told him yes."

"You told him yes?" If Ruth's voice rose any higher, soon only the dogs would be able to hear her.

"I was curious and embarrassed. I thought Bo thought I was you, so I said yes, thinking that was what you would do."

"You could have said *nae*."

Omi pulled her shoulders back. Might as well confess everything, even though her actions didn't paint her in the best light. "I didn't want to say *nae*."

Ruth's eyes nearly popped out of her head.

"I've wanted to kiss Bo ever since fifth grade," Omi said. She clasped her hands in front of her. "I've always been interested in Bo. I was weak, and I'm sorry."

Ruth didn't seem inclined to accept Omi's apology. "You kissed my boyfriend, sneaked around behind my back, told Bo about Elam and his car. It's disloyal, Omi. It's the worst kind of betrayal."

Omi stiffened her spine even as a shard of glass pierced her heart. "We didn't sneak behind your back. I know you believe that, but you were out riding with Elam so often that we didn't need to sneak. You were gone a lot. It gave us opportunities to be alone together."

"You should have stayed away from each other. You're my *schwester*. You should have stayed away." Ruth stomped her foot to emphasize all the injustice she had suffered.

"I suppose I should have," Omi said, but she hadn't been able to resist being near Bo. She had loved him for so long, and she wasn't strong enough to stay away. "I'm sorry. It just happened."

In a heartbeat, Ruth's anger exploded. "It just happened? How convenient."

Bo pressed his hand to his forehead. "Ruth, I'm sorry you're upset. But can you see your part in all of this?"

"*Nae*."

"You played a trick on me, you rode all over Shawano with Elam, and you accused me of trying to keep you from having fun. I had no reason to believe you were interested in me anymore."

"Quit trying to justify yourselves. You don't care about Omi. You just want revenge." She turned to Omi. "I thought you loved me. We always promised to be completely loyal to each other. But now you've betrayed my trust, and I don't know how you'll ever get it back. I don't even know who you are anymore."

Omi was no match for Ruth's tears and accusations. Ever since that kiss from Bo, the guilt had been gnawing at Omi like a dog on a bone. "I'm sorry, Ruth. You've always been my best friend. You are the person I love and trust most in the world."

Ruth folded her arms as if to guard herself against any more apologies. "I wish I could say the same about you. A friend loveth at all times. You are my *schwester*. We should love each other better than anything, especially a *bu*. You need to do the right thing, Omi. You need to do the right thing by me."

Bo stepped toward Omi. "It's going to be okay, Omi. We're all very upset right now. Let's go home and cool down, and we can talk about it later."

Omi slid next to Ruth and grabbed her hand. "I'm sorry, Ruth. Please don't be mad at me forever."

Ruth lifted her chin. "Bo is right. We should talk about

this later when we've all cooled down." She wiped more tears from her face. "I missed the Green Bay fireworks. The least you can do is come watch the Shawano fireworks with me." She glanced at Bo. "Without any boyfriends getting in the way."

Omi's heart was torn in half. "Okay. We can do that. I'm sorry, Ruth. I never meant to hurt you."

Ruth slid her arm around Omi's shoulders and nudged Omi toward the space between two cars. "*Cum.* The fireworks are about to start. Let's watch them together with our family." She gave Bo a pointed look, and her meaning was clear. Bo was not family. He wasn't welcome to the party.

Omi had never felt so despondent in her life.

# Chapter 15

"I'm very cross with you, Omi," Ruth said, her gaze glued to the small mirror while she pinned her *kapp* into her hair. "Hold it a little higher."

Each morning, Omi and Ruth held the mirror for each other while the other one put on her *kapp* and made sure stray hairs weren't sticking out from under it. The community considered it vain to spend more than a few minutes looking in the mirror, so Omi and Ruth's mirror was about the size of a dinner plate, and they kept it in the drawer with their underwear so they wouldn't be tempted to use it more than necessary. Since it wasn't hanging on the wall, someone had to hold it for you when you put up your hair or straightened your *kapp*. Ruth thought it was all a bit silly because she enjoyed looking at herself in the mirror, but Omi had never seen the need for more mirror time. She saw herself every day when she looked at Ruth.

After Omi had gotten hit in the forehead with a two-by-four, she'd looked in the mirror much more often than was necessary, trying to decide how ugly she was with a scar, wondering if it would fade more than it already had. She should probably feel bad about sneaking a look in the mirror several times a day, but she couldn't bear not knowing how the scar made her look. What did people see when they peered at her? Was it a girl who was pretty enough, but not as pretty as her *schwester,* or a seriously disfigured *maedel* who would never be able to find a husband?

Ruth must have read her mind. Or maybe just her face. "Don't worry about the scar, Omi," she said. "You have always been wonderful pretty. Now you just have a permanent line across your forehead. I can hardly see it anymore."

Omi smiled hesitantly. "That's nice of you to say, especially since I know you're mad at me."

Ruth smoothed down a piece of her hair. "All this time I thought it was something I did to drive Bo away, and it was your fault the whole time."

Omi had apologized so many times, the words felt meaningless in her mouth. "I'm sorry."

"I know you're sorry. If I had a dime for every time you said you're sorry, I'd be rich."

"Then maybe you should quit bringing it up," Omi mumbled. That was just wishful thinking. Ruth wouldn't let it go for a long time. She liked reminding Omi about every sin she'd ever committed.

"I always think it's better not to make the mistake in the first place than to say you're sorry a hundred times later."

Omi couldn't speak to that because her feelings for Bo were not a mistake. She was sorry Ruth had gotten hurt, but she didn't know that she would have done anything differently—except maybe not fall in love with Bo way back in the fifth grade. Her feelings couldn't be stopped now. Maybe if she had loved her *schwester* better, she wouldn't have let her emotions run away with her. Maybe she wouldn't have let Bo kiss her. Maybe she wouldn't have told Bo about Elam. She sighed. "Maybes" got her nowhere. All she could do now was try to accept losing Bo. It was the price she paid for being in a family, the sacrifice she would make for her dearest *schwester* and friend. But it still stung like a thousand angry bees. Right or not, she resented Ruth for making her choose.

"I'm still sorry," Omi said, because despite her protests, that was what Ruth wanted to hear.

Ruth took the mirror from Omi and held it closer to her face. "You should be sorry. Bo has been avoiding me ever since the fireworks. At *gmay* last week, he pretended like I was invisible. He didn't even smile at me or try to get close enough to talk."

It was no wonder. The way Ruth had treated Bo at the fireworks, of course he didn't want anything to do with her. Maybe he was trying to send a message to the whole *gmayna*. He and Ruth were no longer dating. Ruth seemed to be the only one who didn't believe it.

Ruth smiled at her reflection. "I finally gave up waiting for him to come over and apologize, so I went to his house."

Omi raised her eyebrows but didn't say anything. Ruth was a terrible flirt, and she'd do anything to get Bo to come back to her.

"I marched right out to his field. I was determined to make him at least acknowledge I'm alive. Do you know what he did? He dropped his hoe, turned, and stomped off in the other direction. His *bruderen* Ben and Titus were both there and saw how Bo humiliated me. Titus said, 'He probably had to go to the bathroom.' But Ben said Bo wouldn't be back as long as I was there. How rude is that?"

Rude, for sure and certain, but Ben was also as honest as the day was long.

Ruth shoved the mirror back into the drawer. "This is your fault, Omi. Bo loves me. I know he does. But you confused him. You made this mess, Omi. You've got to help me fix it. You've got to help me get Bo back."

Omi loved Ruth dearly, but she had no desire to help her *schwester* win Bo's heart. "What do you think I can do? The last time I *helped* you, Bo ended up kissing me and breaking up with you. Short of tackling him if he tries to run away from you, there's not much I can do. Don't you think it would be better for everyone if I just stayed away from him?"

Ruth eyed Omi. "I suppose that's true, but true repentance means regretting what you've done and trying to undo the damage you've caused. That's what a true *schwester* would do."

Omi slumped her shoulders. "Maybe, but I just can't do it, Ruth. I told you several weeks ago that I won't be your go-between. If you two get back together, it won't be because of me. I have to stay out of it. Surely you can see that's best."

Ruth huffed out a breath and pulled a canvas bag from under her bed. "Fine, Omi. But you've truly got to stay out of the way. At least quit looking at Bo like a starving puppy looks at a bowl of dog food. You're just embarrassing yourself and me."

Omi turned her face from her *schwester*. "I don't look at Bo like that."

"Of course you do. What *bu* can resist a girl who adores him?"

"He's resisted you so far." Omi bit her tongue. "I'm sorry, Ruth. I didn't mean to be snippy."

Ruth didn't seem offended. "I do adore Bo, but a girl has to be sneakier than that. If a *bu* thinks you adore him, he doesn't try as hard. You always want to keep them guessing. They love it when you keep them guessing."

That didn't sound like Bo at all, but Omi wasn't going to contradict her *schwester* again. Maybe Ruth was wrong. Maybe she was right. She was the one *die buwe* buzzed around like honey. Omi never would be.

Ruth glanced out the window of their upstairs bedroom. "Will you do me a favor and make the beds, Omi? I've got to go."

Omi narrowed her eyes. "Where are you going?"

Ruth hemmed and hawed for a few seconds. "Until Bo and I are back together, I might as well have some fun."

"Ruth," Omi said, adding a threatening tone to her voice. "Where are you going?"

It was then that Omi noticed how something bunched and bulged beneath Ruth's dress. Ruth saw where Omi was looking and giggled. "*Ach*, Omi, don't look at me like that. Mrs. Welles gave me a big tip last week, and I bought a T-shirt, a pair of jeans, and a swimming suit with some of my cleaning money." She lifted her dress to reveal a rolled-up pair of jeans and a lime-green T-shirt with a big yellow smiley face on the front.

Omi gasped, her already bruised heart sinking to her toes. "How could you?"

Ruth rolled her eyes. "*Ach*, Omi, don't get bent out of shape. You're not my *mater*."

"I thought you wanted to get Bo back. If he finds out . . ."

"Don't tell him, Omi. You said you'd stay out of it."

Omi lifted her chin. "I'll stay out of it." That was true enough. She would never, ever chastise Ruth again. If Ruth was too blind to see how her actions hurt herself and Bo, it wasn't likely she'd listen to Omi anyway.

"Besides, Elam is going through a hard time right now. His *dat* doesn't like that he drives up here every week instead of helping on the farm. He really needs *gute* friends. Raymond and I are helping him."

"I'm sure you are." Omi kept any hint of sarcasm from her voice.

Ruth stuffed her flip-flops into the canvas bag. "We're going to Shawano. Elam wants to buy interior lights for his car. You put them underneath the dashboard, and they light up the inside of your car." She grinned and gave Omi a swift hug. "The boys sit in the front, and I just slip my dress over my head while I'm in the back. Nobody can see anything. Then I take off my *kapp* and let my hair out. I look just like an *Englisch* girl. Nobody can tell. I've got my swimming suit underneath the jeans. Raymond wants to go do the rope swing. He's anchored it so it goes out farther over the pond and won't break the tree limb. Doesn't that sound fun?"

Omi didn't particularly enjoy swimming. She'd rather curl up with a *gute* book or make a batch of shortbread. But rope swinging into the pond sounded like just the thing Ruth would love to do. No wonder she liked to spend time with Elam. Ruth just couldn't see how going off with Elam would make Bo even less likely to get back together with her. For someone who harped about loyalty, Ruth was being extremely disloyal to Bo, her supposed boyfriend.

"It sounds fun," Omi said, because she truly was done arguing with her *schwester*. There was already so much friction between them.

"Tell Mamm that I'll be back before . . ."

Omi shook her head. "If you want Mamm to know something, tell her yourself."

Ruth stared at Omi as if she'd never seen her before.

"Omi, don't you even love me anymore? Come on. Help me out. It's what *schwesteren* do for each other."

"You said it was best if I stayed out of it, and I agree."

"I only meant stay out of things with Bo. I didn't mean my whole life. You're my best friend. I don't want to keep you out of my life. We've always helped each other."

Normally, an argument like that would have made Omi feel guilty enough to give in, but today, she wasn't in the mood. "Sorry, Ruth. I'm staying out of it."

Ruth stuck out her bottom lip in a pout, but she must have decided not to push it. She knew Omi was mad at her, but she probably didn't care why. "You don't have to tell Mamm anything."

"*Denki* for your permission."

Ruth laughed. "Okay, okay. I'll quit being bossy, but you should quit being so contrary. What *gute* is it having a *schwester* if we can't cover for each other?"

Ruth gave Omi a peck on the cheek and practically skipped out of the room. Ruth always seemed content with her place in the world. Omi wanted things that were completely out of her reach. She peered out the window. Elam drove up in his faded red car but didn't honk, obviously wary of attracting attention. She heard Ruth open the front door. Raymond Fisher climbed out of the front passenger seat and opened the back door for Ruth. He smiled at her and said something that Omi couldn't hear.

Omi plopped down on her unmade bed, ache, loneliness, and despair creeping into every corner of her heart.

On top of the heartache, the guilt, the shame, and the deep sense of loss, Omi was profoundly lonely. Up until two weeks ago, Bo had taken up every thought, every hope, every hour of the day. When she hadn't been with him, she'd thought about him, dreamed about him, and foolishly planned a possible future together. Before Bo had come between them, Omi had always been able to confide in Ruth. They were so connected that it was almost as if they could feel each other's feelings and know what the other was thinking. When Omi had been sick with the flu, Ruth had stayed by her side every minute, even sleeping with her in the same bed and sponging off her head when she was feverish. When Ruth cut her foot swimming, Omi had held her hand while the doctor gave Ruth three shots and some stitches.

Now Omi felt disconnected from everybody. Mamm had no idea what was going on between Ruth and Omi, and LaWayne didn't care about anything but his scooter and his next meal. Marilyn was in Pennsylvania with her boyfriend. Ruth had always been her closest friend. Without her, Omi truly was lost.

Then there was the part of herself Omi was deeply ashamed of. What she and Ruth shared was special, but Omi's love for Bo felt different, like a raging forest fire that consumed everything in its path. She wasn't proud of it, but there were times she wanted to marry Bo no matter the consequences, no matter if she lost Ruth. Bo didn't love Ruth, but Ruth's selfish heart wouldn't allow Bo to find happiness with Omi. They were rivals for Bo's love, and on dark days, Omi couldn't stand to look at Ruth, let alone love her.

But whenever Omi had those thoughts, she felt as if she should take a shower or pray for forgiveness. She couldn't love Bo without being disloyal to Ruth.

Then there was Omi's biggest fear, one that made it impossible to sleep at night. Less than four months ago, Bo was madly in love with Ruth. Ruth had betrayed his trust, and he'd been hurt. No matter what Bo said, Ruth could easily make him fall in love with her again. She was too *wunderbarr* for words, and compared to Ruth, Omi was plain and uninteresting.

It seemed inevitable that if Bo gave Ruth another chance, she'd make him fall in love again.

The prospect of Ruth's happiness should have made Omi just as happy. She felt nothing but pain.

# Chapter 16

Ruth hooked her arm around Omi's elbow and tugged her close. "*Ach*, Omi, I'm so excited I can barely breathe. Can you feel my heart beating? You look so pretty tonight. I wish my eyes were as blue as yours."

"You're too nice," Omi said. "But they'll all look at you first."

Ruth's eyes sparkled playfully. "Not if you do your elbow trick. *Die buwe* love your double-jointed elbows."

Omi laughed in spite of herself. Ruth had been out of sorts in one way or another for weeks. It was nice to see her acting more like the old Ruth—merry, enthusiastic, and agreeable. It felt almost like earlier days when they loved each other unconditionally and wanted nothing but the best for each other. "They come in handy when I play volleyball."

They walked arm in arm into the Helmuths' backyard where at least a dozen of *die youngie* had already congregated. Ruth squeezed Omi's arm. "For sure and certain, Bo's going to be here tonight."

Ruth's heart wasn't the only one racing. "Are you sure?" Bo had missed the last two gatherings, most likely to avoid Ruth, but this gathering was at his parents' home, and he couldn't very well miss it without seeming rude. But he probably didn't care if people thought he was rude if he could avoid Ruth.

"*Jah*," Ruth gushed. "I saw Anna Helmuth at the country store yesterday, and she told me to be sure to come because Bo was going to be here." Ruth squeaked in delight. "Omi, even Anna wants Bo and me to get back together, and she's got a reputation for being a *gute* matchmaker."

Omi frowned. Should she have stayed home? If Bo was going to get back together with Ruth, the last thing either of them would want was for Omi to make a pest of herself. "Maybe I should go. I don't want to be a nuisance."

Ruth grunted in displeasure. "Nonsense. There are other *buwe* for you to fall in love with, and Anna insisted that both of us needed to come." She grinned as if the excitement was almost too much to bear. "I think she's got someone in mind for you already."

Omi couldn't be excited about any other *bu*. If Bo didn't want her, she was determined never to marry.

Bo's *mamm*, Sallie Mae, ran back and forth from the house carrying plates of pretzels and cookies, while Emma Helmuth filled paper cups with lemonade. Anna and Felty sat on their camping chairs near the eats table watching six *buwe* play volleyball.

Ruth made a beeline for Bo's grandparents. "*Hallo*, Anna and Felty. *Denki* for especially inviting us to the gathering." Ruth drew out "especially" so Anna would catch her meaning.

Anna lit up like an *Englisch* Christmas tree. "Omi! Ruth! I'm *froh* you're here. There is so much to do tonight and barely enough time." She looked around the yard. "Now where are those nice friends of yours? Elam and

Raymond? I just adore those two *buwe*. Raymond is wonderful *gute* at Popsicle sticking. He has a mechanical mind, that one. And Elam made a bookmark. He's going to go far in life."

Ruth's smile stuttered. "I . . . I didn't know they were coming tonight."

"*Ach*, they're already here somewhere." Anna pointed to Elam's car, which was parked on the far side of the lawn right on the grass next to the clothesline.

"He shouldn't park on the Helmuths' lawn," Omi said.

Anna sighed. "Of course he shouldn't, but I get the feeling that Elam doesn't have much sense about such things. Raymond didn't want to miss the gathering, so Elam brought him. I know Elam is your special friend, Ruth, but you should really talk to him about appropriate places to park."

Ruth obviously didn't want Elam to be in the same place as Bo. "Elam isn't my special friend. I met him because he's Raymond's cousin."

"Of course," Anna said, giving Ruth's hand a pat. "But I wanted them to come because it's always more fun when the two of them come to things. Remember that catapult Raymond made at our Popsicle sticking party? I asked him to bring it tonight so he could show all *die youngie* how to make one."

"*Ach*! Don't get hit!" Felty shouted.

A volleyball came flying toward Anna. Omi blocked it with her fist and sent it flying in the other direction.

Anna scrunched her lips together. "Felty, I think we need to move back a bit."

"*Gute* idea, Annie."

Anna grabbed Omi's hand. "You saved my life. Please let me know when I can return the favor."

Omi giggled. "I will."

Anna and Felty stood and moved their chairs back about a foot. It wasn't going to make much difference, but it obviously made them feel better. Anna sat down and motioned for Omi to come closer. She pointed to the volleyball game, which had now grown to eight players. "There are those two boys I was telling you about, Raymond and Elam. Will you go get them? I have some presents I need to give them."

Raymond and Elam were standing in the thick of the volleyball game. Omi didn't want to get hit by the ball, but she'd do just about anything for Anna, so she tapped Raymond on the shoulder and stepped back. Raymond turned around. "Omi. Do you want to be on our team? Where's Ruth? She should play too."

"Anna Helmuth says she has a present for you and Elam. Can you leave the game for a minute?"

Raymond nudged Elam, and they both followed Omi back to where Anna and Felty were sitting. Anna seemed to be engrossed in a deep conversation with Ruth, but she stopped talking when she saw *die buwe*. "Ruth, I think you know Raymond Fisher and Elam his cousin."

Raymond looked extremely happy to see Ruth, probably because she was fun and exciting, and she played volleyball better than any girl in the *gmayna*. "Ruth, you should come play volleyball. Will you be on my team?"

Ruth smiled. "For sure and certain. I like that you don't hog the ball."

Was Raymond blushing? "I don't need to hog the ball when I play with you. You never miss." He pointed to Elam. "Elam hogs the ball."

Elam raised his eyebrows as if the "why" should be obvious. "I want to win."

Anna cocked her head to one side and eyed Elam. "Elam the Cousin, I don't know your last name."

Elam looked mildly irritated, as if he would rather be in his car. "It's Nelson."

"That's a fine name, Elam Nelson. You have a very nice cousin. Raymond can fix anything."

"*Jah*," Elam said. "He works on my car all the time."

Anna pulled Raymond to kneel next to her. "Did you bring it?" she whispered loudly. Omi could hear every word, even though she felt guilty about listening in on their private conversation. Ruth wasn't paying attention, searching for Bo amongst *die youngie*.

Raymond's blush deepened. "*Jah*, but if I get it out, people will say I'm showing off."

Raymond had always been quiet and shy. He clearly hated to draw attention to himself. Everybody liked him but treated him almost as an afterthought, as if they didn't mind having him around but didn't notice when he didn't show up.

"Stuff and nonsense," Anna said. "You're a mechanical genius. There's nothing wrong with that."

"Should I go get it?"

Anna shook her head. "I'll tell you when. It's only in case of an emergency." Anna looked at Elam and made her voice louder. "I have a very special present for both of you." A chunky canvas bag hung over the back of Anna's chair. She rummaged through it slowly and pulled out a bright, furry red knitted rope with the ends attached together. It formed a circle about the diameter of a large dinner plate. She handed it to Elam. "This is a steering wheel cover. I made it for you because steering wheels get hot in the summer and cold in the winter, and it makes driving quite unpleasant. At least that's what I've been told."

Elam looked as if he had no idea what to say. He was either astounded that Anna had made him such a beautiful and useful gift or horrified that she expected him to put that thing in his precious car.

He stammered and stuttered and choked on his own spit, then took the steering wheel cover from Anna's hand and smoothed his fingers along the cheery red yarn. "*Denki*, Anna. This is really something."

Omi suspected he had no intention of putting it on his steering wheel, but at least he knew enough to be polite. Omi wasn't quite sure what to make of such a gift. Making it had taken an extraordinary amount of time for someone Anna didn't know very well.

Anna went back to her bag and pulled out a navy blue pot holder and a bright pink one. She handed them to Raymond. "I don't know if you need pot holders when you fix cars, but I felt I should give these to you. If you don't need them, find someone special to share them with."

Unlike Elam, who acted bored and slightly irritated about everything, Raymond seemed truly moved by Anna's gift. "*Denki*, Anna. Your pot holders are famous. I heard they saved someone's life once."

Anna nodded. "Not my pot holders, but one of my scarves saved my grandson Gideon from freezing to death a few winters ago. I was *froh* I could help. *Mammis* like to be helpful."

Raymond stood, and he and Elam each stuffed their gifts into their pockets. Elam glanced back at *die youngie* playing volleyball. "You wanna go for a ride, Ruth? Raymond installed those interior lights, and they look really *gute*."

Raymond frowned. "I guess wc could go for a ride. What do you want to do, Ruth?"

Ruth scanned the backyard. "I want to play volleyball." Omi had come tonight half hoping that Ruth would drive off with Elam when she got bored, but Ruth truly didn't seem at all interested in Elam or his car tonight. No doubt she was hoping Bo would appear and decide he was in love with her. Ruth couldn't make Bo fall in love if she wasn't here.

"We can play volleyball anytime," Elam said. "But you'll want to ride in my car before I sell it."

Ruth's eyebrows inched together. "You're selling your car?"

"Maybe. If I get baptized or join the army."

Ruth's eyebrows crashed into each other. "You're joining the army?"

Elam shrugged. "Maybe. Don't you want to ride in my car one more time?"

Ruth nibbled on her bottom lip. She must have really loved that car. "Bo is coming tonight, and I want to be here for him."

Elam groaned. "Bo? Who cares about Bo? I missed the Green Bay fireworks because of Bo. We're sick of hearing about Bo." He put his hand on Raymond's shoulder. "Aren't we, Ray?"

Raymond's gaze flicked in Ruth's direction. "I like Bo."

Ruth smiled at Raymond and glared at Elam. Omi had always been impressed that Ruth could hold two expressions on her face at once. "*Denki*, Raymond. Elam's just jealous because he knows I like his car better than I like him."

Raymond laughed uncomfortably. Elam pretended not to care one way or the other, but his lips twitched in irritation. "You like it when I take you shopping. You like it when I let you roll down the window so the wind can blow your hair."

Ruth huffed out a breath. "I'm sorry, Elam. You've been very nice to let me ride in your car, but tonight I'm waiting for Bo."

Anna nodded her agreement. "You need to stay and play volleyball, Ruth. And Omi and Raymond too. Elam, I know you're excited to try out your new steering wheel cover, but there are plenty of pretzels to eat, and Ruth wants to play volleyball. The steering wheel can wait."

Elam acted as if the whole gathering was a huge inconvenience, but surely he didn't have anywhere important to go, and there were pretzels. Omi stifled a smile. Elam was handsome and he owned a car, but as far as Omi could see, those were his two best qualities. Ruth was smart. It was plain she had more interest in Elam's car than she had in Elam. That was one of the reasons she was so eager to get back together with Bo. Elam was not a sensible choice for a husband, and Bo was perfect.

Raymond must have gotten tired of waiting. He took both of Ruth's hands and pulled her toward the volleyball game. "*Cum*, Ruth. Be on my team."

Ruth let herself be led into the game. Someone tossed the ball to Raymond, and he handed it to Ruth. She got into position and served. Ruth had a *gute* overhand serve that was hard to return. That's why everyone wanted her on their team. Omi smiled. Raymond wasn't usually the type to take charge. He must have really wanted to play.

Elam shambled over to the game as if he couldn't care less, but soon he was cheering and jumping and spiking the ball with enthusiasm. Maybe he'd have a *gute* time tonight after all, but even if he did, he'd never admit it.

Omi nearly jumped out of her shoes when she heard Bo's voice just inches behind her. "*Vie gehts*, Omi? You are the prettiest girl here."

She didn't turn around, even though she ached to look at him. "Ruth is over there."

"I didn't come to see Ruth."

Her pulse raced at the possibility that he'd come to see her. "She's watching. I can't talk to you," she said.

A long pause. "I know, and I feel like I'm going to die."

Anna turned her attention from the volleyball game. "Who's going to die?"

Bo stepped around Omi so Anna could see him. "No one is going to die, Mammi."

Anna shook her head. "Don't say that. You never know for sure."

"I guess I don't."

Anna still clutched her canvas bag in her hands. "Bo, do you remember when you said you might like to learn a new hobby?"

"*Nae*, Mammi. I don't have time for a new hobby."

Anna's eyes sparkled. "*Ach*, *vell*, maybe you should make time. Tonight."

"Tonight?"

Omi thought her heart would break just standing next to Bo. She couldn't bear it any longer. "I'm . . . I guess I'll go play volleyball."

Anna glanced at Felty, who had fallen asleep, and clutched the arms of her camping chair. "You don't want to play volleyball or learn a new hobby without eating two or three pretzels first. You can't play well on an empty stomach. Both of you get a plate and help yourselves to a pretzel. Then you have to spread mustard on your pretzel, and it takes forever to eat because you don't want to get mustard all over your face or on the volleyball."

One side of Bo's mouth curled upward. "Okay, Mammi. I'll get a pretzel."

"I don't want a pretzel," Omi said. The sooner she accepted losing Bo, the better.

Anna's look of surprise was almost comical. "Of course you want a pretzel. Now get over there and eat one, or I'll have to scold the both of you for being so stubborn."

Omi gave in. The last thing she needed was another lecture about her deficiencies as a person.

Felty and Anna were sitting right next to the eats table, so it wasn't a long walk. With their backs to the volleyball game, Bo and Omi each picked up a plate and put a pretzel on it. Their arms brushed against each other as they reached for the pretzels. Omi forgot how to breathe.

Bo grabbed a knife and stabbed it into the butter. "I miss you."

"I know," Omi said, her voice shaking like a match in the wind. "I'm sorry."

"I'm sorry too, for so many things, especially that I didn't pick you first."

Omi spooned some mustard onto her plate. "Ruth says I need to earn her trust again, but all I can think about is you and how I wish Ruth didn't like you. I feel so guilty, like the worst *schwester* in the whole world."

"Do you feel guilty for liking me?"

"*Nae*, I feel guilty for loving you."

She felt him grow still beside her. "I love you too."

Happiness took her breath away. Despair crushed the air from her lungs. "Ruth will never forgive me if she finds out. She'll say I tricked you. I feel guilty enough for letting you kiss me and for keeping secrets from Ruth and for wishing that Ruth was the one who was miserable instead of me."

"You haven't done anything wrong, Omi," Bo said, but they both knew that wasn't true. She'd done everything wrong. Even talking to Bo at the eats table was wrong. How could she forget him if she kept putting herself in his path?

He spooned mustard from the bowl and slowly dribbled it onto his plate. Then he scooped up a dollop of honey butter and plopped it on top of the mustard. He mixed the two together with a plastic knife.

Omi crinkled her nose. "Um, you like them together?"

He turned and grinned at her. "Maybe I have some of my *mammi*'s taste buds after all."

Omi glanced at Felty, who was perched on his camp chair right next to the eats table. He was asleep, his head dipped to one side, his mouth hanging slightly open. Still, she lowered her voice. "It wonders me if you won't change your mind about Ruth, Bo. Ruth is like the sun. I'm the moon."

Bo glued his gaze to the bowl of honey butter, set his plate down, and curled his fingers around her wrist. "Omi, please have faith in me. I already told you. I will never get back with Ruth."

Omi swallowed her anxiety and licked a dab of mustard from her thumb. "*Denki*. I needed to hear that. Again."

"I would tell you every day if I could." He turned and glanced behind him to the volleyball game. "I'm doing my best to avoid Ruth. I'm very angry with her. I wasn't going to come tonight, but Mammi said it was part of the plan."

"Your *mammi* is very smart, but I don't know if even she can convince Ruth to fall in love with someone else. There's no one like you, Bo. For Ruth and me, you might as well be the only *bu* in the world. Ruth will never change her mind."

He chuckled softly. "Much as I like that you feel that way, it's not true. There are several *buwe* who would suit Ruth better. Ones who would be willing to overlook her selfishness and vanity." He paused. "That wasn't nice."

Omi took a bite of her pretzel, because if Ruth was looking this way, Omi had to appear to be enjoying the eats and not having a serious discussion with Bo. "Imagine how I feel. Whenever I have an unkind thought toward my *schwester*, the guilt buries me."

Omi flinched when she heard Ruth close behind her. "So I guess that was a fake apology."

Both Omi and Bo turned at the same time, which probably made them look even more guilty. Omi accidentally inhaled a piece of pretzel and coughed and gasped while Ruth stood glaring at her. "We're eating pretzels, Ruth. You don't have to get touchy about it."

Ruth narrowed her eyes. "*Ach*, Omi, get off your high horse. I know exactly what you were doing. Maybe you should go home and think on your sins, like how you tried to steal your *schwester*'s boyfriend and how you betrayed my trust."

Omi had been weak, and Ruth was mad again. "I'm sorry, Ruth."

"If you really loved me, you'd stop sneaking around behind my back."

"We weren't sneaking," Omi said. "We were eating pretzels so we'd have enough energy for volleyball."

Ruth folded her arms. "Trust is earned, not given. I don't like you talking to my boyfriend."

Omi could feel Bo stiffen beside her. "Omi should be able to talk to anyone she wants."

Ruth suddenly seemed to remember Bo was standing there listening to every word she said. She softened like butter in July. "You're right, Bo. I'm really trying to protect Omi from getting her hopes up or getting her heart broken. You really are irresistible. And forgive me for assuming the worst about you. Of course you need a pretzel before playing volleyball, but Omi isn't going to play, so she doesn't need to eat anything."

Bo's eye twitched like it always did when he was angry. "You need to be nicer to Omi." He was already walking away before he finished his sentence, as if he couldn't stand to be in Ruth's company for more than a few seconds. Omi pressed her lips together. If his reaction didn't send Ruth a clear message, Omi didn't know what would.

Ruth frowned and looked at Omi. "That was rude of him to say. You're my *schwester*. Of course I'm nice to you. Don't you think I'm nice to you yet?"

"Nice enough," Omi said softly. Ruth deceived herself all the time. Omi didn't try to talk her out of it.

Ruth snatched the half-eaten pretzel off Omi's plate and took a bite. "In the long run, it's nicer to be honest. I'll always tell you the truth, Omi, no matter how bad it hurts. You put our relationship in jeopardy. I knew you'd want to be told so you had a chance to repent of your sins. And I think it's the kind thing to tell you that Bo couldn't truly love someone like you. He fell in love with me because he was attracted to my personality. You and I are too different, Omi. I love you just the way you are, but Bo is not your type." Ruth's eyes pooled with tears. "I've made some mistakes, but I'm still the girl Bo fell in love with. Nothing has changed except that he found out about Elam. Bo will remember he loves me if you just keep away from him." She blinked, and a tear rolled down her cheek. "Do this for me, Omi. Do it for the person you love most in the whole world."

The tears were real, and Omi couldn't help but be moved by such sincerity. She felt worse and worse by the minute because Ruth really was counting on her. "I'll do my best, Ruth, but if I come to the eats table and Bo comes at the same time, it's pretty hard to stay away from him."

Ruth patted her on the arm. "I know you'll try. I couldn't ask for a better *schwester*."

"You could probably ask for a much better *schwester*." One who wasn't in love with the same *bu* Ruth was in love with. It had been Gotte's will to stick them with each other, but if it was Gotte's will that Ruth and Bo should marry, why had He put this love for Bo in Omi's heart? Omi's eyes stung. Was Gotte testing her to prove she would be loyal to her *schwester* or she would find a love worth fighting for?

Ruth's eyes filled with compassion, and she put her arm around Omi. "I hate to see you so unhappy. You're a *gute schwester*. You really are. Now you just have to prove it to me. And Bo. Get out of his way, and he'll come right back to me."

Omi was sick of groveling and apologizing and humiliating herself. She stayed silent.

Ruth's concern lasted for a few seconds, then she glanced behind her at the volleyball game. Bo had joined the game, and that was all the encouragement Ruth needed. "Look, Omi." She grinned with her whole face, as if expecting that Omi would be as happy as she was. "There's room on Bo's team for one more. It's almost as if he planned it."

Ruth skipped over to the volleyball game. She smiled and gushed and simpered in Bo's direction, watching Bo more than she watched the ball. It gave Omi some satisfaction that Bo made a point of ignoring Ruth. Omi shouldn't have felt so smug about that, but she was already the worst *schwester* in the world. A little gloating wouldn't compound her sins by much.

Ruth made a big show of diving for the ball and practically threw herself into Bo's arms, pretending that she was keeping herself from falling. Omi couldn't watch anymore. Could she find someone to take her home? Maybe she should just take the buggy and let Ruth find her own way home. For sure and certain, there were five or six *buwe* just waiting for her to ask. Elam could always give Ruth a ride. If Ruth was clever, she might even be able to convince Bo to take her home.

Omi knelt next to Anna. "I think I'll go home. Will you tell Ruth I took the buggy?"

Anna's wrinkles bunched on top of themselves. "Why on earth would you go home? You just got here."

Omi lowered her eyes. "There's nothing here for me."

Anna grunted. "Bo is here."

"And Ruth won't let me talk to him."

"*Schwesteren* can be so bossy, can't they? Though I don't know that firsthand. I didn't have any *schwesteren*."

Omi stood up. "I shouldn't talk to him anyway. It would be disloyal to Ruth, and I would never intentionally do anything to hurt Ruth."

Anna put on her "wise" face and nodded slowly. "I felt that way about my *bruder* Elmer, and then he started seeing Rosie Herschberger after Rosie had tried to steal Felty from me. But I forgave them both, and they forgave me, and we all forgave each other. Rosie is the dearest soul in the whole world. I'm *froh* I didn't stand in the way of their love."

Felty stirred and opened his eyes. "I'm the one who

tried to stand in the way, and Anna scolded me for being petty. She's always been more forgiving than me."

Anna grinned. "*Ach*, Felty, that's not true. I made you sleep in the barn once."

"And I made our grandson Reuben sleep in the barn after he was rude to you."

Omi loved how honest Anna and Felty were about their shortcomings, which seemed very minor to Omi, especially compared to her transgressions, which included kissing her *schwester*'s boyfriend and telling secrets she should have kept to herself. "Lord willing, Ruth will forgive me, but I'm not staying to find out."

Anna wrapped her fingers around Omi's wrist. "Now, Omi, I told Bo I'd take care of everything, and you've got to trust that I will. But I can't take care of anything if you don't stay. Sometimes you young people are so unmanageable. If everyone would just do what I say, they'd all be much better off."

"But there's no reason to stay."

"I can think of two very *gute* reasons to stay." Anna counted on her fingers. "One, Bo is in love with you. Two, Bo isn't in love with Ruth, and three, if you leave, Ruth will think you've surrendered."

"I have surrendered."

Anna kept counting. "Fourth and most important, the excitement hasn't even begun yet. You do *not* want to miss what I have planned. Ruth will not know what hit her."

A shout, a grunt, and a gasp from the volleyball game got Omi's attention. Ruth was hunched over on the ground holding her nose while Bo, Raymond, and Dade hovered over her. Blood dripped from between Ruth's fingers and onto her apron.

Omi ran to her *schwester*. *Die youngie* parted to let Omi through, and she knelt down and put her arm around Ruth. "*Ach*, what happened?"

"Bo boke my dose," Ruth moaned.

Omi glanced at Bo, who was standing over Ruth grimacing as if he was the one who'd been hurt. "You broke her nose?"

Raymond knelt down, pulled a handkerchief from his pocket, and handed it to Ruth, who was breathing heavily and bleeding profusely, but otherwise seemed in fairly *gute* health. "Ruth was diving for a ball, and she met Bo's elbow. It wasn't on purpose."

"Of course it wasn't on purpose," Bo said. Ruth's attempts to stay as close to Bo as possible had backfired on her.

Omi put her hand on the back of Ruth's neck. "Lean forward. That should help stop the bleeding. And pinch the bridge of your nose."

Ruth waved Omi's hand away. "I'm okay." She pulled Raymond's handkerchief from her nose. The gushing had slowed to a trickle.

"It's looking better already," Raymond said.

Ruth leaned closer to Raymond. "Is my nose swollen?"

Raymond tilted his head to get a better look. "A little, but nobody will even notice in an hour or so. I don't think you broke it."

"*Gute*." Ruth attempted to stand. Raymond and Omi each took an arm and helped her to her feet. "It really hurts, but I didn't hear anything crack, and there's not a lot of blood." She shrugged Omi and Raymond away from her and looked at Bo as if he'd kissed her instead of given her a bloody nose. "You're so quick to the ball, and I got in your way."

Bo frowned. "I'm wonderful sorry. I didn't see you coming from behind."

Ruth gave him a dazzling, if slightly disheveled, smile. "It wasn't your fault, and my nose isn't broken so there's no harm done." She held out her hand. "Bo, could you help me over to sit with your grandparents? I think I should rest for a few minutes."

There really wasn't anything Bo could do but say yes. If Ruth hadn't been genuinely hurt, Omi would have thought Ruth had planned the whole thing to get Bo to hold her hand. Bo would have looked callous indeed to refuse help to a wounded girl. He led Ruth to where Anna and Felty were sitting. Felty stood and offered Ruth his camp chair. Raymond leaped into action and set up another camp chair on Anna's right.

Anna looked surprised and bemused at the same time. She motioned for Omi to come closer and whispered in her ear. "Just so you know, this was not part of my plan. I try to avoid blood whenever possible."

Omi's lips twitched upward. "*Ach*, *vell*, you *did* say Ruth wouldn't know what hit her."

Bo's *mater* ran out of the house with a blanket and a fluffy white washrag. Raymond spread the blanket over Ruth's legs, even though it was eighty degrees outside. Bo's *mamm* handed Ruth the washrag, and Ruth started cleaning the blood off her face.

Felty sat down in the new camp chair, and Raymond hovered around Ruth like a waiter at a fancy restaurant. "Are you okay, Ruth? Do you need anything? Can I get you a drink of water?"

Bo lingered near Ruth for barely a minute, just long enough to seem like he cared, but no longer. Once Raymond took charge of Ruth's comfort, Bo drifted away, as if hoping no one would notice he was going.

Omi caught his eye, and he sidled next to her. There were enough curious *youngie* standing around that Ruth didn't notice. Omi smiled wryly. "You seem to have it out for the Coblenz twins."

He cocked an eyebrow. "Very funny."

"*Vell*, you have made both of us bleed."

He chuckled. "You ran at me unexpectedly, and Ruth refused to keep her distance. What was I supposed to do?"

"Everybody," Ruth announced. "Keep playing. I'm fine."

Bo glanced at Omi. They joined the game, but on opposite teams so Ruth couldn't accuse Omi of betraying her. After not even five minutes, Ruth shed her blanket and went back into the game, standing right next to Bo and oohing and aahing every time he touched the ball.

Bo played for a few minutes when Anna called to him. He turned and left the game quickly, obviously eager to get away from Ruth. Ruth gave him a funny look, but she couldn't very well follow him without seeming like a lovesick teenager or a shameless flirt.

Omi kept playing, but her attention was focused on the same place Ruth's was. Anna patted the chair next to her, and Bo sat down. Anna pulled some yarn and two knitting needles out of her canvas bag and handed them to Bo. He seemed mildly surprised before he burst into a smile. Apparently, Anna was going to teach him how to knit right there in the middle of the gathering. Was this her brilliant plan? Was this the excitement she encouraged Omi to stick around for? What did Anna hope to accomplish by teaching Bo to knit? Omi didn't see how it could make Ruth jealous, but it might make Ruth irritated, especially since she wanted Bo in the game and not knitting with his *mammi*.

When it was her turn to serve, Ruth paused and called to Bo, "Come and play, Bo. You can knit another time."

Bo looked up and smiled. "*Nae, denki*. I'd rather knit."

Whatever Anna's plan, Omi had to smile at the look on Ruth's face. Ruth was trying to show some enthusiasm for the volleyball game, keep an eye on Bo, and do her best not to be irritated with Anna. Ruth thought she loved Bo, but she had always thought he was a little boring. Who would choose knitting over volleyball? Ruth must have been beside herself.

After about fifteen more minutes, Elam complained that he was ready to go, and the game sort of broke up after that. Some of *die youngie* gathered around the eats table. Ruth found another camp chair, set it up next to Bo, and sat down. Bo ignored her by pretending to be very committed to his knitting, which wasn't going well at all. Obviously, learning how to knit wasn't the goal. Ruth rested her hand on the arm of Bo's chair, trying to get his attention without being too obvious. "Do you want to play croquet with me, Bo? Or we could even go skip stones at the pond." She didn't sound at all interested in skipping stones, but it was better than knitting.

Bo shook his head. Ruth blew a puff of air from between her lips and forced a smile. "I don't really care what we do as long as I'm with you."

Anna put down her knitting and clapped her hands. "Everybody, Raymond Fisher has brought something very special he wants to show you. It's one of his own inventions."

"What is it, Raymond?" Suvilla Mast asked.

Raymond, glowing red as a beet, nudged Elam, and they both jogged to Elam's car and came back, not with the tiny Popsicle stick catapult, but with what looked like a long stick, some cut sections of PVC pipe, and a small remote-control box with some wires sticking out of it. Elam carried a cardboard box full of tubes covered in red, white, and blue paper. They looked like mini rockets. Omi grinned. Raymond had obviously invented something very interesting. She glanced at Anna, who gave Omi a conspiratorial nod. Was this the excitement Anna had been talking about? And what did it have to do with Ruth? *Ach, vell,* Ruth loved excitement. At the very least, the rockets would pull her attention from "Knitting Bo."

Elam helped Raymond set up his contraption, jabbing the long stick into the grass and securing a four-inch rocket on top of it. Raymond connected a wire to the base of the rocket and connected the other end of the wire to his remote-control box.

"What is it, Raymond?" Suvilla asked again.

Raymond was fiddling with the wires and didn't look up, probably more out of embarrassment than focus. "This is a sugar rocket. Sugar burns really well when it's mixed with potassium nitrate."

"You made it out of sugar?"

"Sugar is the fuel. Anna wanted me to show you, so I made small rockets with only a little bit of sugar because we don't have a big space. Still, this rocket should go thirty feet into the air. Ruth, do you want to push the button?"

Ruth practically exploded into a smile. "Me?"

Raymond pulled a pair of goggles from his pocket and handed them to Ruth. "Wear these just in case."

Ruth's smile got wider. "Sounds dangerous."

"It shouldn't be too dangerous. There isn't enough sugar to kill you."

"Only if you eat it," Anna said.

Elam motioned for everyone to move back about thirty

feet. The excitement was palpable among *die youngie*. Raymond truly was a genius.

"Okay, Ruth," Raymond said. "Push that button, and let's see what happens."

Ruth did as instructed, and Raymond's PVC pipe rocket shot into the air, trailing a thin plume of smoke behind it. All eyes turned to the sky as the rocket sailed up, arced to the right, and then plummeted back to Earth, landing six feet from the launch point. Everybody clapped and cheered, and Raymond turned redder and redder while Ruth curtsied as if she was the one who had invented the rocket.

Elam put another pipe rocket onto the stick, and Raymond again asked Ruth to push the button. Ruth was so giddy she started giggling. This was obviously way better than skipping stones at the pond. Knitting paled in comparison. She pushed the button again, and the rocket sailed even higher. *Die youngie* laughed and cheered. Raymond couldn't have captured their attention more fully if he'd flapped his arms and flown to the top of the tree.

Ruth bounced on the tips of her toes. "This is the funnest thing I've done in weeks." She glanced at Bo and quickly looked away, her smile faltering for a second.

Raymond, still bright red, checked the wire attached to the remote-control box. "Next time I'll make bigger rockets, and we can go shoot them in an open field."

Ruth nodded. "I'd like that." She glanced behind her. "Wouldn't that be fun, Bo?"

"I guess," Bo said. "But I'd rather knit."

Omi clapped her hand over her mouth. Surely Ruth could see just what Bo and Anna were up to. Bo was a terrible actor, and no one could possibly believe he preferred knitting over anything.

Elam grabbed a red rocket with fins from the box. "Should we try this one?"

"*Jah*," Raymond said. "I'm hoping it will go straight up with the fins to guide it."

Elam propped the rocket on the stick, then Raymond adjusted it so it was pointing perfectly vertical. He jogged to Ruth and nodded. "Okay. It's ready."

Ruth pressed the button, and the rocket shot straight into the air. Ten feet up, it veered wildly to the east and downward. A collective gasp traveled through the crowd as the rocket slammed into the Helmuths' neatly stacked woodpile in an explosion of sparks and hot orange flames. The woodpile caught fire, crackling and spitting ash and smoke in every direction.

Girls screamed. *Buwe* yelled. Squealing at the top of her lungs, Ruth dropped the remote-control box and threw her arms around Raymond's neck. Raymond hooked his arm around her waist and pulled her away from the fire.

Bo dropped his precious knitting and grabbed Omi's hand. "The hose," he yelled.

They ran to the standing pipe at the corner of the house that connected to a green hose. Bo grabbed the end of the hose and pulled it toward the woodpile while Omi turned on the water. The handle was stuck tight, and she gripped it so hard getting it to budge that she peeled some of the skin off her palm.

Three girls ran into the house and ran back out carrying buckets followed by others toting bowls and saucepans and vases and pretty much anything that could hold water. Some containers already had water in them. Three of the boys ran to the barn, no doubt to fill their buckets at the hose there. Elam, of all people, helped Anna from her chair, motioned for Felty, and led them to the back porch where they stood and watched the chaos.

As soon as the water started flowing from the hose, Bo pointed it at the woodpile and the flames lapping at the thick logs. Omi didn't know what to do more than what was already being done, so she kept watch over the hose and said a silent prayer that no one would get hurt. The fire wasn't serious, and the woodpile sat by itself in the yard—not against any structures or fences—so it shouldn't be that hard to put out.

Unfortunately, a floating spark ignited the single sheet hanging on the clothesline, and before anyone even had a chance to flinch, fire curled up and around it and detached it from its clothespins. The sheet spiraled to the ground, and what was left of it smoldered against the wooden clothesline pole. The pole was old and rotting, and the base caught fire like kindling. Suvilla was the first to see it, and she threw her entire bucket of water at the pole. She didn't have much of an aim. The water missed the pole and the sheet entirely and splashed onto Elam's car parked next to the pole. The fire curled higher.

Omi gasped as the pole wobbled then tipped, snapping its lines and tumbling onto Elam's car, hitting his windshield and shattering it into a million pieces. Elam was standing next to Anna and Felty when his car was attacked, and his eyes nearly popped out of his head. He opened his mouth, presumably to scream, but no sound came out.

*Ach.* Omi should had included Elam's car in her prayers.

Elam ran to his car while Suvilla and some of the other girls doused the pole with water. He spread his hands and rested his cheek on the hood in mourning. Ruth and

Raymond tried to comfort him, but with him sprawled across the hood of his car, there wasn't much to do but pat his back.

Omi jogged over to Anna and Felty. "Are you all right?"

Anna nodded. "We're fine. But I feel sorry for Elam. I hope he's learned his lesson about not parking your car on the grass."

Bo and the bucket brigade finally put the woodpile out, then stomped the ground to kill any hot spots. It was impossible not to stare at Bo, moving wood with his broad shoulders and strong arms. Omi knew what it felt like to be wrapped in those arms, and she longed to be there again, no matter what Ruth said. Forgetting Bo felt harder than ever. Omi closed her eyes and thought of Ruth and family ties and enduring love. Omi would do her best not to disappoint her *schwester* or Gotte. She simply had to make herself stay away from Bo. It was too hard to be near him and keep her wits.

Three *buwe* lifted the pole off Elam's car and lowered it to the ground. Bo's *mamm* came out of the house and stood next to Anna and Omi, propping her hands on her hips and surveying the damage. "I never liked that clothesline. I should have chopped it down years ago. Now I can have Titus put up one of those fancy pulley systems that brings the clothes to me just by pulling a rope."

"Most of the wood is still usable," Felty said.

Sallie Mae shook her head. "*Ach*, Dat, we don't even need it. We bought a pellet stove years ago. That wood's been sitting there for over a decade. It's time to get rid of it." She marched across the lawn, barking directions to Bo as she went. "The whole pile has got to go," she called.

Anna straightened her glasses. "Now, Omi, please don't get the wrong idea about me. I told you it was going to get exciting around here, but I was talking about Raymond's rockets. For sure and certain, I didn't plan for things to get *this* exciting. I would never intentionally set a fire. Or break someone's nose or dash Elam's windshield to pieces. I hope you know that."

Omi's pulse was still going a hundred miles an hour, and the fear and chaos and relief of it all made her a little light-headed. Laughter burst from her lips. "Anna, you have a reputation for being the best matchmaker in Wisconsin, and I don't wonder but you can do miracles when you set your mind to it, but I'm absolutely sure you had nothing to do with that fire."

Anna sighed. "I always try to leave the fires and floods and pestilence to Gotte. I'm just not up to it anymore."

*Anymore?*

Omi didn't even want to know.

# Chapter 17

Omi wiped the sweat from the back of her neck and led Sandy back to her stall. It was a late August day, and the heat was stifling. She looked forward to September when the weather cooled and the leaves started to turn. Omi had never been one to wish her life away hoping for better days, but she had nothing in her life to look forward to but more separation from Bo and more disapproval from her *schwester*. The only thing that gave her any joy was the thought of Christmas four months away. Not even Ruth could steal Omi's Christmas joy.

The gathering two weeks ago hadn't accomplished what Anna had wanted it to, though Omi wasn't sure of Anna's plan, so she couldn't be sure that Anna didn't consider the gathering a huge success. Ruth talked nonstop about how Bo had held her hand and helped her sit down after he'd given her a bloody nose playing volleyball. "If Bo didn't care about me, he wouldn't have squeezed my hand so tight. And did you see how concerned he was about my nose?"

"He felt bad that it was his fault."

"*Nae*, Omi, there was more to it than that. He wants to get back together. I can feel it."

Trying to convince Ruth against her will was more frustrating than trying to get the cow to hold still so you could milk her.

The good news, or the bad news, depending on how Omi wanted to look at it, was that Ruth seemed to have dropped Elam like a hot potato. It was bad news because Omi had always held hope in her heart that Ruth might yet decide she was in love with Elam. It was *gute* news because Omi always hated it when Ruth had sneaked off with Elam to go riding in his car. Fortunately or unfortunately, Elam hadn't been able to afford to get his car fixed after it was smashed by a burning clothesline, so he'd sold it and no longer had a way to get from Cashton to Bonduel. It was a three-hour drive and expensive to hire a driver. Even if Elam had managed to get to Bonduel, Ruth didn't want to see him. She only wanted to see his car. Elam no longer held any interest for her.

So now Ruth had nothing and nobody to distract her from her devotion to Bo, even though he completely ignored her and avoided her whenever possible. Ruth, of course, blamed Bo's indifference on Omi, but Omi had been dutifully staying away from him. She had nothing to feel guilty about. *Ach, vell,* nothing to feel guilty about *recently.*

Ruth strode into the barn with her canvas bag slung over her shoulder. It was fat and lumpy, obviously stuffed to overflowing. Ruth was going somewhere. "Omi, I need you to finish the chores by yourself tonight. I'm going to the lake."

Was Elam back? Omi did her best to tamp down the hope that bubbled up like jelly on the stove. "You know I can't lift the hay bales by myself."

"Get LaWayne to help you then." She pressed her lips together. "Please, Omi. Elam is in town, and he and Raymond want to go to the lake." She grabbed Omi's arm. "Here's the best part. Raymond fixed an *Englischer*'s car, and the *Englischer* was so grateful he told Raymond we could use his Jet Skis. That's why I have to go to the lake today. Elam is leaving tomorrow, and the Jet Skis can only be used today."

Omi bit down hard on her tongue. It was always the same with Ruth. She took and she took and got irritated when Omi didn't want to keep giving. But maybe this time would be different. Maybe Ruth just needed one more little push to fall in love with Elam. Now that he didn't have his car, maybe she'd try to get to know him. Maybe the car was getting in the way of their romance.

How badly did Omi want Ruth to fall in love with Elam? Very badly, even though Ruth was more likely to fall in love with the *Englischer*'s Jet Skis.

Ruth had used Elam to get out of more chores than Omi could count. But what did it matter, if Omi could marry Bo without hurting her *schwester*, without being eaten alive by the guilt? Omi didn't even bother asking why Ruth was so eager to spend time with Elam when she was supposedly madly in love with Bo.

She glanced up into the haymow. She couldn't lift those hay bales by herself, and LaWayne was helping Dat in the fields, but maybe there was another way. "I suppose I could push the hay bales out of the haymow."

Ruth nodded so hard she fanned up a breeze. "That's right. You don't even have to lift them."

"Okay. But you're doing all the chores tomorrow, including milking the cow."

Ruth squealed and gave Omi a swift hug and a kiss on the cheek. "I'll milk the cow every day for a week, if you want. *Ach*, Omi, I love you so much. I'll come home and tell you all about it." She ran out of the barn on tiptoes, as if she didn't want to make a sound in her escape.

Omi sighed and sat down on the milking stool. It was funny how Ruth assumed that Omi would want to hear anything about her fun time on the Jet Skis.

Her heart was heavier than a stone. Omi and Ruth used to be inseparable. When they were toddlers, they even had their own language that only the two of them could understand. As little girls, they shared everything. When Ruth scraped her knee, Omi cried too. When Omi got teased by some stupid *bu*, Ruth would chase him around the playground until he agreed to quit teasing her *schwester*. Ruth told the best stories, some true, some made up, and Omi used to love to hear Ruth tell them. They would lie awake in bed and giggle when they should have been asleep. They had never kept secrets from each other, and if one of them had a problem, they both worked on it until they solved it. They had always been happy for each other when some *bu* paid them attention—although it had usually been Omi being happy for Ruth, because *die buwe* liked Ruth better. Omi had come to accept it—that was until Ruth had caught Bo's eye. Omi had been so jealous, she had slowly withdrawn her affection and intimacy with Ruth.

She shouldn't have let a *bu* come between them, but there was nothing Omi could do about her feelings except bury them. She and Ruth could never be what they once were to each other. And it made Omi very sad and very ashamed.

She looked up at the haymow again. She needed to bring down five bales, which wasn't many, but when each bale weighed sixty pounds, it was definitely a bit of a chore. She turned her head in the direction Ruth had gone and stuck out her tongue like a five-year-old. Nobody saw, and the gesture made her feel oddly better. She was outrageously angry with Ruth, more than a little disgusted with herself, and completely in love with Bo Helmuth. The only thing she could hold on to was a thin thread of hope that Anna Helmuth was truly the best matchmaker in Wisconsin. If Anna couldn't help her, no one else could.

Omi quickly climbed the ladder into the haymow. There was also a set of stairs against the far wall, but the ladder was closer and more convenient. Dat had just done a hay cutting two weeks ago, and the haymow was filled to the ceiling with bales. After one more cutting, they'd have plenty of hay for the winter plus some left over to sell. After putting on Dat's work gloves, Omi took a bale by the twine and dragged it off the top of the stack. Then she opened the loft door, folded back the guardrail, and pushed the bale out the door. It tumbled through the air and hit the ground below with a satisfying thud.

Omi sneezed twice and brushed a piece of hay from her sleeve. Moving hay bales was heavy, dusty work, and it always made her eyes water and her nose run. No wonder they called allergies "hay fever." Choosing the shortest stack of bales, she slipped her fingers under the twine of the top bale and dragged it off the pile. It fell to the floor, wrenched Omi's shoulder, and made the whole loft shake. She stood up straight and kneaded the muscles in her arm. This was much easier with two people. LaWayne was already three inches taller than Omi and much stronger. He could have done this by himself.

Omi stuck her head out the loft door and eyed the lone hay bale on the ground. It had taken her almost a full minute and all her muscle power to shove that bale out the door. Should she wait for LaWayne to help her?

She huffed out a breath. This was *dumm*, and she was acting like a *buplie*. It was five hay bales, and she could work out her anger by pushing all the weight across the floor. She bent over and put her back into it. Halfway to the door, she rested by lying flat on top of the hay bale and taking some deep breaths. She finally got to the loft door and pushed the bale over the edge. Too late she noticed that the fabric of her dress had somehow gotten tangled with the twine around the hay bale.

Her heart lurched as she lost her footing, and the hay bale dragged her over the edge with it.

# Chapter 18

Omi would never take breathing for granted again. Or moving. The slightest attempt to roll over or scoot farther up in her bed sent pain shooting across her chest and down her left arm. Her right arm wasn't much better. They'd poked an IV in one of her veins and secured it with fluorescent pink medical tape, but a big purple bruise was already beginning to form under the skin because they'd poked her about four times before they'd found a *gute* vein.

Omi tried to shift her weight from one hip to the other in the hospital bed and couldn't stifle the groan that escaped her lips. *Ach*, getting conked in the head with a two-by-four stung something wonderful, but this pain was even worse, constant and intense.

"Are you okay, *heartzley*?" Mamm asked, placing a hand on Omi's shoulder.

Omi hissed. "Mamm, I love you, but please don't touch me. Even my skin hurts."

Mamm jerked her hand away. "I'm sorry."

"It's okay," Omi said. "The nurse said the pain pill would kick in anytime."

Mamm sat at Omi's bedside, her eyes brimming with

concern. "I keep telling your *dat*, the heavy work is for *die buwe*. But will he listen to me?"

"It was my own fault, Mamm. I wasn't being careful."

Mamm reached out to touch Omi's face but thought better of it and pulled back her hand. "*Ach*, my sweet Omi. You're always blaming yourself for things that aren't your fault."

"This one was my fault."

Mamm pursed her lips. "Ruth has a part in it."

Omi didn't want to think about Ruth. She didn't want to talk about Ruth or even see Ruth right now. Because she wouldn't be able to hold her tongue, even though the fall from the haymow hadn't been Ruth's fault. Ruth had put Omi in a difficult position—again—and Omi wasn't ready to forgive her just yet. "Is she here?"

"*Nae*. Still off on Raymond's Jet Skis."

Omi took a perverse sense of satisfaction in thinking how bad Ruth would feel about the accident and how bad she would feel that she had been having fun all day while Omi was lying in the hospital. Then again, maybe Ruth wouldn't feel bad at all. Maybe she'd think Omi deserved a broken arm for daring to love Ruth's boyfriend.

"Can I come in?" Bo stood at the open door, hat in hand, hair disheveled, with a smudge of dirt across his cheek. His fingers curled around the brim of his hat, but Omi could see his hands trembling as if he'd just had a terrible scare. His face was lined with worry, even though Omi could tell he was trying to act casual about it. It was what you did with sick people. If you acted too concerned, the patient got worried that there really was something to be concerned about, and panic set in.

Her heart thumped against her aching chest. He was handsome no matter how badly he needed a bath. She shouldn't let him in. Her loyalty was to Ruth, after all, but she just couldn't resist that tentative smile and those dark, intelligent eyes. "*Jah*, come in."

Mamm's gaze traveled between Bo and Omi. "I need to go find a vending machine," she stuttered, standing up and offering Bo her chair. "I have a hankering for a Twinkie."

Omi started to laugh but sucked in the air when the pain slammed into her. Mamm hated Twinkies. Bo winced as if he was in as much pain as Omi. "Are you okay? Is the pain terrible? Omi, I'm so sorry." He intertwined his fingers with hers, and it didn't even hurt. In truth, it was the best feeling in the world.

She laid her head back on the pillow. "The pain pills are helping, but it still hurts something wonderful."

He exhaled a deep breath and closed his eyes. "I'm so sad you're hurt but so *froh* you're alive!" When he opened his eyes, she saw profound gratitude and overwhelming love. She could barely breathe. "Ben and I were in the field working the horses when Emma ran out and told us there'd been an accident. I got here as soon as I could." He frowned and squeezed her fingers tighter. "I . . . was . . . really afraid. What happened?"

Omi felt her face get warm. "*Ach*, Bo, I'm ashamed to admit how careless I was, and now my parents will have to pay a huge hospital bill."

"Don't worry about the money right now. Gotte will work everything out. Tell me what happened."

"I was throwing hay bales from the loft, and the hem of my dress got tangled in the twine. The hay bale took me down with it. Thank Derr Herr, I landed on top of the hay bale, or it would have been worse."

Bo took a shuddering breath. "Much worse. But it's bad enough. Your *dat* said you broke your arm."

Omi motioned toward her cast with her head, because moving any other part of her body was out of the question.

"Broke my arm, three cracked ribs, and you can see the whole right side of my face is scraped up. I don't dare look in the mirror."

He tenderly smoothed his thumb down the back of her hand. "You're just as beautiful as ever." His lips twitched playfully. "Even with pus oozing out of every pore in your face."

She rolled her eyes. *Ach*, even that hurt! "For sure and certain it's very attractive. With the scar on my forehead, the welts on my face, and the crooked ear, I'm not even fit for the circus."

"The crooked ear?"

"They had to sew my ear back on."

Bo's eyes popped wide open, and his mouth nearly fell off his face. "Your ear? *Ach, du lieva.*"

Omi carefully lifted her hand and pulled away the hair that fell over her ear. "Not my whole ear, just the very back part." She tilted her head so Bo could get a better look, though there wasn't much for him to see but a bandage. "It's called the helix, and it got torn away from my head when I landed on the hay bale. I limped into the house covered in blood. Mamm nearly fainted."

"I don't wonder but she did."

"I told her where Ruth hid her cell phone, and she called an ambulance. I'm *froh* Ruth didn't take her phone Jet Skiing or we would have had to run to the neighbors."

He bent down and kissed her knuckles. Omi would have floated off her bed if she hadn't been attached to an IV. "When Emma said they'd taken you to the hospital, I was dizzy with fear," he said, his voice cracking in about a dozen places. "I'm *froh* you're safe. Gotte is *gute*. So *gute*." Bo glanced toward the door. "I know I shouldn't be here. I know you want to be loyal to Ruth, but I had to see with my own eyes that you are okay. I'm sorry if this hurts Ruth's feelings, but I couldn't stay away."

Omi didn't feel one bit guilty about Bo's being here. Right now, she needed him more than she needed air. She wouldn't shut Bo out simply because Ruth might be irritated. "Maybe Ruth can show her *schwester* a little compassion. I'm in a lot of pain. Besides, she's not here. If she really cared that much about me, she wouldn't have left me with the hay bales." It was unfair to say, but Omi was irritated enough to say it. She lifted her arm to brush some hair from her face and winced.

Bo drew his brows together. "I wish I could take some of your pain. Next time you need bales from the haymow, come and get me. I'll be happy to move every heavy object in your barn."

"I shouldn't have tried to do it myself. Ruth was supposed to help me."

Bo frowned. "But she went Jet Skiing."

She couldn't meet his eye. "With Elam and Raymond. Raymond's *Englisch* friend let him borrow the Jet Skis. They only have them for one day."

Bo's expression darkened like a storm cloud. "Ruth keeps saying she wants to get back together with me, but she's with Elam so often, she wouldn't have time for me even if I wanted to date her again." He held up his hand as if stopping traffic. "I don't want to get back together with Ruth. I will never get back together with Ruth."

"I didn't say anything."

"I saw it on your face," he said. "Doesn't she see how selfish she's acting?"

"She didn't think you'd find out."

"I can't figure her out. I don't even think she's interested in me anymore. Why won't she quit this emotional manipulation and let me marry you?" He scrubbed his hands through his hair. "I hate that you won't marry me unless Ruth gives permission."

It broke Omi's heart seeing him so upset and knowing she was the cause of it. "She loves you. She feels betrayed."

He shook his head. "She wants control. And you're letting her control you." Bo let go of her hand. "I can't stand it, Omi. I can't stand seeing how Ruth uses you and convinces you to do her chores and makes you feel guilty about loving me. Can't you see how this tortures me?"

Every piece of Omi ached with longing. "Can't you see how this tortures me?"

"Does it?" Was he questioning her sincerity?

"We just need to give Anna more time. For sure and certain she'll find someone for Ruth. Then you and I can be together."

"I hope for that. I pray for that, but what if Mammi can't find anyone?" His eyes flashed with despair, and he swiped his hand across his mouth. "You don't love me enough."

"What do you mean by that?"

Lines of anger etched themselves into his face. "If you loved me more, you'd stand up to Ruth."

How could he doubt her love? How could he ask her to choose between him and Ruth? "Ruth said if I truly loved her, I'd give you up for her sake. How can she ask me to choose? How can *you* ask me to choose?"

"Are you going to let Ruth treat you like this forever?"

Bo just didn't understand, and she wasn't in any shape to explain it to him. "I'm not letting Ruth do anything to me. Ruth and I have always been closer than *schwesteren*, and I want to be loyal to her just like she's loyal to me."

"You believe that Ruth is loyal to you, but if she were, she wouldn't have left you with the hay bales. If she were, she wouldn't have talked you into pretending to be her. If she's so loyal, why won't she let you love the *bu* you want to love?"

Her tongue tasted like bile. "You mean, Ruth doesn't care about me?"

"*Nae*, she doesn't. She only cares about herself."

Omi was already in so much pain, she could barely hold herself together. She couldn't keep a tear from trickling down her swollen cheek. "Am I that unlovable?"

The hard lines of Bo's face softened, and compassion pooled in his eyes. "That's not what I'm saying at all." He reached out to her.

"Don't touch me," she said. Everything hurt too much, especially Bo's fake sympathy.

His hand froze halfway between them. "Omi, you are the most lovable person I know."

"I'm not. I stole my *schwester*'s boyfriend, I've put my parents in financial trouble, and I've made your life miserable."

"You haven't made my life miserable. I'm happier than I've ever been because of you."

"Really? Because not three minutes ago you told me it's torture to live like this."

"That's not what I meant."

Omi was crying so hard, the tears threatened to choke her. The right side of her face stung with the salt of her falling tears. "I don't know what you meant, Bo, but I know that you're unhappy, even if you deny it. I can't bear to be the source of that unhappiness. I know how deeply I've hurt you with my indecision and my doubt. I've been trying to make everyone happy, but I just can't carry it anymore."

"Omi, please," he said. She'd never heard such tenderness or such despair.

"Maybe you're right. Maybe I don't love you enough.

But trying to choose between you and my *schwester* is tearing me apart."

"I'm sorry, Omi. I shouldn't have said . . ."

"Why don't you just forget about me? Find someone who doesn't have a twin *schwester* or seven ugly scars or a huge hospital bill. That's the kind of girl you should marry."

Bo pressed his fingers to his forehead. "I should have . . ."

"Omi! *Ach, du lieva*, I came as soon as I heard." Ruth blew into the room like a hurricane, her hair on top of her head in a hasty, damp bun covered with a blue bandanna. Omi didn't miss the look Ruth gave Bo before she crowded next to him by the side of Omi's bed. "*Ach*, Omi, you've been crying! Where does it hurt?" she asked, as if she was in charge of Omi's recovery.

Omi closed her eyes and turned her face from both of them. "Everywhere," she whispered. She swallowed her tears, though she suspected she hadn't seen the last of them. When the pain didn't take her breath away, she might indulge in crying again.

Bo stood up. "I need to go."

Omi couldn't look at him, so she didn't know if he was happy to be going, angry, or just weary. He sounded weary.

"Don't leave," Ruth gushed. "I just got here."

"Omi needs her rest."

"I'll walk you out," Ruth said.

Bo gave Omi one last, regretful look, but there was nothing he could say with Ruth standing there. Omi stared straight ahead and tried not to disintegrate into a puddle. Ruth followed Bo out the door like an obedient puppy, and a few minutes of blessed silence followed. Omi closed her eyes and laid her head back on her pillow. If she pretended to be asleep, would Ruth just go away?

No such luck. Ruth came back and sat in Bo's chair.

Omi opened her eyes. Ruth gazed at her with a look of horror on her face. "I didn't know it was this bad. Mamm didn't say it was this bad. You look like you got run over by a truck."

"How was Jet Skiing?"

Ruth hesitated. "If I had known you'd gotten hurt, I wouldn't have stayed on the lake for so long. You know I would have come straight to the hospital, right?"

Omi knew no such thing.

Ruth scooted the chair a little closer. "I told you to get LaWayne to help you with the hay bales," she scolded.

"I thought I could do it myself."

"Mamm's irritated with me for leaving, but I told you to ask LaWayne for help."

"It's my fault completely," Omi said. Anything to get Ruth to stop talking.

"Does it hurt bad?"

"Really bad."

"I'm sorry, Omi. The *gute* news is that you didn't die or break your neck. That would be terrible if you broke your neck, don't you think?" She patted Omi's hand. "Mamm thinks they'll let you come home today."

"I think so. Right now they're just keeping an eye on my levels."

"Whatever that means." Ruth glanced around the room. "Lord willing you'll come home today. I invited Bo to visit you anytime. He won't be able to avoid me so easily if I'm the one taking care of you. Maybe some *gute* will come of this accident if Bo and I can get back together. At least we can start talking and maybe really communicate with each other."

Omi didn't take any comfort in any such thing.

Ruth pointed to the IV in Omi's arm. "Does that hurt?"

"No more than everything else."

"I know I agreed to do all your milking this week, but since you're hurt, for sure and certain everyone will pitch in to do your chores. I don't wonder that LaWayne will feel sorry enough that he'll be eager to milk." Ruth took the bandanna off her head and pulled the pins from her bun. Her hair fell around her shoulders. "My hair is soaked. I didn't have time to let it dry. As you can see, I rushed over as soon as I heard." She combed her fingers through her hair a few times, wrapped it back into a bun, and pinned it in place. "I wish you would have come with me. Then you wouldn't have had the accident. It was so much fun. There was a Jet Ski for each of us, and Raymond taught me how to drive it. I was so nervous I thought I'd die, but then I got good at it, and the three of us had races."

Omi closed her eyes and didn't even try to listen as Ruth went on and on about the best day of her life and how sad she was that Omi had missed it.

Omi's heart was as heavy and cold as a block of ice. Bo was right. Ruth truly didn't care about her. Maybe Ruth had never loved her. Bo was finished with her, and Ruth couldn't see past the end of her nose.

Omi truly didn't have a friend in the world.

# Chapter 19

Bo hiked up Huckleberry Hill, his steps heavy, his heart broken. He had always come to Mammi and Dawdi for advice and comfort, but he'd made such a mess of things, he feared that not even Mammi and Dawdi could help him. But he didn't know where else to turn, and he was willing to try anything for Omi.

His mind went back to Omi in that hospital bed, and he momentarily forgot to breathe. He could have lost her. He might have lost her. Farms were dangerous places, and people died falling out of haymows. Omi's *dat* shouldn't expect any of his *dochters* to do the heavy work. LaWayne was old enough and strong enough to do that kind of work. Ruth most certainly shouldn't have left Omi to do it by herself.

But deep down, he knew he couldn't cast stones at Ruth, because he hadn't treated Omi any better. He'd been so frustrated that day at the hospital that he'd hurt Omi's feelings when all he'd wanted to do was help her recognize Ruth's selfishness. But he'd been the selfish one, because he'd used his own pain to cause pain. Omi had been devastated, her heart broken into pieces she didn't know how to put back together.

He had been to see Omi every day this week, mostly because Ruth allowed and encouraged it, but his visits had been frustrating at best. After only a few words with Omi, Ruth would take over the conversation and leave Omi out completely, or else Ruth would whisk Bo out of the sick room and try to engage him in conversations he didn't want to have. He was torn between being nice to Ruth for Omi's sake and giving Ruth the sternest, most spiteful scolding he'd ever given.

But a lecture wouldn't help. Ruth didn't listen. She hadn't listened in all the times he'd tried to break up with her. She certainly wouldn't listen again, and Bo was tired of trying to convince her.

An old grayish silver car Bo didn't recognize was parked in front of Mammi and Dawdi's house. He tromped up the porch steps and tapped on the door. "*Cum reu,*" Mammi called.

Bo opened the door. Mammi and Dawdi and Raymond Fisher were sitting at the table with pieces of notebook paper in front of them. "*Ach*, Bo," Mammi said, beaming from ear to ear. "I'm so *froh* you're here. You can help me with my oregano."

"It's pronounced origami," Dawdi said.

Mammi nodded cheerfully. "That's what I said, Felty dear." She patted the empty seat next to her. "*Cum*, Bo. Sit. We're trying a new hobby, and it's nice because it doesn't cost any money, and you can make beautiful swans and frogs and butterflies. It's called orgumbi, and it's the Japanese art of folding paper. Raymond is already on his second animal."

Raymond glanced up from the paper he was folding. "*Hallo*, Bo."

Mammi patted the chair again. "I'd say your coming here today is serendipitous."

"What does that mean?" Bo said, sitting down. Mammi was just about the smartest person Bo knew. She was always using big words that Bo didn't know the meaning of.

"It means that we've been wanting to get you and Raymond in the same room for weeks, and it happened without even planning it." Mammi winked at Dawdi. "More proof that Gotte approves." Mammi showed Bo the origami she was working on, which looked very much like a piece of paper folded in half. "Raymond came to fix the generator that runs our homemade ice cream maker, and I asked him to stay and help with the orgumbo. He's very talented. Show Bo your frog, Raymond."

Raymond smiled sheepishly and slid a cleverly folded paper frog to Bo's side of the table. He pressed on the frog's bottom, and the frog hopped forward several inches. Bo grinned. "That is *wunderbarr*, Raymond. How did you make it?"

Raymond shrugged. "I've done origami before, though I never knew it was called 'origami.'"

"Oregano," Mammi corrected.

"Once you learn how to fold frogs, they're easy," Raymond said. "I can also show you how to make a bird that flaps its wings or a snake that strikes."

Mammi clapped her hands. "Felty loves snakes, don't you, Felty?"

"*Jah*, I do." Dawdi handed Raymond his paper. "Can you make a massasauga?"

Dawdi knew lots of big words too.

Raymond hesitated. "Is that a snake?"

Dawdi nodded. "A venomous one."

"That your car outside?" Bo asked.

"*Jah*." Raymond picked up Dawdi's paper and examined it. "I bought it yesterday. I'm going to fix it up. I have a buyer who will pay two thousand more than I got it for."

Mammi folded her paper in half again. "Raymond is very *gute* at fixing things. That's why I've wanted to get you two together. You need Raymond's help, and he needs yours."

"Okay?" Bo said. He really wanted to talk to Mammi and Dawdi about Omi and Ruth, but if Raymond had a problem, Bo could set his own troubles aside for a few minutes. But he didn't know anything about cars.

Raymond frowned. "I just came to fix the generator."

Mammi abandoned her origami, went behind the counter, and took the lid off the cookie jar. She retrieved four dark-brown lumps from inside, set them on a plate, and brought them to the table. "Eat up. You're growing boys, and this is one of my best recipes."

Bo suspiciously eyed the burnt golf balls. Mammi's gingersnaps could break your teeth if you weren't careful. He grabbed a cookie and licked it. Yep. Hard as a rock. Raymond picked up a cookie and scraped his teeth against it to test its hardness. He also took to licking it like a lollipop.

Mammi sat down and scooted her chair in. "We need to talk about Ruth and Omi Coblenz."

Bo glanced at Raymond. Mammi was definitely the smartest person Bo knew. Raymond was Elam's cousin. If anybody could influence Elam to get together with Ruth, it was probably Raymond.

Raymond looked down and fiddled with the paper Felty had given him. "I'm wonderful sorry about your woodpile, Bo. I was trying to . . . *ach*, *vell*, it doesn't matter what I was trying to do. I shouldn't have been so cocky about my rockets. Someone could have gotten seriously hurt."

Mammi laced her fingers together. "Nobody was hurt, and your heart was in the right place. Ruth loved them."

He slumped his shoulders. "Until I started that fire."

She waved away his concern. "It was more excitement than most of us have had all year, except for Omi's accident, though I wouldn't call that exciting. I'd call it horrifying."

Bo shuddered, thinking about what could have happened. "It was horrifying."

"Terrible," Raymond said. "I'm *froh* Omi is going to be okay. Ruth is taking *gute* care of her."

Bo resisted the urge to roll his eyes. "I suppose, though Ruth seems more concerned about herself than Omi. I have to admit I'm having a hard time forgiving Ruth for what she did."

Raymond's brows inched together. "It wasn't Ruth's fault."

Mammi's eyes twinkled. "I like how loyal you are to Ruth, Raymond. It's something every girl wants in a husband."

"If Ruth had been there, Omi wouldn't have fallen. Ruth was supposed to be helping Omi move hay bales, but Omi had to do it herself because Ruth was Jet Skiing with you and Elam."

Raymond hesitated. "I'm sure Ruth feels bad, but we can't be hard on her. She couldn't have known Omi would get hurt."

Mammi nodded. "How could she have known? I'm sure she feels bad. It's nice of you to defend her."

Bo scrubbed his hand down the side of his face. "She didn't know Omi was going to get hurt, but that's no excuse for her behavior. Ruth knew there were chores to do, but she talked Omi into doing them for her so she could go Jet Skiing. Ruth has been treating Omi like this for months, taking her for granted, handing off her chores, putting her own desires above her *schwester*'s well-being."

Frustration made Bo obstinate. "It seems like you and Elam don't even care that Omi suffers because of Ruth's selfishness. You take Ruth wherever she wants to go. You indulge her."

There. He'd said it, even though Raymond wasn't the one who needed to hear it. None of this was Raymond's fault. Raymond was kind and unassuming, and he'd rather speak in front of a whole room of people than argue with anybody.

Raymond fixed his gaze downward and pressed on his frog. It hopped to the middle of the table. "I care. I'm sorry if you think I don't care."

It was the second time in as many weeks that Bo had let his mouth run ahead of his brain. "I'm sorry, Raymond. I shouldn't take my frustration out on you."

Raymond studied Bo's face. "I thought you and Ruth loved each other. Why are you so mad at her?"

Mammi picked up a cookie and tapped it against the table as if she were trying to crack an egg. "This is exactly the reason you two need to talk. You're working on different ends of the same problem."

Bo studied Raymond's face. "You know Ruth and I aren't dating anymore."

Surprise clicked in Raymond's eyes. "Um. *Nae*. I didn't know that. Ruth says you're her boyfriend."

"I'm not."

Raymond fell silent as a smile slowly grew on his lips. "You're not dating?"

"We're not dating." It seemed both Raymond and Ruth had trouble grasping the truth.

"Well," Raymond said, leaning back in his chair and grinning like a cat. "Well. I thought you were dating." His smile faded. "She talks about you all the time."

"I broke up with Ruth weeks ago, but for some reason, she won't let me go."

Raymond made a face as if it should be obvious. "She loves you."

Mammi huffed out a breath. "She doesn't love Bo. She loves the idea of being in love with Bo. I don't blame her. Bo has nice hair and straight teeth. Unfortunately, Ruth is making Omi miserable, and I think you can help."

Raymond leaned forward as if he hadn't heard Mammi correctly. "Help make Omi miserable?"

Mammi giggled. "*Nae*, Raymond. I think you can help solve Omi's problem. And Bo's."

"I can't believe Ruth is making Omi miserable. They're *schwesteren*. Ruth is fun and kind, and she would never do anything to hurt Omi. She would never dream of harming a soul."

Mammi didn't argue, even though Raymond had a very stilted view of Ruth's virtues. "Have you given Ruth those pot holders yet? I told you to give them to someone special."

Someone special? Raymond and . . . Ruth?

The heat traveled up Raymond's face. "I . . . I . . . *ach*, Anna, I want to give them to Ruth, but she's not interested in me. She's pretty and nice, and she could marry any *bu* she wanted to."

Mammi reached over and patted Raymond's hand. "She doesn't like just any *bu*. She likes you."

"*Nae*," Raymond said. "She likes Bo."

"But what about Elam?" Bo said, completely confused.

"She doesn't like Elam," Raymond and Mammi said at the same time.

Mammi gave Bo a grandmotherly smile that said, *I love you, but you don't really know very much.* "Elam is a nice *bu*, but Ruth is too smart for that." She glanced at Raymond. "No offense."

"No offense taken. Elam's my cousin. I love him, but he's really annoying sometimes, and he's a terrible driver. Ruth liked his car, but he doesn't have it anymore. I fixed Elam's car so he'd let me go on all his rides with Ruth, but Ruth isn't interested in Elam. She only likes Bo."

Mammi shook her head so hard, Bo felt a breeze. "Ruth only thinks she likes Bo, but Bo is very boring. Ruth needs more excitement in her life, and you, Raymond, are exciting."

Bo was slightly offended at Mammi's opinion of him. "I'm not boring."

Mammi gave him a pointed look. "Of course you're not. We just need Ruth to think you're boring. You can go back to being interesting after Ruth is engaged. It's all part of the plan." She shook her finger at Raymond. "You need to be more diligent in following my instructions. Give Ruth those pot holders. That's the most important thing."

Bo had a hard time believing Raymond could be interested in Ruth—mostly because he had a hard time believing that anyone could be interested in Ruth. Then again, he had once been interested, and Raymond was much better suited to Ruth than Bo had ever been. Raymond was always ready for adventure, even adventure that flirted with the edge of the rules. He was content to let Ruth be the center of attention because he hated any attention on himself. He was patient and forgiving, and Ruth needed both qualities in a husband. "You really like Ruth that much?"

"I do," Raymond said.

They all fell silent. Bo saw a tiny light at the end of the long, dark tunnel. His heart skipped a beat.

Raymond folded and unfolded the paper in his hand. "What if she doesn't really like me? I think I'll die if she rejects me to my face. I couldn't stand to be embarrassed like that. I'd rather be single."

The look of horror on Mammi's face made Bo smile. Raymond's attitude was a matchmaker's worst nightmare. "Bite your tongue, Raymond Fisher. You don't want to die an old bachelor. Unmarried men are a menace to society."

Bo swiped his hand across his mouth to hide a smile. "My *mammi*'s right, Raymond. Don't take this the wrong way, but I would be very happy if you took Ruth off my hands."

Again, Mammi tapped her cookie on the table, leaving a small indentation in the wood. "I'm disappointed in you, Raymond. You fix cars, drive Jet Skis, and shoot off rockets, but you're afraid to tell Ruth Coblenz how you feel. If you're not willing to fight for love, you don't deserve it."

Dawdi sat back and folded his arms. "Don't you think the risk is worth the reward? It could mean a lifetime of happiness for you and Ruth."

Bo didn't want to sound callous, but he needed to be honest. "With the added benefit that it would get Ruth out of my hair."

Raymond sat in stunned silence, his eyes fixed on his frog. "I just . . . I never considered it before because Ruth is so set on marrying Bo. I didn't even let myself have the tiniest bit of hope."

"You can now let your hopes run amok," Mammi said.

Raymond shook his head. "*Nae.* Even if Ruth stops liking Bo, that doesn't mean she could ever like me."

Mammi pinned Raymond with a stern eye. "You young people are all the same. You won't believe a word that comes out of my mouth. I'm smarter than you think, and if you give Ruth those pot holders, you have a chance. Besides, what have you got to lose?"

Raymond's Adam's apple bobbed up and down. "My dignity."

"Not at all," Mammi said. "If Ruth embarrasses you, you'll just be joining a long line of *buwe* who have made fools of themselves over a girl. It's like a club, and there's no shame in belonging to it."

"I belong to the ASPCA," Dawdi said.

Mammi took the last cookie off the plate and rolled it across the table to Raymond. "We are all here to help you, Raymond. We'll do everything in our power to make Ruth fall in love with you."

A smile grew slowly on Raymond's lips. "Do you really think I could persuade her to love me?"

Bo hated to bring it up, but he wouldn't feel *gute* about himself unless Raymond knew everything. "But, Raymond, don't court Ruth out of obligation to me or Mammi. You shouldn't sacrifice your future just for my benefit."

Raymond gave him a puzzled look. "How would I be sacrificing my future?"

"Ruth is selfish. She uses people to get what she wants. More often than not, she makes Omi feel guilty until Omi does Ruth's bidding. She used Elam for his car. She used you for your Jet Skis. I just want you to be sure you really want a relationship with Ruth. She's not very nice."

Raymond's eyes flashed with indignation. "Ruth isn't like that. I know she tricked you by trading places with Omi, and you didn't like her taking rides with Elam, but she has a *gute* heart, and I'd be blessed indeed if she agreed to be my *fraa*."

Bo almost breathed a sigh of relief. He'd told Raymond the truth. If Raymond chose to ignore it, Bo didn't need to feel responsible for Raymond's happiness. Bo could concentrate on his own happy ending.

"Well then, for goodness' sake, give Ruth those pot holders. You're not getting any younger and neither is Bo. It's time both of you settled down. No grandson of mine is going to be a menace to society."

# Chapter 20

Ruth wiped a trickle of sweat from her neck. "Why do we have to host *gmay* in August? It's too hot for yardwork. I'd much rather host in January when you don't have to clean up the yard at all. The snow covers everything, so no one can tell if you haven't weeded or planted flowers."

"But then we have to wash the walls and scrub the baseboards," Omi said, not feeling sorry for Ruth. Omi only had one *gute* hand for weeding, the skin under her cast itched something wonderful, and her ribs were still sore. Besides, Ruth had more than her fair share of leisure time, and it didn't hurt her one bit to weed the flowers in preparation for *gmay*. At least Dat had given the hay bale job to LaWayne and forbidden Ruth and Omi from even climbing into the haymow. Omi suspected that Mamm had put her foot down about the girls doing the heavy jobs, though Dat probably would have come to the decision on his own. After a few weeks, Omi would convince Dat to at least let her climb into the haymow. It was a *gute* spot when she wanted to be alone.

Ruth made a face. "We wash the walls and scrub the baseboards anyway. There's always work to be done, but there's extra for *gmay*."

Omi concentrated on a stubborn shoot of bindweed wrapped around one of Mamm's petunias. "I wish it wasn't at our house this week. I look like a monster."

Ruth set down her trowel and propped her hands on her hips. "You do not, Omi. We're all just *froh* you're alive. Those scabs will heal."

Dr. Patel, the plastic surgeon, had given Omi a jar of cream to rub on the scabs and scratches on her face every day. She said it would help prevent scarring. Omi hoped so. She was looking less like Ruth every day, and Bo had fallen in love with Ruth's face, not one pocked with scars.

Omi's heart sank. What did it matter if she were beautiful ever again? She had driven Bo away. For sure and certain he wouldn't have her now even if she was pretty. Omi couldn't stand up to Ruth, and Bo blamed her for it. Omi was weak, and Bo needed a strong *fraa*, one who wouldn't give in to Ruth every time Ruth got her feelings hurt or made unreasonable demands. Besides that, why would Bo want to be married to the *schwester* of a girl who had made his life miserable? It would be better for him if he just forgot the Coblenzes altogether and found someone else to love.

Of course Omi didn't want that, didn't want that at all, but she feared Bo had already given up on her. She hadn't seen him for a week.

"Besides, you don't have a boyfriend, so you don't need to impress anybody tomorrow." Ruth always made it a point to remind Omi that Bo was Ruth's boyfriend and Omi had no business thinking about him. Ruth tucked an errant lock of hair behind her ear. "I need to impress Bo, and if I'm out here much longer, I'll be sunburnt to a crisp. *Ach*, I hate weeding."

A silver-gray car pulled up in front of their house, and Raymond got out of the driver's seat. Ruth caught her breath, shot to her feet, and bounded across the grass. "Raymond! I didn't know you could drive."

Raymond's face was beet red, but he gave Ruth a wide smile. "I got a license so I could buy this car. I'm going to start a new business fixing cars and reselling them."

Ruth clapped her hands. "That is a *wunderbarr* idea. You know how to fix anything."

Raymond came around to Ruth's side of the car, and they both strolled over to where Omi was weeding. "It's a nice car," Omi said. "Where's Elam?"

Raymond kicked at the grass at his feet. "After he lost his car, he decided to go to Kansas to find work. He wants to earn enough to buy another car and then join the army."

Ruth's eyebrows inched up her forehead. "It wonders me how his parents feel about that."

"They're not happy, but Elam thinks he'll earn enough money to buy a house and get married."

Ruth frowned. "Does he have a girlfriend?"

"*Nae*, but he's planning on finding one once he gets out of the army."

Omi grinned. "At least he has a plan."

"Elam is a nice *bu*," Ruth said. "But he was too attached to his car. I don't see how he'll ever give it up to be baptized."

Ruth obviously didn't hear herself. She was just as attached to Elam's car as he was. And now it was Raymond who had the car. Omi bit her bottom lip. It was best not to hope.

Raymond's face got redder as he pulled a handful of pink yarn from his pocket. It was one of Anna's pot holders. "Ruth, Anna asked me to give this to you. She said you liked pot holders."

Ruth studied the pot holder in puzzlement. "That's nice

of Anna, but I don't have any feelings for pot holders one way or the other."

Raymond acted as if Ruth had just backed a car over his heart. "*Ach*. Okay. I'm sorry. She said you'd like it."

A giggle burst from Ruth's mouth. "You don't have to be so sad about it. It's just a pot holder."

Omi tried to smooth things over, though she wasn't sure why Raymond seemed so dejected. "We can always use another one. It was thoughtful of you to bring it over."

Ruth eyed Omi, and realization dawned on her face. She nodded enthusiastically. "It's wonderful nice. We use pot holders at every meal to protect our table from getting scorch marks. It's probably the most useful gift I've ever received."

Raymond sprouted a small smile. "Anna said you'd like it."

"I love it," Ruth said, gushing a bit too much in an effort to make up for hurting Raymond's feelings, even though she and Omi had no idea why Raymond's feelings were hurt in the first place. He was obviously more sensitive than they realized.

Ruth set the pot holder on the porch step. "I'll put it there until I'm ready to go into the house."

"Mamm will be thrilled with a new pot holder," Omi added.

That was exaggerating just a bit, but Raymond's smile widened and took over his whole face. He jiggled the keys in his hand. "It wonders me if you want to go for a ride, Ruth. I'm finished working on this car, and I want to make sure there are no strange noises coming from the engine before I deliver it to the buyer."

Ruth's eyes lit up with delight. "Does it have air conditioning?"

"It sure does."

Ruth squealed happily. "I love air conditioning." She glanced at Omi, and her face fell. "Do you mind finishing the weeding? I really want to try out Raymond's car."

Raymond's expression clouded over. "If you need to do the weeding, I can come another time."

"But I want a ride before you sell it. It looks fast." Ruth stuck out her bottom lip in an attractive and irresistible pout.

"There will be more cars," Raymond said, his gaze traveling between Omi and Ruth. "And I'm sure you want to help Omi with the weeding."

Ruth waved her hand around as if swatting flies. "Omi doesn't care. She doesn't have anything better to do anyway. You don't mind, do you, Omi?"

Omi's heart hardened like cement. Of course she minded, but Ruth would be irritated and even downright angry if Omi didn't give in.

Raymond spoke before Omi could. "But, Ruth, Omi has a broken arm. She needs help."

Ruth glued her gaze to Omi's face, urging Omi to say yes. "You don't mind, do you, Omi?" she repeated. "You only need one hand to weed."

A dark storm brewed on Raymond's face. He drew his brows together and stared at Ruth as if troubled by her very existence. "But, Ruth . . ." He scoured his hand back and forth over his jawline. "I don't know what to think," he said softly. "Bo was telling the truth. I thought he was exaggerating, but he was right."

Ruth stiffened. "Right about what?"

He stuffed his keys into his pocket. "Bo told me that the day I took you out on the Jet Skis, you left Omi to move hay bales by herself. He said that's why Omi fell."

Omi's mouth went dry, as if she'd eaten a scorched piece of toast.

Ruth gasped out her indignation. "How could Bo say such a thing? The accident wasn't my fault." She looked at Omi. "Tell him, Omi. Bo can't blame me for the accident."

Omi didn't know what to say. The accident wasn't Ruth's fault, but Omi's weakness and Ruth's selfishness had certainly been part of the reason it happened.

Ruth gave up waiting for Omi to free her of responsibility. "I told Omi before I left that she shouldn't move the hay bales by herself. I told her to get LaWayne to help her. It's not my fault she didn't listen."

"That's true," Omi said. "I should have waited and had LaWayne help me."

Raymond shook his head. "It's not your fault, Omi. Ruth was supposed to help. It was her job to help."

Ruth sighed in exasperation. "What, Raymond, are you my *mater* now? I don't need a lecture."

"If you had told me that you were supposed to move hay bales, I wouldn't have taken you Jet Skiing. Or I would have come and helped move bales first."

"Of course I didn't tell you. I wanted to go Jet Skiing. You only had them for that one day." Ruth glared at Omi, even though her words were directed at Raymond.

Raymond didn't like confrontation. He and Omi had that in common. But he seemed determined to convince Ruth to take some responsibility for the accident. "If you had been there, Omi wouldn't have fallen."

Ruth folded her arms. "I can't believe you're blaming me. If you want to feel guilty for taking me Jet Skiing, that's your problem, but I don't feel guilty for going. I had fun, and I'm sorry Omi got hurt." Ruth *was* sorry Omi had gotten hurt, but not especially sorry. Her concern had been outweighed by the fact that Bo had come to visit every day for a week after Omi had come home from the hospital.

Omi pressed her lips together and closed her eyes. How petty and unforgiving her thoughts had become!

Raymond didn't seem satisfied. "Bo told me something else I didn't want to believe, but now I'm beginning to wonder. He said he loves Omi."

For one breathless moment, Omi was as light as a feather. Bo still loved her?

Her heart crashed to the ground when she saw the anger on Ruth's face. "He's mad at me and punishing me by pretending to be in love with Omi. He's not. He loved me first, and he'll love me again."

Raymond backed away, holding his hands up in surrender, but to Omi's surprise, he didn't back down, even though he lowered his voice and looked extraordinarily sad. "Bo says that Omi loves him, and that you are the one keeping them apart. That you've made Omi choose between you and him. It hurts my heart to know that you would purposefully ruin Omi's happiness. I've always thought of you as one of the kindest, sweetest girls I know."

Ruth's face turned bright red. "Bo is exaggerating, and Omi loves me too much to let herself fall in love with my boyfriend. We're *schwesteren* first. Omi would never betray me like that."

It was the explanation Ruth always fell back on. *If you love me, Omi, you'll stay away from Bo.* But maybe it wasn't a question of whether Omi loved Ruth. Maybe it was a question of if Ruth loved Omi as much as Ruth loved herself. Omi couldn't lift her gaze. She couldn't bear to discover the answer in Ruth's eyes.

Were she and Ruth close or just pretending? Did she trust Ruth's love or not?

She took a deep, shuddering breath. Of course she didn't trust Ruth's love. She was barely clinging to the hope that Ruth still cared for her. If Ruth loved her, why would she make Omi choose between her *schwester* and the *bu* she loved? She'd asked the same thing of Bo. Did anyone really care about what she wanted?

Raymond was full of shocking surprises. He stepped close to Ruth and took her hand. Ruth froze, obviously stunned by Raymond's boldness. "Ruth, I care for you a great deal. You are so much fun. I'm never happier than when I'm with you, riding in Elam's car, shooting off rockets, making crafts out of Popsicle sticks. I couldn't have imagined that you could be so selfish and so cruel as to keep Omi and Bo apart." He lowered his eyes and shook his head. "I just couldn't have imagined it." He pulled his keys from his pocket. "Stay here and help your *schwester*. She needs you. Maybe I'll see you later."

He turned and walked slowly to his car, and Ruth stood like a statue and watched him drive away. Then she sat down cross-legged in the grass and rested her elbows on her knees. Omi couldn't look at her, didn't know what she was thinking. If she was mad, it was best to stay out of her way until she calmed down. If she was surprised, then she should be left in silence to sort out what had just happened.

Omi concentrated faithfully on the bindweed climbing up the flowers, even though getting rid of it was always a losing battle. Soft sniffles from Ruth's side of the flower bed drew Omi's attention. She sneaked a look at Ruth out of the corner of her eye. Ruth silently stared straight ahead while a river of tears flowed down her cheeks, as if the moisture coming from her eyes wasn't a part of her. As if the real Ruth was just sitting there while the Ruth deep inside was bawling like a baby.

No matter how badly Omi had been hurt or how frustrated she was with Ruth, she couldn't let Ruth cry alone.

She laid down her trowel, slid off her gardening gloves, and sidled next to Ruth on the grass, putting her good arm around Ruth's shoulder and pulling her close. Without saying a word, Ruth lay her head on Omi's shoulder and sobbed even harder. There were no words, so they simply sat together while Omi tried to make sense of the emotions tumbling around in her head.

# Chapter 21

Not five minutes later, a buggy pulled in front of their house, and Felty and Anna Helmuth climbed out. Ruth was still crying, her eyes puffy, her cheeks wet, and at the sight of visitors, she let out a little sob. Omi patted her on the arm. "It's okay." She didn't know why Anna and Felty were here, but maybe they'd popped in to visit Mamm and Dat to see how preparations for *gmay* were coming. Maybe they wouldn't even notice Ruth's tears as they passed.

Unfortunately, Bo's *mammi* and *dawdi* clasped hands and headed straight toward Ruth and Omi. Anna had a delighted smile on her face, as if Ruth and Omi were her favorite girls in the whole world and she was so happy to see them. Omi wasn't sure what Felty was thinking. He carried a long canvas bag and seemed to be intensely focused on making sure Anna didn't trip as they walked across the grass.

Omi thought it best if they stood up to greet Anna and Felty, and she sort of pulled Ruth up with her. Anna stopped on the sidewalk and caught her breath, her eyes twinkling. "How wonderful that you girls were just sitting right here. We came to pay you a visit."

Omi gave Ruth's hand a squeeze. "This is kind of a bad time."

Ruth shot her a grateful look.

"*Ach*," Felty said. "A bad time is the best time to come."

Omi raised an eyebrow doubtfully. The best time? Ruth was a mess, and Omi wasn't much better. This was the worst time for a visit from Anna and Felty.

Felty propped the canvas bag against his leg and loosened the drawstring. He pulled a camp chair from the bag and set it up on the grass next to the flower beds as Ruth and Omi watched in awkward silence. Anna smiled and sat down. Felty motioned to the ground. "Now that Anna is comfortable, let's get to this weeding."

"Weeding?" Omi said.

Felty bent over, braced his hand on the dirt, and sat down right next to the petunias. "You have *gmay* tomorrow, and this flower bed isn't going to weed itself."

Anna nodded. "Felty is the world's best multitasker. He can weed and have a deep conversation at the same time."

Omi grimaced. Felty wanted to have a deep conversation? She didn't think she could bear it. Ruth would probably march into the house and lock herself in her room.

"My knees creak something wonderful," Anna said. "It's like a little drum solo when I get out of bed in the morning. If I sit on the ground, I can't get back up. That's why we have this camp chair, for when Felty needs to multitask, and I need to sit. We bought it when our granddaughter Mary Ann decided to leave her husband and camp in her backyard. We felt we should camp with her just to show our support."

One side of Omi's mouth curled upward. No doubt Anna had a thousand amazing stories of her adventures as a matchmaker.

Ruth glanced at Omi, shrugged, then sat down next to

Felty. She dabbed her face with her apron and sniffled softly. It wasn't what Omi would have expected from Ruth. Maybe Ruth didn't want to make a fuss in front of two old people. Maybe she was so upset from Raymond's visit that she didn't have the energy to resist Felty's offer to help. Whatever the reason, she concentrated on the dirt and started pulling weeds.

Omi sat on the other side of Felty and found another shoot of bindweed to wrestle.

Anna patted the arm of her camping chair. "We're *froh* we caught you on such a bad day." Her smile faltered. "We're not *froh* that it's a bad day, but we're *froh* we caught you."

"We came to talk about Gotte," Felty said, stacking another weed on the small pile of weeds he'd already pulled.

Omi faked a smile. "Gotte?" Ruth was about to disintegrate into another puddle of tears, Omi's heart was a lump of coal, the weeds were choking Mamm's beloved petunias, and Felty wanted to talk about Gotte?

Felty plucked a tiny weed from under a pebble. "Our grandson is sure he'll never be happy again, you're completely miserable, and Ruth is so afraid of being wrong, she's forgotten what love is. I think Gotte is a *gute* place to start."

"That's not true." It seemed Ruth was done with being long-suffering. "I know what love is. I know that Omi's stealing my boyfriend is not love."

Felty held up his hand. "Let's not get ahead of ourselves. We need to talk about Gotte."

Anna leaned forward in her chair. "By the way, Ruth, did Raymond ever give you a pot holder?"

Ruth pressed her lips together and blinked back fresh tears. "*Jah*. He gave me a pink one."

"*Gute*. It was one of my prettiest ones."

Felty smoothed out the dirt in front of him. "Let's talk about Gotte. Omi, what do you think of Him?"

Omi drew her brows together. "I don't think I'm supposed to have an opinion. The bishop says Gotte is incomprehensible."

"Everybody has an opinion, even if they don't say it out loud. Gotte knows how you feel about Him, and He loves you whether you like Him or not."

Ruth swiped at a tear trickling down her face. "I don't think we're allowed to dislike Gotte."

Felty nudged Omi with his elbow. "What do you think about Gotte?"

Omi drew from her memory of every sermon she'd ever heard. "He created the world. He died for our sins. His wrath is kindled against those who break His commandments."

Felty sighed. "*Ach, vell*, it's *gute* this flower bed is so big. We have plenty of time to sort out our feelings." He scooted forward to reach another weed. "Ruth, what do you think about Gotte?"

Ruth held up her fingers and ticked off her answer. "He is eternal and incomprehensible. He was the Word made flesh. He created the world and suffered on the cross. If we get baptized and keep the commandments, we'll go to heaven to live with Him, and we'll be eternally happy. The wicked will go to hell and burn forever."

Would Felty let Omi try her answer again? Ruth's answer had been better only because she'd had more time to think about it.

Felty tilted his head and studied Ruth's face. "Are you afraid of going to hell?"

Ruth lowered her eyes. "I . . . I don't know. Sometimes I think I'll never be good enough for heaven. Sometimes I don't even want to try because it's so hard. Even Raymond says I'm mean and selfish, and I thought he liked me. I thought he was my friend. My boyfriend can't stand the sight of me, and Gotte always seems to be mad at me. Maybe I am going to hell."

"Aha!" Felty said, raising his voice. "Now we come to it. *Denki*, Ruth, for being so honest."

Omi frowned. Had Felty not liked Omi's answer? He seemed to be overly pleased with Ruth.

Anna clicked her tongue and cooed sympathetically. "*Ach*, Ruth, it's hard to be happy with the thought of hell hanging over your head."

"*Jah*," Felty said. "There's no joy in living when you fear Gotte is mad at you all the time, or you think He's finding fault with every choice you make. Do you ever push Him away because of it?"

Ruth's face drained of color. "We're not supposed to push Gotte away. That would be wrong and wicked. We're supposed to worship Him."

"Gotte is tough enough to take your anger, Ruth. And He loves you no matter how you treat Him or how you feel about Him."

Omi wasn't sure Felty should be talking about Gotte that way, as if Gotte was Felty's friend instead of the Eternal and Incomprehensible.

Ruth, on the other hand, seemed to hang on Felty's every word. "Sometimes I ignore Gotte or pretend He doesn't exist." Worry lines etched themselves into her face. "I'm going to hell, aren't I?"

Felty shook his head. "It's not for me to judge, but I don't think Gotte is finished with you yet, and I know He loves you, even with all your flaws."

Ruth took a shaky breath. "I don't like thinking He's looking over my shoulder, judging me for my mistakes.

I just want to have fun. I just want to be happy, and I feel like Gotte disapproves of my happiness."

A lump lodged in Omi's throat. If she had been a better *schwester*, she would have known how Ruth was feeling. Maybe she could have helped her find the happiness she so desperately wanted.

Felty looked at Omi. "What about you? Do you feel like Gotte is always mad at you?"

Omi nibbled on her bottom lip, thinking hard on the perfect answer. "I'm careful not to make mistakes so Gotte has nothing to be angry about."

"Everyone makes mistakes," Felty said quietly.

"I know, but I try hard to make as few as possible. Gotte expects more from me. I try not to let Him down."

Ruth drew her brows together. "Are you saying Gotte doesn't expect as much from me?"

"I don't think He does, because you don't expect better of yourself. You don't even try, Ruth. Maybe I'm just more . . ."

"Righteous?" Ruth folded her arms and huffed out a breath, but it wasn't indignation Omi saw in Ruth's eyes. It was anguish. "Gotte loves you better."

"Aha!" Felty said again. This time louder. "Ruth thinks she is a hopeless case, and Omi thinks she's perfect."

"I do not," Omi said, her heart rebelling against such an unfair appraisal.

Felty peered at Omi, his warm eyes piercing her skull. "I'm not scolding you. You must be exhausted trying to meet Gotte's expectations. It wonders me if you beat yourself up every time you fall short?"

Omi wanted to protest that she made sure never to fall short of Gotte's expectations, but that excuse sounded prideful and dishonest. She suddenly felt the weight of Gotte's demands on her shoulders. But maybe they weren't

Gotte's demands, and maybe that was what Felty was trying to get her to understand.

Felty turned to Ruth. "I'm not scolding you either. Not yet. You are two of my favorite girls in the whole world, and Heaven knows, we all have plenty of flaws." He yanked a stubborn weed from the ground and shook the dirt off the roots. "I'm going to tell you something I haven't told anyone outside our family. When I was a much younger man, I killed another soldier in battle."

Omi gasped. "You did?"

He pointed at Ruth. "Do you think Gotte will send me to hell for that?"

"I . . . I don't know."

He turned to Omi. "Do you think I'll ever be able to meet with Gotte's approval?" Felty smiled at Ruth. "I've made some serious mistakes in my life. Do you think Gotte is mad at me? Do you think He'll lock me out of heaven?"

Omi frowned. "Everybody knows what a godly man you are. If you can't get to heaven, I don't think anyone can."

Felty leaned back on his haunches and stroked his beard. "Gotte is not waiting for you to do something wrong so He can punish you, and you don't have to be perfect to earn His love. Gotte loves you just the way you are, and He wants you to be in heaven so badly He died for you."

Ruth was crying again. Omi felt confused, unsettled, and hopeful all at the same time. Was that really what Gotte was like? Could she trust Him to love her no matter what?

Felty stood and moved five feet to the right and sat down again by the next patch of unweeded flowers. Ruth and Omi scooted next to him, but this time they sat by each other with Felty on Omi's right. "Now," Felty said, "let's talk about being a twin."

Okay. The talk about Gotte was over. It was a nice talk, but Omi couldn't see why Felty and Anna had felt the need to come all the way to their house to share their feelings about Gotte.

"Talk louder, Felty," Anna said. "You're farther away now, and I still want to listen in. Things are getting exciting."

Felty started another pile of pulled weeds. He was the fastest weeder Omi had ever seen. He'd obviously had years of experience. "Okay, Ruth, what do you think about Omi?"

To Omi's surprise, Ruth's eyes filled with tears once more. She wasn't usually this emotionally delicate. "She stole my boyfriend."

"Let's not talk about Bo just yet," Felty said. "Tell me what you think about Omi."

Ruth took a deep breath. "She's always been a *gute schwester*. She used to be my best friend."

"And?"

"She spoke the truth when she said she is more righteous than I am."

"That's not true," Omi said, even as a shard of glass pierced her heart. The truth was what Ruth thought it was, and Omi had unintentionally made Ruth feel inferior.

Felty held up his hand. "You'll get your turn, Omi."

Ruth folded her arms and turned her face away. "Omi never does anything wrong, never has a bad feeling about anybody. She always tries to make everyone happy, even if we take advantage of her for it. She seldom wants to do anything fun, and she feels like she has to repent if she sings the wrong note in *gmay*. She disapproves of me and everything I do."

"Do you ever feel like she judges you, maybe condemns you for not being a better person?"

"All the time," Ruth said.

Omi clamped her teeth and stayed quiet. It was so unfair of Ruth to say such things, but if she wanted Ruth to listen to her, she needed to listen to Ruth.

Felty nodded, adding another weed to his pile. "In a way, you see Omi the same way you see Gotte."

Ruth opened her mouth and promptly closed it again.

"Now, Omi," Felty said, and Omi knew what he was going to say before he said it. "What do you think about Ruth?"

Maybe some things were better left unsaid, but if the two of them were going to come to an understanding, Omi would have to be as blunt with Ruth as Ruth had been with her. "Ruth is never satisfied with what I do for her. She is always asking for more and more, and if I resist, she says I don't love her. She talked me into trading places with her, even though I was mortified about it. She still leaves me to do the chores so she can go riding with Elam or Raymond."

"You never asked to go with us," Ruth said. "We would have let you come."

Omi ignored Ruth. That was just an excuse, and Ruth knew it. "Ruth insists that Bo loves her and says I betrayed her. I've tried to make it right. She forced me to choose between her and Bo, and I chose her, even though she doesn't appreciate it. I gave up the *bu* I love to make Ruth happy, but she doesn't care that I'm miserable."

Nothing Omi had said seemed to shock Felty. Maybe he was too old and wise to be shocked by much of anything. "It sounds like you see Ruth the way you see Gotte, demanding and expecting perfection. You feel you have to earn Ruth's love." He gave Ruth a piercing look. "Do you make Omi earn your love?"

*Ach.* That was why Felty wanted to talk about Gotte.

They sat in silence, while Felty plucked weed after weed from the flower bed. Ruth and Omi had both abandoned the job several minutes ago. Ruth was staring at her hands. Omi stared at Ruth.

Ruth laced her fingers together. "Do you think you have to earn my love, Omi?"

"I don't think there's anything I could do to convince you to love me."

Ruth studied Omi's face. "Are you really that miserable?"

Omi felt momentarily ashamed of herself, but for the first time in her life, she was unwilling to make things easier or soften the truth for Ruth. "You know I am."

A quiet moan escaped Ruth's lips. "You stole my boyfriend, Omi. I wanted to make you pay. I wanted you to be just as miserable as I was. I'm a horrible person."

"You're not a horrible person," Omi said, forcing the words out of her mouth. Her resentment ran deeper than an insincere denial.

Ruth hiccupped softly. "You're so righteous, Omi. Mamm loves you more because you never give her anything to worry about. I gave up trying to be perfect years ago." Ruth scooted around to face Omi directly. "But then you did the worst thing of all. You stole my boyfriend. I was upset at losing Bo, but it was also a chance for me to feel more righteous than you, to feel like I was better than you. I've made a lot of mistakes, but I would never, ever go so low as to steal my *schwester*'s boyfriend. Do you know how betrayed I felt, especially when you made it out to be my fault?"

Omi couldn't breathe. Ruth had been selfish and insensitive, but Omi had clung tightly to a sense of righteous indignation that made her resentful and unforgiving. She'd pushed her *schwester* away, abandoning the intimate relationship they used to have and trading it for dishonesty and bitterness. *Now* who was the horrible person? "Ruth, *die buwe* have always liked you better than me. Neither of us is perfect, and Mamm loves us both the same."

"*Jah*. That's why she yelled at me for thirty minutes at the hospital. Her favorite child got hurt, and she blamed me. She didn't even want to hear my side of the story. I told you to have LaWayne help." Ruth sniffed back the tears. "You will always think you're better than me. Your troubles will always be my fault, and you will always believe that Bo couldn't have ever really been in love with me."

"That's not fair, Ruth."

Ruth folded her arms as if she *would not* be convinced. "Maybe not."

Anna didn't seem to notice the dark clouds that loomed over them. "Isn't this *wunderbarr*? You're finally starting to communicate."

"Gotte gives us commandments because He loves us," Felty said. "The commandments save us from a lot of misery. But Gotte also knows that we're going to break the commandments. Often. So He made a way for us to come back to Him, even though we make mistakes. If only perfect people made it to heaven, it would be a very lonely place. That's why He died on the cross. Don't ever underestimate the power of Gotte's love. It is the most powerful force on Earth and in heaven." Moving like a much younger man, Felty pushed himself off the ground and stood up. "Anna, I think our work here is done."

Anna gave Ruth and Omi a kind smile. "I'm *froh* it's all settled. But now we have to go. We're starting a new hobby, and our appointment at the archery range starts in twenty minutes. Just enough time to get there by buggy."

Omi glanced at Ruth. As far as she could see, nothing was settled. She and Ruth were as mad at each other as ever, and the chasm between them had only widened in the last half hour.

Anna stood, and Felty collapsed her chair and stuffed it into the canvas bag. "It's been a wonderful pleasant conversation with you girls." Felty pointed to the flower bed. "Lord willing, you'll figure it all out. There's still lots of weeding to do, and my grandson is still miserable."

Omi frowned. It wasn't her fault Bo was miserable. Ruth was stubborn and selfish.

She caught her breath. Omi had always been eager to blame Ruth for everything because it made Ruth look like the bad *schwester* and Omi seem like the victim. She had made Bo miserable because he thought she wasn't willing to fight for his love. "*Ach*, Ruth, I'm a horrible person."

"Join the club."

Omi grabbed Ruth's hand and gave her a piercing look. "We need to talk, Ruth."

"I don't want to talk anymore."

"We need to talk," she said again. "Really talk. We need to be honest and say all the hurtful things and figure this out together. I can't live like this anymore, thinking of my *schwester* as a stranger, tiptoeing around you, resenting you."

Ruth sighed. "I can't live like this either, but I can't bear your harsh judgment right now."

"I'll do my best not to judge, Ruth, if you'll do your best not to be offended." She wrapped her arm around Ruth's shoulder. "I want my *schwester* back."

Ruth burst into tears. "I do too."

They hugged for a minute, and Omi swallowed past the lump in her throat. "I know this hurts you, but I love Bo with all my heart, and he loves me."

"He only thinks he loves you."

"*Nae*, Ruth, he loves me. I did not steal Bo from you. You drove him away. He doesn't want to marry you."

Ruth pulled back. "You're blaming me and judging me."

"You're pretending there's something between you and Bo. But it isn't real. Even if Bo didn't love me, he wouldn't love you." Omi squared her shoulders. She was no longer willing to sacrifice her happiness to spare Ruth's feelings. It would only lead to bitterness between them. "I'm going to marry Bo whether you approve or not."

Ruth's eyes widened. "Then you don't love me enough."

"I love you very much, Ruth, but I won't give up Bo to prove it. Bo will not come running back to you, no matter how badly you want that, no matter how badly you want to spite me."

Ruth's face clouded with uncertainty. "It's not spite. It's about right and wrong."

Omi tried again to get close to Ruth by laying her hand over the top of Ruth's. "I've offended you," she said gently. "And I'm sorry that you're upset. Does holding so tightly to this grudge makes you feel superior?"

Ruth looked away and sniffed. "That's not the reason."

"You tell yourself I stole Bo so you feel justified and reassured that you are a better person than I am."

Ruth eyed her resentfully. "You don't like thinking that I'm better than you, do you?"

Thanks to Felty, Omi could see where both she and Ruth had gone wrong. "People don't understand how hard it is to be a twin. We feel like we have to outdo each other to be special." She pulled her knees to her chest and wrapped her arms around her legs. "I don't want it to be a competition anymore. I'm sorry that I've criticized and scolded you. I see how wrong I've been to think I had to correct and judge you. That is not my place or my intention."

"You do it all the time."

"I'm sorry, Ruth. Can you forgive me?"

Ruth's mouth twitched doubtfully. "It *is* spite."

"What?"

"I've been holding on to Bo out of spite. You're so deeply *gute*, Omi, and I'm so selfish. You always win. I hated the thought of you winning Bo too."

"It's hard for me to understand how you could ever feel inferior to me. *Die buwe* barely notice me. You light up every room you walk into. People want to be around you because you make them happy. There's no one I want on my team more when I'm playing volleyball. There's no one I want on my side more than you."

"But I never felt *gute* enough in your eyes," Ruth said.

Omi sighed. "It's like Felty talked about Gotte. You push me away because you think I'm always judging you. I *have* judged you, but I'm not going to do that anymore."

Ruth laughed ruefully. "You've been judgmental, and I've been selfish. I demand more and more of you because you always say yes. I get testy when you stand up for yourself."

"*Jah*, you do. I'm going to stand up for myself from now on. And marry Bo."

A single tear escaped Ruth's eye. "But, Omi, I really think I love him. Why do you get the happiness that should have been mine?"

"Why can't we both be happy?"

"Because there's only one Bo, and I'll never be happy again knowing I ruined my chance with him. We'd be together if I hadn't messed up."

"But, Ruth, maybe it is Gotte's will."

"That I messed up? I don't think Gotte likes it when we sin."

"There's a difference between messing up and willfully

sinning. We're human. Gotte expects us to mess up, and He can use our mistakes to create something even more beautiful."

Ruth sniffed and nodded. "Beauty for ashes, I guess."

Omi felt as if she was on the cusp of something important, something she hadn't realized before. "I think deep down, you don't want to marry Bo, even though you feel like you should."

"That doesn't make any sense, Omi. Of course I want to marry Bo." She drew her brows together. "But I want to be a better person, and I shouldn't begrudge you your happiness."

"Why did you go for a ride with Elam that first night?"

Ruth made a face as if it should be obvious. "I like cars. And going fast."

"Why didn't you just invite Bo to go with you?"

"Well, I . . . I didn't think Elam would like it."

Omi shook her head. "Elam was eager to give anybody a ride who wanted one. Remember the day we did Popsicle crafts? Elam offered to take me for a ride. He liked showing off his car."

Ruth cracked a smile. "Except to Vernon Schmucker."

Omi giggled. "Except Vernon."

Ruth pursed her lips. "I didn't tell Bo because I don't think he would have wanted to go."

"Why didn't you ask him instead of cooking up that silly scheme to trade places?"

Ruth sat up straighter and smeared all signs of moisture from her face. "I wanted to have fun."

Omi nodded vigorously. "And you thought Bo would put a damper on the party."

Ruth raised her eyebrows. "Sometimes he's so serious."

"Why do you want to marry someone like that?"

Ruth gave Omi a pointed look. "Why do *you* want to marry someone like that?"

Omi bloomed into a smile. "You know the answer."

"Because he's wonderful handsome." Ruth pumped her eyebrows up and down.

"That too, but Bo is much better suited to me than he is to you. He's quiet and thoughtful, but good-natured and kind. 'Quiet and thoughtful' doesn't appeal to you as much as 'adventurous and fun.'"

Ruth hesitated. "I suppose one reason I want to marry him is because he's a godly man. I would be *gute* enough for Gotte if Bo was my husband."

"You will always be *gute* enough for Gotte."

"I want to believe that," Ruth said.

"There are plenty of godly *buwe* out there who like to have fun. They're different from Bo, but different doesn't have to be a bad thing. You just haven't found the right *bu* yet."

Ruth closed her eyes and winced. "*Ach*, Omi, I think I *have* found the right *bu*."

"Raymond?"

She pointed to the pot holder still sitting on the porch. "He gave me one of Anna's pot holders. It must be love," she said drily.

"It must be."

She huffed out a breath. "We've done so many fun things together. He let me win every Jet Ski race and didn't care if I splashed water in his face. He taught me how to fry an egg on the engine of Elam's car. We bought big blocks of ice from the store and sat on them to slide down the hill. And those rockets! Do you remember the rockets, Omi? He let me light every one."

Omi hadn't seen Ruth smile all day. It was a nice sight. "I remember the rockets."

Ruth took a deep breath. "But I've ruined things with Raymond too. He can't stand me."

"He likes you, Ruth. I've seen the way he looks at you."

"You heard him. He called me selfish and cruel. You don't know how those words stung."

"They stung because you like him, and you hate the thought that he thinks poorly of you."

"I do hate it. Raymond isn't quick to judge anyone. I really messed up this time." She blinked away fresh tears. "It hurts so bad because he was right. I've treated you poorly, Omi. I wouldn't blame you if you never spoke to me again. I've been selfish and cruel and all the things Raymond said. Bo must really hate me."

"He doesn't hate you." Omi's lips twitched upward. "He's frustrated."

Ruth grunted. "I bet he is. He's tried to be patient, and you've tried to be loyal, even though I don't deserve your loyalty or your love."

"You don't have to do anything to deserve my love, remember?"

Ruth laughed through her tears. "*Gute* thing we had that talk with Felty."

"He's wonderful smart. After all, he's Bo's *dawdi*."

Ruth caught her bottom lip between her teeth. "What . . . what should I do about Raymond? Do you think I can convince him to give me a second chance?"

"Raymond likes you. He'll give you more than a second chance."

Ruth sprouted a doubtful smile. "I'd like that. I really would." She stabbed her trowel into the dirt and stood up.

"I'm going to call him. He just got a cell phone, and he gave me his number."

Ruth was halfway to the house before Omi stopped her. "Oh, no, you don't. Come back and help me finish the weeding."

Ruth groaned. "*Ach*, Omi, it's just one phone call."

Omi shook her head. "I'm never letting you wheedle your way out of your chores ever again. Besides, you don't even know what you're going to say."

Ruth folded her arms. "Okay then, help me come up with a plan."

Omi knelt down and stabbed her trowel into the dirt. "Weeding first, boys second." She frowned to herself. "I don't know what I'm going to say to Bo. He may already have given up on me."

"Bo won't give up on you. He's stubborn when he thinks he's right. And he always thinks he's right."

Omi giggled. "He does not."

"*Jah*, and such a know-it-all," Ruth teased.

Omi tossed a shovelful of dirt in Ruth's direction. Ruth dodged it easily. "It's not his fault he's so smart."

"Not half as smart as Raymond. He once fixed a car with duct tape and a Pringles can."

Omi was so happy, she couldn't keep from laughing. Ruth had found someone she could truly love. All was right with the world. "You didn't eat that egg, did you?"

"What egg?"

"The one Raymond fried on the car engine."

Ruth smiled wryly. "It didn't actually touch the engine, silly. He put the eggs in a tinfoil bowl and used the engine as a stove. He's brilliant. He even knows how to make a tinfoil bowl. I bet Bo can't do that."

Omi just grinned and didn't argue. She was convinced

that Bo could do just about anything he set his mind to, including make a tinfoil bowl, drive a car, or invent a catapult out of Popsicle sticks. But what she loved even more was that Bo could chase the clouds away with his smile, make her giddy with just one kiss, and bring her more happiness than she ever thought possible.

# Chapter 22

It took them an hour to finish weeding and talk over a plan. Ruth was sure that nothing she could say would convince Raymond to forgive her and give her a second chance. Omi feared that Bo had given up on her and was already looking for another girl to date. They had to pull each other out of the depths of despair.

Raymond needed to see that Ruth regretted her actions, and Bo needed to see that Omi was strong enough to stand up for herself, even to her *schwester*. They concluded that the four of them needed to have a long, serious talk, but Omi didn't know if Raymond or Bo would agree to be in the same room with Ruth and Omi. There were a lot of hard feelings to sift through.

Omi picked up the weed piles and put them in the garbage can. Ruth swept the dirt from the sidewalk. The flower beds looked better than they had all summer, and Mamm would be proud to hold *gmay* at her house. *Ach*, *vell*, Mamm would do her best not to be proud, but if it wasn't pride, Omi didn't know what it was, because everyone sure got worked up about having a beautiful, well-groomed yard for *gmay*.

The squealing of car tires got their attention, and they

both looked up as a gray-silver car took the corner too fast and came toward them.

Ruth drew her brows together. "Raymond's back."

Their plan to get Raymond and Ruth together wasn't quite ready. This wasn't the right time for Raymond to show up. Omi glanced at Ruth. "Do you think he's come to apologize?"

"He doesn't have anything to apologize for."

The gravel crunched underneath Raymond's tires as the car slid to a stop. Raymond jumped out of the car. "Ruth, I've been calling and calling."

Ruth gave him a hesitant, hopeful smile. "Really?"

"What's the use in having a phone if you don't answer it?"

Ruth's smile disappeared. "Mamm gets a headache when she sees it."

Raymond seemed to be in too big of a hurry to hold on to his annoyance. "Can you two come with me? Bo just called. He says his *mammi* is in the hospital, and she wants to see us. All of us."

Omi's heart lurched. "In the hospital?"

"*Jah*. He said she got shot, but that doesn't make any sense. He was sort of breathless on the phone."

"Oh, no!" Ruth grabbed Omi's hand. "With an arrow?"

"I don't know, but Bo sounded very worried. He said to hurry."

Omi thought she might be sick. Archery was one of Anna's new hobbies. Had she really been shot? "I'll go tell Mamm where we're going."

"Hurry, okay?"

Omi nodded. For all she knew, Anna was dying and wanted to give them her last words. But . . . why would she want to give them to Ruth, Omi, and Raymond? Bo was her grandson, but Omi couldn't imagine that she was one of Anna's top-four favorite people. Didn't you want to talk to your most favorite loved ones when you died? She hesitated for a second, then ran into the house and found Mamm. She was washing walls for *gmay*. "Mamm, Anna is in the hospital, and Raymond is taking us to see her."

Mamm frowned. "The hospital? What happened?" She threw her rag into the bucket at her feet. "And why does she want to see you?"

"I don't know, and I don't know," Omi said. There was no time for more words. She ran out the front door and slid into the back seat of Raymond's car. Ruth and Raymond were already in the front.

As soon as Omi shut the door, Raymond took off and tore down the road. Raymond wasn't usually one to get worked up about things, but he focused intently and silently on the road as he pulled away from their house.

"What else did Bo say?" Ruth asked.

"Not much," Raymond murmured. "He said Anna called Ben's phone and asked us to come to the hospital."

Ben and Emma had a phone because of Ben's MS. "But why does Anna want us to come to the hospital? I can think of about three hundred other people she'd call first."

The car slowed momentarily. Raymond must have let up on the gas. "Hmm. I don't know."

Ruth wrapped her hand around the seat belt across her chest and looked at Raymond. "I don't know about Anna, but I always feel better when you're around, Raymond. You can fix anything."

Did Raymond sit up a little taller? "But she doesn't know me that well."

Ruth shook her head. "She thought that Popsicle cata-pult was the cleverest thing ever. I don't wonder but she thinks you're the smartest *bu* in the world."

Raymond was smart, but unless he had a medical degree he hadn't told anybody about, there wasn't a *gute* reason for Anna to want him at the hospital. Omi would never say that to Ruth or Raymond. They were looking at each other as if they were the only two people in the car. Omi kept her mouth shut. They'd all find out soon enough. She just hoped with all her heart that Anna wasn't seriously hurt, and that she wouldn't waste her last breath on three Popsicle sticking buddies.

They parked at a spot near the emergency room and jumped out of the car. Bo met them coming from the other direction as if he'd just arrived himself. He looked like a wounded animal, frantic and distraught. He was hatless and there was mud smeared down the front of his shirt, as if he'd run from the fields as soon as he'd heard the news. He saw Omi, caught his breath, and immediately ran to her, his arms outstretched, his face etched with worry. There was nothing else for Omi to do but run into his embrace and hold on for dear life. She loved him so much, and she didn't care who was watching or what they were thinking. Bo needed her, and she'd do anything for him, even make a fool of herself on the hospital parking lot.

"*Ach*, Omi," he whispered breathlessly. "I'm scared."

"Me too," she said, her voice cracking. She wanted to stay like that forever, but Ruth and Raymond were standing there staring at them, and Bo's *mammi* might be on death's door. Omi gave Bo an extra squeeze and pulled away. "What do you know about your *mammi*?"

He nodded to Raymond, took Omi's elbow, and nudged her toward the sliding doors. "Not much. She called Ben's phone and asked to talk to me. She said she was in the hospital, something about getting shot, and told me to call Raymond and have him bring you and Ruth. She said not to tell anyone else because she didn't want family to crowd into the emergency room."

"But why did she want us to come?" Ruth asked, which was the question on everybody's mind.

Bo walked up to the desk where a nurse was sitting. "We're here for Anna Helmuth. Can we see her?"

The nurse bloomed into a smile. "What a cute lady! I always wanted a grandma just like her. She hasn't complained about one thing since she's been here, and she asked me if I'm dating anybody."

Bo pressed his lips together. "She does that."

"Is she okay?" Omi asked, feeling better just talking to the nurse. If Anna had been in any real danger, the nurse wouldn't have been so cheerful.

The nurse glanced at Omi, and her eyes widened. "You're the girl who was in here a few weeks ago. I remember you fell out of a haymow. Are *you* okay?"

Omi instinctively put her hand to her face. "I'm okay. The doctor said there wouldn't be any permanent scarring."

The nurse shook her head. "Of course not. In a few weeks, no one will be able to tell."

Omi had heard it before, but the nurse's calm and cheerful demeanor made her feel like it was absolutely true.

"How is my grandmother?" Bo asked.

The nurse grimaced. "I'm sorry. You're worried, and I got distracted. She told me to bring you back as soon as you arrived. Come with me."

They followed the nurse down a corridor lined with curtains. She pulled back the fourth curtain to reveal a small space containing a bed and two chairs. The bed was empty, and Anna and Felty sat in the chairs to the side of it. Anna did not look like she'd been shot, stabbed, or injured in any way.

Until she tried to clap. "You came!" she said, her smile

as wide as the Wisconsin River. Her left index finger was wrapped in several layers of gauze, and there was a strange gray clip attached to the end of her right index finger.

Bo knelt down next to her. "Mammi, what happened? You told me you'd been shot."

Anna frowned in puzzlement. "You thought I said that? No wonder you look as pale as a sheet."

Bo took off his hat and scrubbed his fingers through his hair. "I vividly remember you telling me you'd been shot."

Felty stroked his beard. "She meant she had to get a tetanus shot."

Anna nodded. "*Jah.* I wasn't happy about getting a shot, but the cut was deep enough they wanted to be cautious. The doctor insisted that I didn't want to get lockjaw."

"Cut?" Bo said.

Anna wrapped her three unbandaged fingers and thumb around Bo's wrist. The injured finger stuck out in a permanent point. "Did I tell you we started a new hobby?"

"Knife throwing?" Bo said, not even half joking.

Anna laughed. "Wouldn't that be something?"

Felty smiled at Anna as if she was the most beautiful person in the world. "That would be something, and only slightly more dangerous than archery."

"But probably easier," Anna said. "Shooting arrows is hard. The string is impossible to pull back all the way, and when you let it go, it hits the underside of your elbow and really hurts. I've got a bruise."

Omi could tell Bo was trying very hard not to overreact. "You've got a bruise yet?"

Anna waved her bandaged finger in the air. "It's nothing. Felty was enjoying himself, but I wasn't doing so well shooting arrows, so I gave it up, pulled out my knife, and started whittling a stick."

Bo's eyebrows nearly flew off his forehead. "You have a knife?"

Anna nodded. "It's my all-purpose tool. You can file your fingernails and tighten loose screws, and in a pinch, you can use it as a knitting needle, but I don't recommend that. Your scarves turn out bumpy. It's better to carry your knitting needles with you at all times."

"Whittling is fun." Raymond always tried to be helpful.

"Now I'll have a scar to match Bo's," Anna said. "He nearly cut off his finger when he was a teenager, but that was his middle finger, so I suppose we won't be identical." Anna's mouth fell open. "Felty, we could have used super-glue and saved a trip to the emergency room."

"We should have thought of that, Annie."

Anna shook her head and smiled at Bo. "But then we wouldn't be having such a *wunderbarr* time here with all of you."

"How did you cut your finger, Mammi?"

"My knife slipped, and there was blood everywhere. The doctor gave me three stitches." Anna pointed to her neck. "He also checked this mole at no extra charge."

Omi didn't want to be rude, but she had to ask the question everyone was thinking. "We're *froh* you weren't hurt worse, Anna, but why did you ask us to come? We're not even related to you, and Raymond broke the speed limit twice."

Anna's mouth fell open. "You broke the speed limit? That's very reckless for a young man with such a promising future."

Raymond shuffled his feet. "I was worried about you. We thought you'd been shot."

Anna smiled. "I'm honored to know you would risk getting a ticket for me." She held out her hand to Felty, who reached into his pocket and pulled out four quarters and gave them to her. She handed Bo, Ruth, Omi, and Raymond each a quarter. "Felty and I feel there isn't enough communication going on among the four of you. Go buy yourselves a treat from the vending machine, then come back and we'll decide who is going to marry who. I personally think Bo should marry Omi and Raymond should marry Ruth, but that's just my opinion. There's a lot of unnecessary suffering going on, and Felty and I are putting a stop to it. Aren't we, Felty?"

"That's right, Annie."

Bo frowned as his gaze darted between Omi and Ruth. Omi knew exactly what he was thinking. Or maybe she didn't. He'd given her a hug, so it didn't seem like he was mad at her, but he might have hugged her because he'd been carried away in the emotion of the moment.

The careful plans Omi and Ruth had made hadn't included vending machines, hospitals, or Bo's grandparents, but who knew when they would get an opportunity like this again? And Omi really wanted to make things right with Bo, because every day of not being with him was pure misery.

Ruth overcame her discomfort and shock first. "*Cum*," she said. "Let's go find the vending machines."

The four of them ambled uncomfortably down the corridor. Anna had said too much, but there was still so much left to be said. What was Bo thinking? Would Ruth swallow her pride and apologize? And what about Raymond? He and Ruth hadn't parted on *gute* terms.

Raymond opened his hand and showed Bo his quarter. "Does anybody want to tell Anna that twenty-five cents isn't enough to buy anything at the vending machines?"

"They give away free cookies and water to all emergency room visitors," Ruth said, looking as uncomfortable as Omi had ever seen her. Omi half expected her to run for the exit, but Ruth must have been as eager to make things right as Omi was, no matter the consequences. They trailed after Ruth as she found the magical cupboard with free cookies and pulled out six packages. They each got themselves a cup of water and headed back to Anna and Felty. Omi didn't know whether her dread or her anticipation was greater. Just what kind of communication did Anna have in mind? Surely Omi wouldn't end up engaged to the wrong person, would she?

They walked back down the hall, and Bo hung back to walk beside her. He didn't say anything, but he reached out and brushed his fingers against her hand. Her heart did a tap dance.

Anna and Felty had managed to collect four other chairs, and they'd formed their two chairs and the other four into a tight circle in the small space. Anna motioned for the four of them to sit. "Omi, you sit next to me. Then Bo, then Ruth, and Raymond next to Felty."

The chairs scraped against the floor as they all sat down and stared uncomfortably at each other.

Anna had a look of complete delight on her face. Felty seemed amused. Everyone else had turned a sickly shade of gray. "Now," Anna said, "this is called a trust circle. I read about it in my yoga book. First we all need to put our cookies in our laps so our hands will be free to hold. Let's join hands."

Beads of sweat formed on Raymond's upper lip. "Join hands?"

"*Jah*. It's an important part of the trust circle to feel connected to each other and the universe."

Raymond might not have been comfortable with the trust circle, but Omi was ecstatic, even though she wasn't sure how holding hands would connect them to the universe. But it would certainly connect her to Bo. She pressed her lips together when Ruth and Bo took hands, but surely Anna knew what she was doing. Bo turned to smile at her, and she slipped her fingers into his hand. They couldn't do much more than that with her cast. Her heart overflowed with love for this patient, kind, loving man, who was willing to go along with his *mammi*'s crazy ideas, even when they didn't make sense.

Anna pulled the little clip off her finger to hold Felty's hand.

"Annie," Felty said, "they won't be able to track your oxygen levels if you take that off."

Anna swatted away his concern. "I've gone for eighty-five years without having my oxygen levels tracked. I've been completely fine."

Omi wrapped her hand gently around Anna's. "I don't want to hurt your finger."

"Don't worry, dear. I don't feel a thing. The doctor numbed it up *gute*." Anna scooted back more firmly in her chair. "We will now go around the circle, and each of us will apologize for something. This is a way to seek forgiveness and show our vulnerability. I will start." She cleared her throat. "I am sorry that I didn't bring my knitting because we've been sitting here for two hours with nothing to do but watch my oxygen levels. I could have knitted two pot holders by now."

"Maybe not with your injured finger, Annie-banannie."

Anna shrugged. "I would have liked to try." She looked at Omi. "Your turn. What do you want to apologize for?"

Omi couldn't say what was really in her heart: that she was sorry for hurting Bo and being weak and judging her *schwester*. Her feelings were too tender, and she feared she'd burst into tears. "I'm sorry I tracked dirt into the emergency room."

Anna's smile faded. "That was a *gute* try."

Bo studied Omi's face and cleared his throat. "I'm sorry I thought Mammi had been shot."

"An honest mistake," Anna said.

Ruth frowned. "I'm sorry I didn't put on a clean dress before coming over here."

Raymond eyed Omi. "I'm sorry I broke the speed limit."

Anna's face lost any hint of cheer. "I don't think I explained the trust circle very well. At least three of you should be in tears by now."

Felty winked at Anna. "It wonders me if we should go around again. I just wanted to say that I'm sorry for trying to trick you into giving up matchmaking by pushing you into a new hobby. If I hadn't been trying to distract you, we wouldn't be sitting in the hospital."

"*Ach*, Felty, you didn't trick me. I know you're just trying to protect me, even though I'm perfectly capable of taking care of myself. We all make mistakes. I forgive you." She glanced at Omi. "Okay then, we're going to try this again, and this time I want to hear some real, heartfelt apologies." She furrowed her brow. "I suppose my last apology set a bad example. I'm going to try harder." She gazed at Bo. "I'm sorry for being such a sneaky *grossmammi*. I know that sometimes I can be bossy and stubborn, but it's hard when I know I'm right and I can't get people to agree with me. There's nothing else to do but be sneaky sometimes."

"You don't need to apologize for that, Mammi. Several of your grandchildren are living happily ever after because of you."

Anna nodded. "I'm *froh* you think so, because I may have apologized, but I'm not going to quit matchmaking. There are too many grandchildren yet."

Bo laughed. "Don't ever change, Mammi. I like you just the way you are."

"And so do I," Felty said. He lifted Anna's hand to his lips and kissed it.

Anna sighed in resignation. "*Denki*, Felty. Because my days of trying new hobbies are over." She held up her hand to remind everyone about her injury. "We were going to try making shadow puppets next week, but you can see how impossible that will be. No more hobbies. I'm running out of fingers, and matchmaking keeps me plenty busy."

Omi studied Bo out of the corner of her eye. She didn't think she had the courage to say what she needed to say, which was ironic because she wanted to apologize for being a coward and not standing up to Ruth.

"I'm sorry," Ruth blurted out, even though it wasn't her turn. She squeaked and hiccupped and puckered up her face like a prune and looked at Raymond as if he were the only person in the room. "I've been wonderful selfish. I wouldn't blame you if you never wanted to shoot rockets with me again." The tears seemed to fly out of her eyes like horizontal raindrops. They ran down her cheeks, and she had to let go of Bo's and Raymond's hands to wipe her nose.

Raymond jumped to his feet, found a box of tissues, and brought the whole thing back to the circle. He handed four or five tissues to Ruth. Then he leaned over, took her hand, and whispered soft words to her while she blew her nose. "It's okay, Ruth. I still like you a lot."

She sniffled. "I'm not a bad person."

"I know you're not."

"Omi and I had a long talk. I shouldn't have pressured her to trade places with me. I shouldn't have gone to the lake when she needed my help with chores. I blamed her and took her for granted, but all that is going to stop. I just . . . I just want to be the kind of girl you could be proud of, the kind of girl that you'd like to take for a drive or make Popsicle stick crafts with. I hope you can forgive me for being selfish about Omi and stubborn about Bo."

Raymond handed her another tissue. "You're the only person I want to shoot rockets with."

Ruth brightened. "Really?"

He nodded. "Really. No one is as fun as you, Ruth."

Ruth dabbed at her nose and glanced at Bo. "I want to apologize for trying to trick you by trading places with Omi."

Bo looked at Ruth with so much compassion, it brought tears to Omi's eyes. "I was angry and hurt, Ruth, but I am nothing but grateful now for what you did. It's what brought me and Omi together in the end."

"I know," Ruth said, and Omi couldn't tell if she still regretted Bo or just regretted her behavior.

Bo still had hold of Omi's hand, and Ruth's hands were occupied with her tissues. Omi liked it that way. "It wonders me if it wasn't Gotte's will that you traded places with Omi," Bo said, "because I don't think you and I are suited for each other."

Anna nodded adamantly. "*Jah*, Bo is as boring as a pair of stockings."

Bo pursed his lips. "Um, *jah*, I'm very boring."

Omi almost laughed out loud. She didn't think Bo was boring, and obviously, Bo didn't think he was boring, but he and Anna obviously felt the need to convince Ruth. They didn't know that Ruth needed no convincing. She and Omi had already settled that Ruth preferred Raymond, his car, and his penchant for explosions.

Anna reached across the circle and patted Ruth's knee. "You need someone who will keep you on your toes and knows how to fix a toilet."

"I do," Ruth said, not taking her gaze from Raymond. She pressed the tissue to her nose. "Bo, I'm wonderful sorry

I kept insisting that you loved me and not Omi. I held you hostage and made Omi miserable."

Bo gave her a half smile. "I wouldn't say you held me hostage."

Ruth frowned. "At the very least, I held Omi's love hostage. I told her that if she loved you, she didn't love me. I was cruel, but I was also deeply hurt. Maybe I brought it upon myself, but it felt like a betrayal when you two fell in love with each other."

Bo looked down at Omi's hand intertwined with his. "I'm sorry you felt betrayed."

Ruth huffed out a breath. "Omi and I already worked it out. She's forgiven me. I've forgiven her. I've forgiven you, and I hope you'll forgive me. You and Omi deserve to be happy. Together."

Omi finally found her voice. She tugged on Bo's hand. "I'm sorry that I wasn't stronger. I'm sorry I didn't stand up to Ruth and fight for our relationship. I know I hurt you."

"I'm not a horrible person," Ruth growled.

Raymond handed her another tissue. "Of course you aren't."

Bo's smile was so tender that Omi couldn't help but be warmed by it. "I shouldn't have pushed. I am the one who needs to apologize for putting pressure on you. Ruth was forcing you to choose."

Ruth raised the fist that was clutching three or four tissues. "I'm sitting right here, and I'm not a horrible person."

Raymond handed over the whole tissue box to Ruth. "You are the most wonderful girl in the world."

Ruth whimpered into her handful of tissues.

"Isn't that nice?" Anna said, her smile wide and twinkly. "These are much better apologies than the first ones."

Raymond gave Ruth a sheepish look. "I'm sorry I said all those mean things to you earlier today."

Ruth pulled three more tissues from the box and blew her nose. "You weren't trying to be mean. You were trying to be honest, and I wouldn't like you half as much if you didn't tell me the truth. I hope you always tell me the truth."

Felty opened his cookie package and took out a lemon cookie. "Honesty is the best policy."

Raymond laid his hand over the top of Ruth's. "I just . . . I just wanted you to see . . ."

Ruth put her other hand on top of Raymond's. "I know. *Denki*. You've always been a *gute* friend."

Raymond's face turned red. "I hope to be more than a friend. Much more."

Ruth nibbled on her bottom lip. "I'd like that."

Raymond reached into his pocket and pulled out a piece of paper that had been folded into some sort of design. "I . . . I made this for you. It's a bird."

Anna leaned back in her chair. "We taught Raymond how to do oregano."

Raymond pulled the tail of his paper bird, and its wings flapped back and forth. Omi grinned. Ruth laughed out loud and took the bird from his hand. "I love it. How clever of you."

If the nurse had turned off all the lights, they probably would have been able to read by the glow of Raymond's face. "I've never given a girl a gift, ever."

Ruth was sufficiently gushy. "I've never gotten such a *wunderbarr* gift before, ever." She pulled the bird's tail several more times and made its wings flap and laughed as if she was the happiest girl in the world.

And just like that, Ruth and Raymond were a couple.

*Vell*. That was fast. Ruth and Raymond had gone from being estranged friends to practically engaged in less than an hour. Anna really was the best matchmaker in the whole world. Omi's heart was so full, she thought it might burst.

Anna smiled as if she couldn't be happier. "Do you see how powerful the trust circle is? It's never failed me yet."

Felty looked sideways at Anna. "Have you ever done a trust circle before?"

"That's my point, Felty dear. It works, but people just have to believe in it. I think we all believe."

Omi didn't know about anyone else, but she was a believer.

A nurse in dark blue scrubs ambled down the hallway. She stopped and smiled wryly. "This looks like fun. Are you playing a game?"

"It's a trust circle," Anna said. "The best way to get an apology from someone you love."

The nurse raised her eyebrows. "You think that would work on my husband? He's got a whole lot of stupid to apologize for."

Felty laughed. "I don't wonder but it would."

The nurse handed Anna a piece of paper. "Well, Anna, you're all set to go. The doctor wrote you a prescription for some pain pills if you need them."

"I won't need them," Anna said. "I gave birth to thirteen babies. Everything else is child's play."

"Okay, then, but take the prescription with you, just in case."

Bo and Raymond put the extra chairs back where they belonged, Ruth threw away all her tissues, and Anna and Felty led the way down the corridor to the emergency room exit.

Anna took Felty's arm. "We're all going to be busy with *gmay* tomorrow, but next week, I expect you all to visit and give me a report on wedding plans. I am very helpful during wedding season, and I make *appeditlich* creamed celery with raisins, if you want your guests to have a real treat."

Raymond didn't comment on the possibility of a wedding, but his face was now redder than a gallon of beet juice. Ruth simply smiled. She'd have no problem getting Raymond to propose to her. She was brave like that, and Raymond was smitten.

Bo pointed to his *mammi*'s hand. "Be careful with that finger, Mammi. No heavy lifting until the stitches are healed."

Anna giggled. "I save all the heavy lifting for my grandsons. You'll come over and help with that, won't you?"

"For sure and certain."

Anna and Felty ambled to their buggy, which was parked right next to Raymond's car.

"*Cum*," Raymond said, his voice squeaky and thin. "I'll take you girls home."

Bo jumped all over that. "Omi can ride with me."

Ruth and Omi smiled at each other. Perfect. This day was turning out much better than it had started.

As soon as they were out of sight of the others, Bo boldly took Omi's *gute* hand, and they strolled to his buggy as if they had all the time in the world, which they did. In fact, they had their entire lives to savor being together.

Bo glanced behind him, checking for eavesdroppers. "How did you get Ruth to change her mind?"

Omi grinned. "It was all Raymond's doing. He showed Ruth some disapproval, and she saw herself through his eyes. They really are the perfect match, and Ruth finally realized it."

"My *mammi* knew from the beginning."

"Your *mammi* is a wonder. Is there anything she can't do?"

"Whittle, apparently."

Omi cleared her throat. There was still something she wanted to make sure Bo knew. "I'm sorry for choosing my *schwester* over you."

Still holding her hand, Bo leaned up against the buggy door. "You don't have to apologize for that, Omi. I put you in a terrible position. I'm the one who's sorry."

Omi held up her hand to stop any notion that he should take the blame. "It was not your fault. I let Ruth have too much power over me. Even if she hadn't changed her mind, I had decided to choose you. I was going to tell you that before we were summoned to the hospital. I had decided that I wasn't going to surrender my happiness to Ruth, especially since she was being selfish and unreasonable."

His lips twitched upward. "Until this very moment, I didn't realize how much that would mean to me."

She wrapped her free hand around his strong arm. "I will always choose you, Bo, no matter what. I love you better than I love anyone."

His smile was a raging bonfire. "Don't let Ruth hear you say that."

"I think she already knows. When she marries, I hope she will feel the same way about her husband."

"I don't wonder but she will." Bo looked around once again. He'd parked his buggy in an out-of-the-way parking lot. It was empty except for them and Bo's horse. "Omi, if you agreed to marry me, I would be the happiest *bu* alive."

Her heart did about seven flips. If he was the happiest *bu*, she was most certainly the happiest girl. "Then you'd better hurry and ask."

He cocked an eyebrow. "In the parking lot?"

She nodded. "Why not?"

"It's not very romantic."

"It would be if you'd put your arms around me and whisper in my ear." She felt her face get warm. She'd never been so bold or so mischievous, but Bo had never been *gute* at taking hints. She had to be straightforward.

Bo widened his eyes in surprise, then smiled as if nothing would make him happier. He pulled her close, so close she could feel his heartbeat against the palm of her hand. Inclining his head toward her, he whispered, "Omi, I love you like no *bu* has ever loved a girl. It was torture thinking that maybe I'd lost you. But I can't propose to you in a parking lot."

Omi was so surprised, she giggled. "Why not?"

"Emma would kill me. And my *mamm*. And my *schwester* Lizzy."

Omi frowned in mock disappointment. "Then you'd better find a *gute* place soon, because I'm a very impatient person."

"Omi, I've been waiting for a very long time to ask you to marry me. I've already picked a place. It's not in the hospital parking lot. Nobody likes hospitals."

"I like hospitals. I just don't like being a patient."

He frowned. "I don't like it when you're a patient either. I'll never forget how I almost lost you."

"I'll never forget how I almost drove you away."

"That would have been impossible."

The bishop wouldn't approve, but Omi snaked her *gute* arm around Bo's neck. She couldn't resist the opportunity to be this close. "I love you, Bo, even if you're opposed to parking lots." She propped herself up on her tiptoes and kissed him like they'd never be able to do it again. Bo was taken by surprise, but only momentarily. He clamped his arms around her so tightly that he briefly lifted her from the ground. Indeed, she was floating on a cloud as he kissed her with abandon.

They pulled apart when Omi winced at the pain in her ribs. She wasn't a hundred percent better, and Bo had accidentally held her too tight. "Omi, I'm sorry. I just wanted to get you as close as possible."

She felt as if she was glowing from the inside. "I hope you truly are planning to propose to me, because I'm looking forward to a whole lifetime of pain-free kissing ahead of us."

He looked up at the sky as if thinking about it. "I don't want to give away the surprise, but you should plan on a lot of kissing. I would hate to disappoint you."

# Chapter 23

Nobody counted exactly, but Anna Helmuth was certain that more than four hundred people had come to the wedding. Her creamed celery with raisins disappeared so quickly that not even the brides and grooms had gotten a taste. Of course no one knew for sure if Anna's dish had been eaten or had been disposed of before it even made it out to the table. And the only person who knew for sure wasn't talking.

Four hundred guests were only to be expected when there were two brides and two grooms in the wedding party. Omi glanced to her left where Raymond and Ruth sat sharing a slice of cake. Ruth had never looked prettier, and Raymond seemed as bright and as buoyant as one of his rockets.

Raymond's cousin Elam had pulled up to the house this morning with a pickup truck full of fireworks. He was planning to light them after supper tonight. It promised to be quite a show. Mamm had directed LaWayne to move the woodpile to the other side of the house.

"This cake is *appeditlich*," Bo said, smiling at her. He hadn't taken his eyes off her since they'd stood before the bishop earlier today.

Omi's heart skipped a beat. "Aendi Elizabeth made eight different flavors."

The day after their trip to the hospital, Bo had taken Omi to the meadow with the stone bench where he'd first told her he loved her. It had been the perfect place to propose, which he had done without delay. Then he'd kissed her and given her a paper folded like a frog that jumped when she pressed on its bottom. Raymond had helped him make it.

Raymond had proposed to Ruth on the same day, taking her past the outskirts of town and lighting a rocket that exploded overhead just as he asked the question.

Both Ruth and Omi had said yes.

Omi and Ruth had dreamed of a double wedding ever since they were eight years old. Today was the perfect fulfillment of years of dreams.

Omi's arm was out of the cast, and her ribs had never felt better. The scratches and scrapes on her face were completely healed. The only sign of the haymow accident was the scar behind her ear that no one, including Omi, could see, and a jagged, tiny scar about half an inch below her right eye, which Bo insisted made her face look even more interesting. It also served as a reminder that Omi hadn't lost any limbs, ears, or eyes in the accident. It could have been much worse, and she thanked Derr Herr every day for the blessing of being able to look on Bo's face and hear his low, gentle voice telling her he loved her.

With her two facial scars, most people could easily tell Omi and Ruth apart if they looked closely enough, and Omi found that she liked that people could tell the difference. She no longer wanted to be Ruth. She no longer envied Ruth or coveted Ruth's boyfriend. She didn't care if she was the moon to Ruth's sun.

Omi was the center of Bo's universe, and that was all that mattered.

Anna studied the tiny scar on her finger, the one she'd gotten on the day she decided to give up whittling and on the day Bo and Omi had finally gotten together. "Felty dear, I think it's been a very successful year, don't you?"

"Very successful, Annie. We learned chair yoga, painting, Popsicle sticking, and origami."

"*Ach, vell*, of course we learned all those things. My favorite was oregano. I still have that clever box Raymond folded for me. I keep the sugar cubes in it. But that's not what I'm talking about. I'm talking about the four people who found love because of us."

Felty stroked his beard, smiled, but didn't say anything. It was his signal that he didn't agree.

"*Vell*, Felty, if you have something to say, why don't you come out and say it?" She didn't really need to ask because she knew exactly what Felty was thinking. She'd gotten hurt yet again while scheming to match one of her grandchildren, and she'd ended up in the emergency room for the second time in so many years. Felty just couldn't understand that it was all for the greater good.

Felty took a bite of Elizabeth Mast's carrot cake. Carrot cake was his favorite. "Annie, you did get hurt, but I'm not going to mention it. You always do what you think is right, and I certainly can't scold you for that."

"I'm *froh* you weren't even thinking about my many brushes with death."

"*Nae*, Annie. I was thinking about our great-grandson Menno." He pointed to the far side of the tent where Menno sat with his *bruderen* and *schwester* eating a piece of Elizabeth's butter pecan cake.

Anna nodded. "You should be concerned. That cake is quite dry."

"I want you to help me play matchmaker for Menno."

Felty usually tried to discourage her matchmaking schemes. Now he was planning one of his own? Anna couldn't have been happier. "Why, Felty, you don't even have to ask. I'd be happy to help." She scooted her chair closer to Felty's. "What girl do you have in mind? Lily Ann Mischler is darling . . . a little short, but she has a cute button nose. Sadie King likes dogs, but she hates raisins. It wonders me how Menno feels about raisins."

Felty leaned back in his chair. "I think Menno would be the perfect match for Evie Burkholder."

Anna's throat dried up like a desert, and her heart fell to her toes. "Evie Burkholder will never do, Felty. She's stuck up and full of herself. And she's allergic to strawberries. Can you imagine Menno going without strawberries for the rest of his life? It will never work."

Felty was right about almost everything, except for thinking that Anna would like painting, but he was wrong about this. He should leave the matchmaking to the expert and stick to making Popsicle stick bookmarks.

"I think they'd be perfect for each other," Felty said.

Anna's shock turned into a hot flash. She pulled one of Raymond's oregano fans from her bag and waved it back and forth in front of her face. She must protect Menno at all costs. No *bu* should have to live without strawberries.

# Glossary of Amish Words and Phrases

| | |
|---|---|
| *ach*: | oh |
| *Ach, du lieva*: | Oh, my goodness |
| *ach, vell*: | oh, well |
| *aendi*: | aunt |
| *appeditlich*: | delicious |
| *bruder, bruderen*: | brother, brothers |
| *bu, buwe*: | boy, boys |
| *buplie*: | baby |
| *cum*: | come |
| *Cum reu*: | Come in |
| *Dat*: | Dad |
| *Dawdi*: | Grandpa |
| *deerich*: | foolish |
| *denki*: | thank you |
| *die buwe*: | the boys |
| *die kinner*: | the children |
| *die youngie*: | the young people |
| *dochter, dochters*: | daughter, daughters |
| *dumm*: | dumb |
| *Englisch, Englischer*: | A non-Amish person |
| *fraa, fraaen*: | wife, wives |
| *froh*: | glad |
| *gmay*: | church services |
| *gmayna*: | the Church |
| Gotte: | God |
| *grossmammi*: | grandmother |

| | |
|---|---|
| *gute*: | good |
| *Guter nammidaag*: | Good afternoon |
| *Guter owed*: | Good evening |
| *hallo*: | hello |
| *heartzley*: | sweetheart |
| *jah*: | yes |
| *maedel*: | girl |
| *Mamm*: | Mom |
| *Mammi*: | Grandma |
| *mater*: | mother |
| *nae*: | no |
| *onkel*: | uncle |
| *rumschpringe*: | running around time |
| *schwester, schwesteren*: | sister, sisters |
| *Vie gehts?*: | How is it going? |
| *wunderbarr*: | wonderful |

# Omi Coblenz's German Apple Pancakes

> 6 tablespoons butter, divided
> 2 large apples, peeled, cored, sliced
> 3 tablespoons lemon juice
> ¼ teaspoon cinnamon
> 5 tablespoons powdered sugar
> 3 eggs, room temperature
> ¼ teaspoon salt
> ½ cup flour
> ½ cup milk

Preheat oven to 425 degrees.

In a glass pie plate, melt 4 tablespoons of the butter in the microwave. In a separate bowl, mix apples, lemon juice, cinnamon, and powdered sugar. Pour apple mixture into pie pan with butter and mix. Microwave 2–4 minutes (until apples are tender). If you're Amish, you'll want to fry the apples in a pan over medium heat on the stove because Amish people do not have microwaves.

Melt the remaining 2 tablespoons of butter. Mix the melted butter, eggs, salt, flour, and milk together in a separate bowl. Pour egg mixture over apple mixture in the pie plate. Bake at 425 degrees for 20 minutes. Serve with maple syrup (optional).